Fiction Crosby,

HARVEST
of
SECRETS

HARVEST
of
SECRETS

ELLEN CROSBY

Minotaur Books
New York

HARVEST OF SECRETS. Copyright © 2018 by Ellen Crosby. All rights reserved. Printed in the United States of America. For information, address St. Martin's Press, 175 Fifth Avenue, New York, N.Y. 10010.

Map © 2018 by Peter de Nesnera

www.minotaurbooks.com

Library of Congress Cataloging-in-Publication Data

Names: Crosby, Ellen, 1953– author.
Title: Harvest of secrets / by Ellen Crosby.
Description: First edition. | New York : Minotaur Books, 2018.
Identifiers: LCCN 2018025708 | ISBN 978-1-250-16483-4 (hardcover) |
    ISBN 978-1-250-16484-1 (ebook)
Subjects: LCSH: Montgomery, Lucie (Fictitious character)—Fiction. |
    Vinters—Fiction. | Vineyards—Virginia—Fiction. | Murder—
    Investigation—Fiction. | GSAFD: Mystery fiction.
Classification: LCC PS3603.R668 H37 2018 | DDC 813/.6—dc23
LC record available at https://lccn.loc.gov/2018025708

Our books may be purchased in bulk for promotional, educational, or business use. Please contact your local bookseller or the Macmillan Corporate and Premium Sales Department at 1-800-221-7945, extension 5442, or by email at MacmillanSpecialMarkets@macmillan.com.

First Edition: November 2018

10 9 8 7 6 5 4 3 2 1

In memory of Catherine Reid Kennedy,
who fought so hard to keep the beast at bay
and always made time to read my books
long before they were books.

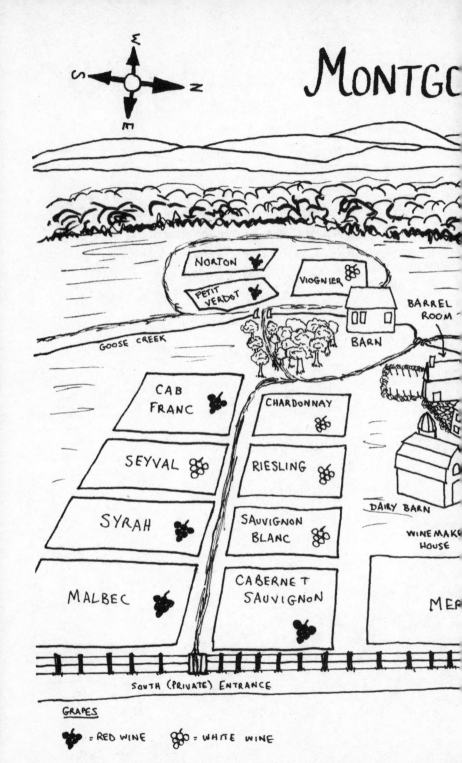

RY ESTATE VINEYARD

CEMETERY

SUMMER HOUSE

HIGHLAND HOUSE

SMOKEHOUSE

...ILLA

CARRIAGE HOUSE

GOOSE CREEK

FARM MANAGER'S HOUSE

PINOT NOIR

CHARDONNAY

MEV

MAIN ENTRANCE

ATOKA ROAD

ROUTE 713

In water one sees one's own face, but in wine one beholds the heart of another.

—ANONYMOUS, FRENCH PROVERB

The blood of your parents is not lost in you.

—MENELAUS, *The Odyssey*

HARVEST
of
SECRETS

One

"You found a human skull?" I said to Antonio. "*Just* the skull?"

"It turned up when we had to dig up part of the tree root," he said.

"Why were you digging?" I was irked, hot, and tired, and Antonio knew it. All he and Jesús were supposed to do was cut up the branches of a tulip poplar that had split in two after lightning struck it during a storm the other day and tote everything away. The tree, which had been at least five feet in diameter and probably seventy or eighty feet tall, had come crashing down onto the old brick cemetery wall. It had also taken out the roof and one side of an old fieldstone storage shed.

The storm, with its lashing rain and fierce wind, had been a warm-up act to Lolita, a Category 5 hurricane with a beguiling name and enough scary "worst-ever" attributes hung on it like ornaments on a Christmas tree to prompt mass evacuations in the Caribbean in anticipation of her arrival. Forecasters predicted Lolita would eventually come roaring up the Atlantic coast and barrel through Virginia, scaring the bejesus out of anyone in her path and making everyone at my vineyard more tense and edgy than usual at harvest time.

"We had to dig." He sounded testy as well. "You'll see why when you get here."

Antonio gets prickly when he thinks I'm telling him how to do his job, or if I seem to doubt his word, though he is always respectful. Still, he has some cause to be annoyed because most of the time when it comes to running the vineyard or taking care of our equipment, he's dead-bang right. He's also one of the best and smartest farm managers I've ever known.

The Montgomery family cemetery sits on a bluff where it commands a breathtaking view of the Blue Ridge Mountains—especially at sunset—which is the reason my ancestor Hamish Montgomery, who received our land as a grant for his service in the French and Indian War, chose that site. Generations of my family have been laid to rest there since the late 1700s. Both of my parents were buried inside the low redbrick walls along with Hamish, and I had no doubt someday I'd join them.

"I'm on my way," I said to Antonio. "In the meantime, don't do anything or move anything, okay? Are you sure the skull doesn't belong to one of the graves? Are you sure it's human?"

"Don't worry, Lucita. Jesús won't go near it." He spoke as if he were calming an upset toddler, instead of his boss. "He says it's *mala suerte*—bad luck. Finding a skull means someone's going to die. I'm sure it didn't come from the cemetery and yes, I'm sure it's human." He added in that placating tone, "You'll see."

"Tell Jesús no one's going to die. That's just an old super-stition." I didn't mean to snap at him, but just now I couldn't afford to have either of them—or any of our crew—get spooked. Not in the middle of harvest, our busiest time of year.

But as I spoke a gust of wind rushed past me, icy fingers caressing my neck and making me shiver. My grandmother, my father's mother, used to tell me that was the sign a soul was leaving this world on its way to the next.

Now *I* was imagining things. It was probably only a stray blast of cold air from the air-conditioning.

Antonio muttered something ominous-sounding under his breath and then hung up. All I caught was the word *boda*. Wed-ding. He and Valeria, the mother of his baby daughter, were getting married the week after next at the vineyard, my wed-ding gift to the two of them. Maybe there were also Hispanic superstitions that involved weddings and skeletons. Dear Lord, I hoped not. Antonio was already jittery enough about this marriage.

I'd been in the barrel room when he'd called me—during harvest we work all hours, seven days a week. Partly because I'd wanted to escape the brutal heat, but also because the lees on last year's barrels of Cabernet Franc needed stirring. The process is called *bâtonnage* and we do it to extract more flavor from dead yeast cells and other sediment that slowly sifts to the bottom of a wine barrel. I closed the bung—the stopper—to the barrel I was working on and put the bâton back where it belonged.

Then I texted Quinn.

Going to check on Antonio and the tree. Almost done with bâtonnage. Back soon.

Quinn Santori had been the winemaker at Montgomery Estate Vineyard ever since I returned home from France five years ago, and as of a few months ago, he was my fiancé. Just now he was out in the south vineyard measuring Brix for this year's harvest of Cab Franc, a test that determined the sweetness of the grapes and whether they were ready to be picked.

Quinn knows me so well. He texted right back. *What's wrong?*

Not sure. I climbed into a dark green ATV that was parked outside the barrel room. I nearly hit Send on my reply and then reconsidered.

They found a skull.

Quinn pulled up beside me in a fire engine–red ATV about thirty seconds after I arrived at the cemetery. I had known he would come once I told him what Antonio and Jesús had discovered. He climbed out of his ATV and walked over to mine. Side by side the two vehicles always made me think of Christmas. Or stoplights.

Anvil-shaped clouds the color of dull pewter moved across the Blue Ridge Mountains and streamed toward us like freighters. We were in for another storm later on, a big one. Lolita, sending us one more warning of what was to come. At least the birds were still singing and the wind hadn't whipped up yet, blowing through the trees until their branches rustled and swayed like dancers.

Quinn slid an arm around my waist and his kiss landed in my hair, which I'd twisted into a knot to keep it off my neck in the soupy heat.

"They really found a skull?" he asked.

"That's what Antonio said."

We walked over to where limbs from the huge tree had already been cut into smaller pieces with a chainsaw. The back of the Superman-blue pickup that had belonged to Antonio's predecessor and had logged nearly two hundred thousand miles was piled high with leafy cut-up branches. Jesús sat on the tailgate smoking, the chainsaw lying on the ground next to him, while Antonio paced back and forth, his phone clamped to his ear. He was talking to Valeria. I could tell by his body language and that low, solicitous tone of voice.

Antonio was lanky, slim, dark-haired, with skin a warm russet brown, and the kind of soulful brown eyes and easy seductive smile that melted women's hearts. Tears would flow the day he married Valeria. He had walked across the border from Mexico into Texas when he was twelve and never went back—though he did send money to his mother faithfully as clockwork—and taught himself how to do just about anything that had to do with farming equipment and how to repair it.

Jesús was a short, plump spark plug, strong and dependable, born in El Salvador, possessing a swarthy complexion and a silver tooth that glittered when he laughed, which was often. I always knew when he was around, because there'd be laughter among the rest of the men—he was a joke-cracker—and maybe someone would be singing in Spanish, a song remembered from home. Heart of gold, that was Jesús. I couldn't imagine how we'd get along without either of them, and Benny, our other full-time worker.

Jesús slid off the tailgate. Antonio stopped pacing and disconnected his call, shoving his phone into his back pocket.

"It's back there," he said. "In the shed."

The four of us walked over together, though Jesús hung

back a few paces. The girth and height of the tulip poplar had obscured the little stone shed. It had been built by one of my ancestors as a place to keep shovels, rakes, and other garden implements used to care for the cemetery and the graves. I used it to keep flower vases and a collection of little American flags I put on the graves of my ancestors who had fought in our country's wars on Veterans Day, Memorial Day, and the Fourth of July.

With the roof gone and the interior of the shed now exposed to the outdoors, it was clear why Antonio and Jesús had discovered the skull. When the tree split and toppled over, part of the trunk had landed on the roof and a couple of large tree roots had pulled out of the ground, leaving behind a sizable hole. The skull lay there on its own. My first thought was, *where's the rest of it?*

It was human, all right. All of the teeth were intact. Whoever it was, he or she appeared to be grinning at us, perhaps surprised—or pleased—to be discovered in such an unexpected way.

"I wonder if the rest of . . . it . . . the body is here, too," Quinn said, echoing my thoughts. "Maybe we should dig a little more and find out."

I shook my head. It was already creepy enough to realize I'd been walking over a buried skull all these years every time I used the shed. How had I never sensed its presence?

"We have to call the Sheriff's Office," I said. "These are human remains. No more digging."

"It's next to a cemetery," Quinn said. "People are dying to get in."

Jesús and Antonio grinned.

"You're not funny," I said to Quinn.

"Sorry. But, seriously, it's true. Why wouldn't you find human remains here?"

"The skull is outside the cemetery. It can't have moved or shifted under the wall, and certainly not this far away," I said. "Not *inside* the shed."

Antonio shrugged. "Don't look at me. If you want to call the Sheriff's Office, Lucie, call 'em. Maybe they can tell you."

"I wonder how old it is," Quinn said. "I mean, how long it's been here."

"I don't know," I said. "What I wonder is why there's no coffin."

"There's an easy enough explanation for that." Quinn gave me a meaningful look. "It would also explain the skull being outside the cemetery."

I knew where he was going with this and I didn't like it one bit.

"What do you mean?" It was the first time Jesús had spoken and he sounded ill at ease. "You think it's *el diablo*?"

"Don't worry, Jesús. Quinn's not talking about anything supernatural. No ghosts. No devil," I said.

He nodded, seemingly reassured. "Okay. That's good."

I knew what I said next would upset him all over again. "Not exactly. What he means is that whoever this is was murdered."

Two

Murder. The word settled over the four of us like thick, dark smoke, reducing everyone to uneasy silence. Maybe whoever this was wasn't laughing after all. Maybe it was a grimace of pain or a final agonized scream.

Quinn cleared his throat. "We could be getting ahead of ourselves here. Maybe . . . the ground did shift. Maybe the roots of the tulip poplar caused it to heave, and the body ended up out here instead of inside the cemetery. It happens all the time at old graveyards."

"Thirty feet?" I said, giving him an incredulous look. "Inside the shed?"

"Okay, so that's a crazy idea. Unless the shed was built after this person was buried." He shrugged. "But why do it right next to a cemetery? That's weird, don't you think?"

I did.

I pulled out my phone. "I think it's time to call nine-one-one."

THERE ISN'T A LOT of crime in Atoka, Virginia, population two hundred and sixty, give or take. The town—village, really—is located in the middle of the affluent heart of Virginia's horse-and-hunt country next door to better-known Middleburg. Around here everyone knows everyone else, and we know each other's business, as well. Very little happens—good, bad, a scandal, a celebration—without becoming the number-one topic of conversation the next morning around the coffeepot at the General Store. Six months ago we'd finally installed an alarm system at Highland House, my home, at my brother Eli's insistence after someone walked in one night that shouldn't have been there. But before that we'd rarely locked the doors and no one who dropped by to visit ever used the doorbell. Mostly folks opened the front door, stuck their head in, and yelled "Yoo-hoo."

On a quiet, sultry September afternoon it didn't take long for a tan-and-gold Loudoun County Sheriff's Office cruiser to drive up Sycamore Lane, the private road that wound through our land, and park at the bottom of the hill below the cemetery. Right behind it was an EMT van. I was grateful they didn't arrive with lights flashing and sirens blaring, which would have alarmed the winery staff and any visitors to the tasting room. Right now, though, what worried me more were the jangled nerves of our migrant grape pickers, even the legal ones. Lately the men had gotten so edgy in this new immigrant-unfriendly era that I knew every one of them would be dead certain ICE had arrived.

The discovery of a body at Montgomery Estate Vineyard wouldn't remain a secret for long, but just now the fewer people who knew about it the better. A man climbed out of the cruiser and a woman got out of the van.

Quinn squinted at them and said, "Don't we know that deputy? Looks and walks like a bear? What's his name?"

"Mathis," I said. "Biggie Mathis. He's been here before, remember?"

Quinn nodded. "Hope he doesn't think we make a habit of this," he said under his breath as we waited for Deputy Mathis to lumber up the hill along with the woman.

Biggie Mathis took off his cap when he reached us and appraised the four of us like we were waiting for the detention hall monitor to show up after school. "Ms. Montgomery," he said, nodding at me. "Good afternoon. I understand you called nine-one-one about a body. Someone found human remains."

From his matter-of-fact tone he could have been talking about the weather. At least he didn't say *again*.

"That's right." I indicated Antonio and Jesús. "This is Antonio Ramirez, the farm manager here, and Jesús Echeverría, another of our full-time employees. The two of them discovered the skull inside an old storage shed when they were removing a tree that came down on the shed and the cemetery wall. You already know Quinn Santori."

Biggie pulled out a notebook. The EMT, an athletic-looking woman with short steel-gray hair, headed for the shed.

"*Ustedes hablan inglés?*" Biggie asked Antonio and Jesús.

"We do," Antonio said and Jesús nodded.

"Tell me what happened," Biggie said.

They finished their story as the EMT came over to Biggie. "I called the M.E., Big. He can have the honor of filling out the paperwork. I don't know why I got called out on this one. That skull is DOA. Desiccated on Arrival. Whoever this is has been here for years. Looks like the body was dumped, too. The grave's not really that deep." She surveyed the four of us and said in a brisk voice, "Well, bye all. I'm taking off. I've got a family barbecue tonight and I need to get home and make cole-slaw. Have a nice day."

As she left, a dusty station wagon the color of mint ice cream with two-toned wood-grained paneling on the sides drove up and parked at the bottom of the hill, taking her place.

Quinn let out a long, low whistle. "Will you look at that?" he said. "A Ford Country Squire, probably 1972 or '73 or there-abouts. Haven't seen one of those for ages. Looks like it's in just about perfect condition, too."

"Who is that?" I asked Biggie as a man with thinning white hair, a slight stoop, and a bit of a paunch climbed out of the car. He had a neatly trimmed goatee and wore a pair of horn-rimmed glasses.

"That," he said, "is Dr. Winston Churchill Turnbull. Brand-new county medical examiner. Lives over in Purcellville. Just got back from service in Iraq." He pronounced it *Eye-rack*.

"Iraq? Seriously?" I stared at Dr. Turnbull. "He's got to be in his seventies."

"Seventy-four. Came out of retirement to volunteer as a sur-geon in one of the local hospitals over there. Felt it was some-thing he needed to do. He came home after serving a year and a half and signed up as a Loudoun County medical examiner.

Said what he saw over there turned his stomach—especially the little children caught in the crossfire in that hellhole. He told me after he'd already seen the worst man could do to his fellow man, examining dead bodies and figuring out the cause of death back home would be a piece of cake. A relief, even, because when you're dead the suffering has ended." Biggie spoke with a mixture of awe and admiration.

"He sounds like an amazing man."

"You got that right," he said and waved an arm at Dr. Turnbull. "Hey, Doc. Up here."

Winston Churchill Turnbull waved back and sprinted up the hill toward us.

"Afternoon, everyone," he said, before turning to Biggie. He didn't seem at all winded from his little jog. "What have we got here, Othello?"

Othello? I cast a sideways glance at Biggie, who looked flustered, but said in a calm voice, "Thanks for coming so quickly, Doc. These folks found a human skull. Apparently dug up by accident when a tree root exposed it. Also looks like it's been here for a while."

Dr. Turnbull turned his gaze on Quinn, Antonio, Jesús, and me. His eyes fell on my cane, which I use because of a car accident ten years ago. In spite of three surgeries and a lot of physical therapy my left foot is still partially deformed. The doctors said I'd never walk again. I don't think of my cane as a sign of disability. I think of it as a symbol of victory because they were wrong. I'd bet good money the man standing in front of me had seen a lot of young people with canes or in wheelchairs or worse—limbless—in Iraq.

"I'm Dr. Winston Turnbull," he said, zeroing in on me. "Everybody calls me Win. And who are all of you?"

We introduced ourselves and after I said my name, he said, "You make mighty fine wine, Ms. Montgomery."

"Thank you. And it's Lucie." I hesitated and then said, "Will you be able to tell us anything about who this is? Male? Female? How long he or she has been here?"

"Let me take a look first. I'm just a country doctor," he said, which sounded like a whopper of an understatement after what we'd just heard about him. "First, I need to be sure that these are human remains."

"They are," Biggie said. "I guarantee it."

Win nodded like he agreed, though he seemed like a trust-but-verify kind of doctor, so he went on. "Well, then, the next thing to determine is how long they've been here. If they're old—decades, maybe older—then a forensic anthropologist ought to take over and handle the excavation. Or a taphonomist. In other words, if I determine that it's not a criminal investigation that involves law enforcement, you need expertise beyond mine."

The explanation went completely over Jesús' head and even Antonio looked baffled. "Why would you need someone who stuffs dead animals?" Antonio asked.

Win Turnbull smiled. "Sorry, I guess I wasn't very clear. I'm talking about a taphonomist, not a taxidermist. An individual who studies human remains from the time of death until the time they are discovered—what just happened today, for example. A taphonomist focuses on what impact the environment had on the body—the soil, the interaction of the remains with plants, insects, or other natural causes that could result in decomposition. He or she decodes how the remains came to be where they are, what happened, hopefully in order to identify who this person was, if that's possible," he said. "Families wait in hope forever if they never see a loved one who has mysteriously disappeared, if they don't have a body to bury and grieve for. Sometimes you can finally give closure to a nightmare that has lasted years. Decades. Not a happy ending, but at least an ending."

"How do you figure out all this stuff?" Antonio asked. "From just a bunch of old bones."

"Bones talk," Win said, with a somber smile. "That is, if you know the right questions to ask, what to look for. Come here, I'll show you."

Biggie looked like he wanted to object to us tramping over the area surrounding the grave, but Win gave him a long stare and said, "Their footprints are already all over the place anyway. It would be better if they understand this. Trust me."

Biggie pursed his lips and nodded, but he still didn't seem happy. He followed the rest of us over to the newly unearthed grave site. Win went down on one knee and the rest of us formed a semicircle around him.

"Well," he said, after a moment, "this is definitely a human skull."

"What else can you tell about it?" I asked.

Win knelt on both knees and bent over so he could study the skull more closely. Then he straightened up and twisted around so he could look up at us. "Probably in her late teens, maybe early twenties."

Someone young, a girl, who should have had her life ahead

of her. I caught my breath and Win's eyes met mine once again. He had just transformed this vacant-eyed skull into a person, giving her a history.

"Of course I can't tell you the cause of death," he said. "There's no corpse to examine—no tissue, no organs."

"How do you know how old it . . . I mean, she . . . was?" Quinn asked.

"Because of the number of bones. An adult human has two hundred and six bones. A child has significantly more."

"Why?" Jesús asked.

"Because a child's bones haven't fused together yet. It's a process known as ossification, which develops gradually from childhood until adulthood," Win said. "Look here."

He pointed to the skull and everyone, including Biggie, leaned in to see what he was indicating. "In a young human skull, there are a series of zigzag lines that separate the various plates that protect and encase our brains. These lines are called sutures and as we get older, the sutures disappear as the plates fuse together. Hence, fewer bones."

Win began sketching imaginary lines on the skull with an index finger. "Across the top of the head we have the sagittal suture. From the back of the head to the temple is the coronal suture. The squamosal suture more or less follows the shape of the ear where the temporal plate is located. There are others, but you get the idea."

"Since you can't see any sutures," Quinn said, "is that how you knew her age?"

"As I said, it's just a rough guess. I'd have to examine the skull more closely. Don't forget the bones have decomposed while they were in the soil. But I do think she had outgrown puberty. I also believe she was probably Caucasian, based on the eye orbits and the nasal cavity."

"You can tell it's female?" I asked. "Just like that?"

"The clearest indication would be to see the pelvic bones," he said. "Obviously. Which may or may not still be here."

My eyes strayed to a patch of earth below the skull where more bones might still lay under the soil. It was still within the perimeter of the shed. Was the rest of the skeleton intact? Had the shed served as protection for a body?

"However," Win went on, "it's still possible to make some determination of sex from the skull. Males, for example, have larger, squarer, and more pronounced jaws than females. They also have a more prominent supraorbital ridge—in other words, the brow." He traced a finger where the forehead would have been and then sketched in the eyes over two black, sightless holes. "Males also have more rectangular eye sockets. In general, their bones are more robust than the delicate bones of a female."

"You're pretty sure about this?" It was the first time Biggie had spoken in a while. "It's a young female? I mean, she."

"I'd want to do a more in-depth examination to confirm it, but yes, I'm reasonably certain."

There was more silence while we absorbed that information. Young. A woman, just barely. Buried outside the walls of my family's cemetery in an old shed. Deliberately? To hide her? My stomach churned. For some reason it seemed more disturbing, more . . . shocking . . . to know the remains were female, not male.

"Can you tell how long she's been here?" I asked.

"I'm afraid not," he said. "Determining time of death—

especially when you're talking about years, or in this case, I would venture to say decades—is a lot more complicated."

"What about DNA?" I asked. "Is there any way to collect it from bones that are this old, when there's no hair or skin left?"

I tried to keep my tone nonchalant, asking as a matter of curiosity. Quinn cast a quizzical glance in my direction but I pretended not to see it.

Win began to get to his feet. Quinn put out a hand and pulled him up. "Thanks." Win brushed the dirt off the knees of his khakis. "You can obtain DNA from teeth, Lucie. This young woman has a very good set of them left. You'd be surprised what we learn."

"So you might even be able to identify her?"

"If you're wondering if she's related to you, my dear, we can swab your DNA and see if we get a match," he said in a kind voice. "If she's not, then it depends whether any of her relatives are in our DNA database. Sometimes we get lucky. Other times not."

Quinn shot me another puzzled look and said to Win, "So what happens now?"

"Right now," Biggie said, interrupting the conversation, "we've got a storm coming and I need to put yellow tape around what's left of this shed. Until we know more, this is a crime scene. That means everyone needs to keep away. No trespassing. Let Doc Turnbull do his work until we get some more answers about who we've got here."

A clap of thunder boomed directly above us, as if Biggie had planned it to go with his voice-of-God "keep out" edict. I looked up at the sky. Angry black-and-gray clouds swirled like a boiling cauldron clear to the Blue Ridge. The mountains themselves were partially swallowed up by the menacing darkness. The wind picked up and everyone began to move.

"Let's get this grave covered up so nothing washes away before the storm hits," Win said, his voice rising to be heard above the wind.

The first fat drops of rain started to fall. "Come on," Biggie shouted as a devil's pitchfork of lightning lit up the sky over the Blue Ridge. "We've got to get her covered up and get out of here."

Her.

I wondered who she was.

UNFORTUNATELY NEITHER QUINN NOR I had put the roofs back on the ATVs so we were both soaking wet and chilled by the time we pulled in to the old dairy barn where we kept the equipment. We drove back to the house in my Jeep looking like something someone forgot to shoot, showered together, and changed into dry clothes. The storm passed almost as swiftly as it had come, leaving behind a cloudless sky, clean, fresh, cool, air, and a Technicolor late-summer sunset that turned golden yellow, then vivid orange, and finally a fierce red over the Blue Ridge. Tonight Hurricane Lolita seemed impossibly far away.

We ate dinner outside on the veranda so we could watch the sun go down. In a few weeks it would be too cool to do this, but for now I reveled in these Indian summer evenings before autumn and chillier nights arrived for good. Persia Fleming, our housekeeper, had left us dinner—Southern fried chicken, homemade potato salad, and green beans picked ear-lier today from the garden tossed with crunchy slivered almonds sautéed with butter. Apple pie à la mode for dessert. Also homemade.

"I never get tired of this view," I said as the mountains slowly changed to the color of an old bruise and the sky faded to a deep violet. A few stars winked like tiny lights that had just been turned on. When I was little my mother used to tell me that the Eskimos believed the stars were really openings to heaven that allowed the love of those we'd lost to pour through, shining down to let us know they were happy. After she died, I often looked up and wondered which star—which opening in heaven—she had chosen to send her love back to me.

"Me, neither." Quinn settled back in his chair, resting his wineglass on his chest. "Want to do some stargazing tonight? We could dry off the Adirondack chairs and finish the bottle of wine at the summerhouse. It's so clear we'll be able to see the Milky Way since the moon doesn't rise until after midnight. Plus it's probably one of the last opportunities for seeing the summer triangle."

Of all the unexpected things I discovered about my fiancé, the biggest surprise was his passion for astronomy, along with a far-reaching and eclectic knowledge of outer space, stars, planets, meteors, comets—actually, any phenomenon that occurred in the night sky. He was especially fascinated by the Messier Objects, a collection of 110 astronomical objects consisting of star clusters, nebula, and galaxies. The original list, compiled in 1771 by a French astronomer named Charles Messier, had consisted of forty-five items. Over the years, however, astronomers continued adding to it until what had become the most famous list in astronomy totaled 110 items. Every year on a designated night between mid-March and mid-April—when the entire collection of Messier Objects was visible in the night sky—Quinn took part in the "Messier Marathon," a competition organized among amateur astronomers to locate as many items on the list as possible that one night.

The first year Quinn moved to Virginia from California my father had let him set up his telescope at our summerhouse, which was on the other side of my mother's rose garden. There he had an unencumbered view of the night sky that stretched above an expanse of farmland, pastures, and rolling hills bounded by the Blue Ridge Mountains. It had grown to be one of our habits to sit out there at night in a pair of Adirondack chairs with a glass of wine or an after-dinner drink as Quinn would teach me about the constellations and planets, show me long-tailed comets or a flurry of meteor showers, a galaxy I'd never seen, the beauty of the Milky Way—until I learned the cycle of what was visible in the northern hemisphere at different times of year.

A few days ago while we were cleaning wine barrels on the crush pad he told me about the recent discovery of a planet that apparently had water and an atmosphere similar to Earth's.

"It's only thirty-nine light years away." He'd sounded as excited as if he'd made the discovery himself. He was keen on space travel, too, following the developments of commercial projects that would someday let regular folks take a trip to the moon and back. If he ever won the lottery I knew he'd use the money for a round-trip ticket in a heartbeat. *Sign me up. Fly me to the moon.*

"Does that mean it's pretty close to Earth?" I'd asked.

"Relatively speaking, it is," he'd said. "There are a little over ten thousand earth years in a light year."

"That's three hundred and ninety thousand years. I guess it wouldn't be the next stop after a moon visit."

He'd grinned. "Not for you or me."

"Lucie?" Quinn said just now, bringing me back to the present. "Earth to Lucie. Anybody home?"

I looked up from my wineglass. He was staring at me, a puzzled expression on his face.

"What?"

"I asked if you wanted to do some stargazing. Are you all right? You seem like you're in another world tonight."

"I'm sorry. Yes, of course, I'd love to. I just can't stop thinking about that girl."

"The skull?"

I nodded.

"Want to talk about it?" he asked. "Today when we were with Win Turnbull, I could tell there was something on your mind."

My older brother, Eli, always says I can't lie for beans. My face gives me away. Just now I was glad for the darkness and the flickering light of the two pillar candles that burned in hurricane lamps on the table. Hopefully the dancing shadows wouldn't betray me because I didn't want to tell Quinn the truth. At least not yet.

"Don't worry, I'm okay. I just wonder who she is," I said. "And whether she's related to me."

WE WALKED OVER TO the summerhouse together. In the darkness I brushed against my mother's David Austin roses, releasing a fragrant scent that drifted into the night air. Quinn set up his telescope while I dried off the chairs, still wet from the afternoon downpour.

"The sky's so clear you can already see a lot of stars and planets without the telescope," he said.

By now I knew where to look. One of the first things Quinn had taught me was how to locate the five bright planets—Mars, Mercury, Jupiter, Saturn, and Venus—all of which could be seen, depending on the time of year, just by looking up at the sky. I spotted Mars, Saturn, and Venus right away, along with Altair, Vega, and Deneb, the three stars of the summer triangle.

"Come and take a look at Mars through the telescope," he said. "It's really beautiful tonight. Reminds me of a campfire in the distance."

I went over and peered through the eyepiece. "I see it," I said and there was Mars, pale red, a strong steady light that didn't twinkle like the surrounding stars.

"Now find Saturn," he said, "and you should also should be able to see Titan, Saturn's biggest moon. Look about four ring-lengths to the east of the planet. It's sort of orange and looks like it's surrounded by smog."

After a moment I said, "I found them."

"Okay, look below Saturn and you should see Antares," he said, "in the constellation Scorpius. It's the brightest star near the head of the scorpion. This is probably one of the last nights you'll be able to see it forming a triangle with Mars and Saturn. It only happens in summer. Pretty soon Mars will start to fade and the other two will disappear below the horizon."

"What's so special about Antares?" I asked. "It's not a planet like Mars or Saturn."

"No, but it's an important star, a supergiant nearing the end of its life," he said. "Once it has no more fuel left to burn, it's going to collapse and explode into a supernova. Some astrophysicists say it will be brighter than the entire rest of our galaxy put together."

I straightened up and imagined a scene from an end-of-the-world movie. Earth would be scorched by the explosion he'd described and enveloped in a filmy cloud, except for the few brave souls who managed to survive. "I hope it isn't going to happen anytime soon," I said.

"Time is relative when it comes to outer space." He moved behind me and wrapped his arms around my waist, kissing my neck. "You've got to wonder how anyone can look at a night sky like this one and say the earth is flat."

"People still believe that?"

"Sure. They're some of the same folks who swear the moon landing was faked," he said. "You know what I want to know?"

"What?"

"If they're right, where is the edge?"

I started to laugh and he said, "No, I'm serious. If the earth is flat there's got to be an edge, so why don't those guys know where it is? Advertise, even. 'Visit the edge of the earth.' Hell, I'd sign up in a heartbeat. The first thing I'd do is hang over and see what was underneath."

I laughed again. "You're crazy," I said and shivered.

"And you're cold. We should have brought sweaters. It's getting chilly."

"I know." I leaned into his body for warmth. "I think I left my grandmother's quilt in the summerhouse."

"You did. I saw it on the rocking chair."

I let the screen door bang behind me and a moment later returned with the scrappy bright-colored nine-patch quilt my grandmother—my father's mother—had made. I'd been visiting her for a few weeks the summer she'd put it together, a curious nine-year-old fascinated by the vast collection of colorful fabrics heaped as if they were snowdrifts on every flat surface of her sewing room. Once she realized my interest she'd let me pick out the fabrics for this quilt, teaching me about value and color and even sneaking in a few sewing lessons. Ever since then I'd loved quilts; someone's labor of love, the colorful fabrics and hundreds of patterns and blocks to choose from, stitched together in a unique creation that was a work of art.

"Quilts," Granny Montgomery had told me, "are meant to be used. Years ago women used fabric from worn-out clothes or other fabric scraps for the tops and stitched together Domino Sugar bags for the undersides so they had something to put on their beds, or hang across windows and doors to keep out the cold. A quilt can last a hundred or more years if you take care of it. Don't keep yours tucked away in a drawer or an old trunk."

I wrapped the quilt around me and settled into the Adirondack chair. Quinn handed me a glass of wine. "Something is on your mind. It's more than just that skull by the cemetery."

"It's nothing, really."

"Your nose is growing." He waited me out.

I sighed. "Okay. It has to do with something you said when we were out here one night a couple of weeks ago."

"It's hard to keep track of all the memorable stuff I say,

since I'm so profound most of the time," he said in a teasing voice. "How about giving me a little hint?"

I grinned. "You said the air we breathe right now is the exact same air as everyone who ever lived on earth, all the way back to the beginning of time. Cleopatra. Michelangelo. St. Francis of Assisi. Jack the Ripper. It hasn't changed."

In the darkness a match blazed as he lit up one of his Swisher Sweets cigars. "Ah," he said. "That."

The cigar tip glowed like an orange minimoon. "It's true," he said. "What does it have to do with that skull?"

Somehow he always managed to connect the dots at lightning speed. "It got me thinking about my family—my ancestors, I mean—everyone who lived in Highland House ever since Hamish built it two hundred and fifty years ago. Thinking about them as people, instead of names listed in the family tree in the Montgomery family Bible or headstones in the cemetery. Wondering what they said, how they felt, who they loved . . . what made them happy or angry."

"Where are you going with this, Lucie?"

I sipped my wine before I answered him. "Nowhere, really," I said, which wasn't true. "But when I saw that skull today I had a feeling . . . actually more than a feeling that she and I are related."

That part was God's truth.

"I already figured that out," Quinn said. "Look, you heard what Win Turnbull said. He can take a sample of your DNA and they can match it against the skull, so you'll know for sure. The family record information in the Bible could probably help you figure out who she is once you know more or less when she lived. Plus there might be something in what's left of your father's genealogical records that didn't get burned in the fire."

The summer I moved home from France, a fire had destroyed part of the downstairs of Highland House—the library and the foyer took the brunt of the damage. The library, with my father's valuable collection of rare first editions—mostly books on colonial American history and Virginia history—and many of his papers, had been almost completely gutted, except for his hand-carved gun cabinet.

"I know," I said to Quinn. "In the meantime, there's something wrong about that skull being where it is. I hope she didn't . . . suffer when she died."

"I know you do." He reached for my hand across the narrow space between our chairs. "You do realize you might never know what happened to her or who she is?"

I nodded. "Even if we don't find out, I want to have her properly buried in our cemetery. It doesn't matter if she's related to us or not. She deserves a decent burial."

He squeezed my hand. "You're a good person, sweetheart. Maybe you could talk to B.J. about how to handle something like this. I'm sure he'd know what to do."

B.J. Hunt owned Hunt & Sons Funeral Home in Middleburg. He and three generations of Hunts had buried practically everyone who lived in Middleburg and Atoka for the last one hundred years.

"I'll call B.J. once we find out whether there's . . . more . . . of her to bury," I said. "I hope we find out who she is. I'd hate to think of her ending up like The Urn."

The Urn was a local legend; an ornate silver funerary urn

containing the ashes of an unknown soul who had ended up
in the vault of Blue Ridge Federal Bank in Middleburg. No one
had ever claimed it and the record of the person who had originally left the ashes had mysteriously vanished. Every night
the bank employee who locked up always stopped by the vault
and wished The Urn good night. The practice had been going
on for decades and by now folks believed something bad
would befall the first person that forgot to wish The Urn sweet
dreams.

Quinn grinned and stubbed out his cigar in an ashtray
next to his chair, snuffing out the tiny orange flakes of fire
until they were gone. "Want some more wine? Bottle's almost
empty."

"Sure."

There was one thing I hadn't told him, something I wasn't
ready to discuss. At least not yet. After that remark he made
about everyone breathing the same air—it was five weeks ago,
to be precise—I'd sent away for a DNA ancestry test kit from
the Genome Project. I also hadn't told Eli, my older brother,
or my younger sister, Mia, who lived in New York City. Mia
would probably flip out and Eli was one for letting sleeping
dogs lie. Knowing him, he'd warn that we might end up learning that one of our relatives was an ax-murderer or a serial
killer.

I'd made sure I picked up the mail until the test kit came
a few days later. That evening I'd locked myself in the bathroom, spitting until I filled a vial with enough saliva for the
lab to test. Surprisingly it had taken longer than I expected to
produce that much spit. Afterward I'd sealed it shut with a
stabilizing ingredient that was supposed to keep the sample

viable even if the return package detoured through the Sahara Desert or the North Pole.

The results, according to the Genome Project website, came by email in four to six weeks. That meant I should be receiving a notification any day now.

"There's something else that might help figure out who she is," Quinn was saying.

"Pardon?"

"Lucie. Are you listening to anything I said?"

"Sorry. I'm still thinking about her. And that grave, the way she was hidden in the storage shed."

"That's what I'm talking about," he said. "The grave. Didn't you say almost every one of your ancestors is buried in that cemetery?"

I nodded. "That's right. Everyone who lived in Highland House, as well as some of our close relations."

"Well, if she ends up being related to you, we could probably figure out who she is by process of elimination."

"You're right," I said. The mystery woman wouldn't have a headstone in the cemetery, if she were a Montgomery.

Which meant we might be able to solve the riddle of *who* she was. But not *why*. Why bury her just outside the cemetery, without a coffin?

That question intrigued me even more. And the more I thought about it, the more it seemed to me there were no good answers.

Three

During harvest we work flat-out, late nights and pre-dawn mornings, seven days a week until all the grapes are picked and moved to either oak barrels or stainless steel tanks. Usually we start in August and finish in mid-to-late October. Because it's our busiest time of year and everything else that happens depends on how well harvest goes, tempers have been known to grow frayed and sharp words get exchanged.

This year had been more difficult and more combustible than any I could remember. First we had a couple of rainy weeks at the end of August when we were supposed to pick many of the white wine grapes, which threw off our schedule—and every other vineyard in northern Virginia. What was worse, everyone was short of help because so many of the migrant workers had returned home or else were keeping a low profile for fear of deportation. The combination of lousy weather and not enough workers was bad all around. Everyone was scrambling. You couldn't get a crew to come back and pick the next day if it had rained the day before. They had already moved on and were picking somewhere else and that vineyard wasn't going to let them go.

There is an unwritten code of ethics among vineyard owners in our region that we help each other out, share advice and resources, rearrange schedules when possible, sell extra grapes if they could be spared and you needed a few more tons of some varietal to make your wine. Sure, we were competitors, but the Virginia wine industry was still in its fledgling stages and a rising tide lifted all boats. More to the point, the next time someone was in trouble it could be you.

But the altruism and help-thy-neighbor do-gooding seemed to dry up as soon as it became a problem to find enough workers to pick all the grapes. This year's harvest had turned into a free-for-all, everyone for him- or herself, whatever it took to get the fruit picked. Quinn and I were getting ready for bed later that night when he mentioned the subject of picking our Cabernet Franc, which was the next grape that would be ripe enough to bring in. I'd forgotten all about it until he reminded me that he'd been testing Brix on the Cab Franc just before we met Antonio and Jesús at the cemetery.

"Depending on the weather over the next few days, the Cab Franc might be ready by Sunday at the earliest," Quinn said as he slid into bed next to me. "But right now, with what the forecasters are saying about Lolita moving up the coast and heading our way over the weekend, I think we ought to pick on Saturday—get a crew in—rather than take our chances."

We live and die by the weather and what Mother Nature

does or doesn't do, but weather forecasters are only human. Sometimes I think they've got one of the few jobs in the world where you can be wrong so often and still remain employed.

It's painful to pick grapes before they're ready, especially after the hard work you've done all season to care for and nurture them to this stage. Pick too early and they've got a high pH and low sugar. In other words, they're not sweet enough.

"It's only Monday," I said. "The forecast could change half a dozen times between now and Saturday, especially if Lolita stays out to sea and downgrades to a lesser category or makes landfall farther up the coast and hits New York and New Jersey. I'd hate to pick early if the Brix is too low. The weather might still be warm enough afterward that the grapes could survive the rain. They'd be riper. Better."

"I don't disagree, but we don't have the luxury of waiting to see what Lolita does and then get caught with no crew available. And if the weather cools off instead, we'll have diluted the fruit by waiting. I say we line up guys to come in on Saturday and take our lumps."

There is a saying among vineyard owners and winemakers that great wine is not made in the cellar; it's made in the vineyard. It's all about how you care for the grapes when they're still on the vine that matters. Our job as winemakers—if I'm strictly honest—is not to screw up what nature and hard work in the field have given you once it's time to make the wine. It's less about the magic we perform to get the wine into a tank or a barrel—and eventually into a bottle.

I sighed. Quinn was probably right. So much of grape growing and winemaking was a crapshoot. Lolita would take whatever capricious or deadly turn she wanted to take. Plan for the worst, hope for the best.

"Okay, we'll pick Saturday," I said. "But if we're going to get that entire block done in a day, we need to hire at least one more person. Our crew is beat, you know that. No one has had a day off in weeks. We need someone competent, in addition to our guys and the migrant workers Antonio hires. Someone who can drive the tractor, weigh the grapes, do everything. I wonder if La Vigne could spare Miguel as a favor after all the help we've given Toby?" I paused and added, "I could ask."

Quinn rolled over onto his side and propped himself up on one elbow. In the darkness I could just make out his profile limned by silvery moonlight. "You mean ask Jean-Claude, don't you? Not Toby."

I felt the heat rise in my cheeks. "Jean-Claude is the winemaker now. Plus Miguel's a good worker. He knows what he's doing, unlike some of the other guys. And since he and Antonio are practically related—or will be, after Antonio marries Valeria—the two of them work together really well."

"You sound awfully defensive, sweetheart. Sure, go ahead. If you want to ask Jean-Claude, go ask him." He lay down again and turned over so he was facing the wall, instead of me. "Fine by me."

It wasn't fine by him. I should have known.

Three months ago Tobias Levine, a retired diplomat with a career that included serving as secretary of state, U.S. ambassador to the United Nations, and ambassador to France, had bought the two-hundred-and-fifty-acre estate next door to us. In addition to the Greek Revival mansion, swimming pool, tennis courts, extensive manicured gardens, and guest cottages, the property also had a working vineyard and an elaborate complex of stables, offices, and training facilities for about twenty horses. Toby moved in with Robyn Callahan, his longtime partner, brought his own Thoroughbreds and polo ponies, and renamed the vineyard La Vigne Cellars, which was clever and catchy.

A few weeks after they had settled in, Toby and Robyn threw a lavish garden party to meet the neighbors. Toby also took the opportunity to introduce Jean-Claude de Merignac, La Vigne Cellars' new winemaker. Somehow Toby had managed to keep the news that he'd hired someone from one of France's oldest winemaking dynasties under wraps until that evening and it had the bombshell effect on everyone at the party that I somehow suspected was the intention. For me it had an especially devastating effect.

I'd been in love with Jean-Claude. Once.

Jean-Claude de Merignac had been my first big crush. I'd been thirteen. He was twenty-eight. He'd taken about as much notice of me as if I'd been an overly rambunctious puppy that kept getting in the way. Instead he saw me as my older cousin Dominique's little American cousin: a gangly, awkward kid who still hadn't gotten rid of all her baby fat, wore braces on her teeth, and had just started dealing with the agonies of teenage acne. My brother, Eli, and I had been sent to France for the summer, told by our parents that it was an adventure and an opportunity to spend time with our grandparents and cousins while improving our French. But both of us knew— as children always do—that we were being exiled abroad because Mom and Leland, who never wanted us to call him "Dad" or "Daddy," weren't getting along and hadn't been for a while. Eli, who was fifteen, and liked to act as if he were already a man of the world, told me bluntly that having us out of the house and sending Mia, who was five, to Granny Montgomery's in Charlottesville, would give our parents a chance to work things out. Or else they'd probably be getting a divorce.

Maybe that was why I clung to my fantasies of a love affair with Jean-Claude, because it kept me from thinking about the bleak prospect I might be facing back at home. Why I fell head over heels for Baron Armand de Merignac's handsome, dark-haired, wealthy son, even though I knew he had a reputation as a playboy, an outrageous flirt, and a heartbreaker. If only he'd wait a few years until I got a little older, I could change him and he'd settle down.

The de Merignacs were one of the best-known families in the French winemaking world; they had owned their ivy-covered château in Bordeaux as far back as the reign of one or another Louis—the thirteenth or fourteenth, I could never remember—and their wine was on a par with such famously expensive *premier cru* vintages as Haut-Brion, Lafite Rothschild, d'Yquem, and Pétrus. Jean-Claude's father was the tenth-wealthiest man in France, having also built an empire in the media world, as the owner of a successful Formula One race car team, and, most recently, as the new owner of The Flying Squirrel, the hottest cult vineyard in the Napa Valley.

Quinn didn't know anything about my adolescent school-girl crush the night Toby introduced Jean-Claude, but it hadn't taken him long to figure it out. For one thing, Eli—who was also at the party—told him.

"She was totally goo-goo-eyed for him," he said. "You should have seen her. I practically had to drag her to the airport to get on the plane for Washington when it was time to go home." Finally when Quinn wasn't looking I punched my brother lightly in the arm and told him under my breath to knock it off.

It hadn't helped, either, that Jean-Claude noticed me right away and once he realized who I was, his eyes had followed me all evening. To my surprise, he was just as devastatingly handsome as I remembered from nearly twenty years ago. Older, of course, and more rugged-looking, some gray at the temples, but it suited him. And still single, though over the years I'd heard through members of the family in France that there had been affairs, lots of them. Also a scandal—I didn't know what—that had been kept under wraps, the story being that Armand de Merignac had bought off the right people in return for agreeing to exile his son from Bordeaux for the foreseeable future.

"Lucie, *ma belle—mon amour*—you look absolutely stunning," he told me, his smile still dazzling as he handed me a glass of champagne. "You've changed since the last time I saw you. I hardly recognized you at first."

I could feel Quinn's eyes boring a hole through the two of us. "I hope so," I said, my cheeks turning pink. "I was thirteen. And I'm engaged now, you know." I held up my left hand with Quinn's grandmother's beautiful antique diamond engagement ring like a talisman warding off his fatal charm and attraction. "Let me introduce you to my fiancé."

The meeting between Quinn and Jean-Claude had gone about as well as I could expect, especially since everyone already had a few drinks. The two of them shook hands, sizing each other up.

"I hope you appreciate what you've got," Jean-Claude told Quinn. "Lucie is a precious and beautiful hothouse flower. I had my eye on her for a long time. I knew she would grow up to be a beauty."

Which was a load of crap, though he winked at me as though we had a conspiratorial secret, some passionate tryst in the long-distant past. And I let *hothouse flower* go, as if I were some delicate creature that needed pampering. He really didn't know me at all.

"Believe me, I know just how lucky I am," Quinn said in a smooth don't-mess-with-me-or-her voice. "And I know exactly what I've got." He kept emphasizing the word *I*.

After Jean-Claude had moved on, Quinn said in my ear, "What in the hell is he doing *here*? Why isn't he out in Napa at The Flying Squirrel? Something doesn't add up. La Vigne, a new vineyard with only thirty acres under cultivation, isn't his kind of place. I wonder what the real story is."

"Toby knew Jean-Claude and his father when he was the U.S. consul in Bordeaux, long before he became ambassador to France," I said. "Robyn told me just now. Apparently he and the de Merignacs have been friends for ages. Maybe Jean-Claude is doing this as a favor, sticking around for a year or two until he gets La Vigne going in the direction Toby wants. Toby's been saying he wants to make world-class wines."

"Don't we all," Quinn said with an edge in his voice that almost sounded like jealousy.

Later that night, Jean-Claude did a good job of answering Quinn's question himself, saying all the right things about why he had come to Virginia, and specifically to La Vigne Cellars. Besides his family's friendship with Secretary Levine, he saw Virginia as a challenge, a place where he was excited to put his stamp on relatively unknown New World wines using his Old World clout, expertise, and influence, which he was certain would make the international wine world take note of our *terroir*. He had joked that like Toby, another American ambassador to France in a different century—who had also been a friend and client of the de Merignac family—had believed in Virginia's potential, certain that we could make wine as good as anything produced in Europe. Not necessarily better, but doubtless as good. Of course everybody at the party knew he was talking about Thomas Jefferson and Toby had been surprised and flattered by the comparison.

But it soured Quinn on him even more. "So he's here to be the savior of the Virginia wine industry because the rest of us aren't up to it," he said. "Good luck with that."

From then on, there wasn't much love lost between the two of them, something Jean-Claude figured out immediately. So telling Quinn that I wanted to ask Jean-Claude if we could hire Miguel for a day to help with harvesting our Cabernet Franc had been like rubbing salt in a wound.

"Oh, come on." I tugged on Quinn's arm, pulling him so he turned over in bed and faced me again. "We could use the help, and Miguel and Antonio work really well together. The two of them get as much done as any four other workers we have. Can't you forget that you don't like Jean-Claude just this once?"

"He's a narcissist with an oversized ego. No."

"Quinn."

"What?"

"Look, you're not worried I still have a crush on him, are you? Come on, I was a kid."

"Of course not. But the guy is a notorious womanizer and you're a very beautiful woman. I wouldn't put anything past him."

I kissed him on the lips. "I love you and I promise you have nothing to worry about. I can handle Jean-Claude. Besides, from what I hear he has a girlfriend. I think he's seeing Nikki."

"Our Nikki?"

"Our Nikki."

"Isn't she a little young for him? She's . . . like twelve."

"She's twenty-two."

Nikki Young was our new events manager. She was young, blond, with a honeyed Southern drawl and pretty, perky cheerfulness: someone you figured could easily have been the head high school cheerleader or every child's favorite summer camp counselor. Customers loved her, especially her charming way of flirting with our older male customers, who adored her. From what I'd heard, she'd caught Jean-Claude's eye as well. To their credit, they were discreet, but it was obvious she was as crazy about him as I'd been all those years ago.

"And Jean-Claude's—what?" Quinn said. "Fifty-five? Old enough to be her grandfather."

"He's forty-five, not fifty-five."

"Old enough to be her father, then."

"They're both consenting adults."

"Yeah, well, I hope she doesn't think she's the only consenting adult he's sleeping with."

"No one said anything about Nikki sleeping with him." I sat up in bed and ran my hands through my hair. "Jesus, Quinn. How did we end up having this conversation? How do you know any of this? What are you talking about?"

He pulled me down next to him and cradled me in his arms. "Gossip," he said in my ear. "Forget I mentioned it."

"Tell me."

"Aw, sweetheart, I shouldn't have said anything."

"Well, you did," I said, now thoroughly wide-awake. "Dammit, he hasn't changed a bit. Still breaking the heart of every woman who falls in love with him. Including Domi- nique. She was seeing him the summer Eli and I stayed in France. By the way, don't bring that up with her. Ever. Jean- Claude dumped her for someone else and never told her. She found out when she saw them together at the Bastille Day fire- works. She was devastated."

"That's cruel. I hope he doesn't hurt Nikki. She's just a kid."

"Are you going to tell me who else he's sleeping with?"

"I don't know if there's anything to it," he said. "I over- heard some talk the other night in the bar at the Goose Creek Inn."

"And?"

I could feel him shrug. "It's Robyn."

"*Robyn Callahan*? Are you serious?"

"'Fraid so."

"She would never do that to Toby. No. No way. She and Toby have been together for ages and she's crazy about him. You can tell. He's crazy about her, too. Those two really love each other."

"Remember when he went up to New York for that Council on Foreign Relations meeting and dinner with the secretary-general of the UN and she stayed here because she was trying to finish a painting someone commissioned?"

"Oh, come on." I paused. "Good God. Was it just that once?"

"I don't know. They aren't putting out a newsletter."

"Very funny. Actually, it's not funny at all. I hope Toby never finds out. If it's true, it's awful."

"I told you the night I met him at Toby and Robyn's party that he didn't belong here. For a lot of reasons. I've done some checking into his background, asked some old friends out in Napa and a contact in Bordeaux. Jean-Claude's not a very nice guy, Lucie."

"What do you mean?"

"His father has been paying people off for years to clean up after his son and keep the family name unsullied. I don't think he came to La Vigne because he wanted to. I think he's run out of places where he hasn't pissed people off or screwed with them."

He rolled onto his back and we both stared at the ceiling.

I hoped Quinn wasn't right. But he wouldn't say things he wasn't certain were true, regardless of how he felt about Jean-Claude.

"The best thing he could do is leave," Quinn said. "Before anyone gets really hurt."

A moment later I heard his breathing, soft and regular, and I knew he'd fallen asleep. Leaving me alone with my own dark and disturbed thoughts.

Four

The house landline rang the next morning precisely at seven-thirty while Quinn and I were downstairs in the kitchen fixing breakfast. I reached for the phone as Quinn shoveled a small mountain of coffee into a filter. It would taste like rocket fuel—or paint stripper—as it always did, although he swore he'd started making it less strong for me. The telephone display showed Detective Bobby Noland's private work number.

Bobby and I go back a long way; we grew up together. My earliest memories of Bobby are of him and Eli deciding I needed to be the Union prisoner they captured and locked up in the burned-out old tenant house we now call the Ruins and use for concerts and plays. I was five, they were seven, and the tenant house was dark and damp and scary. The two of them got to be Confederate soldiers who were part of the Partisan Rangers, the rebel militia group that rode with Colonel John Singleton Mosby, otherwise known as the Gray Ghost. As soon as

Bobby and Eli took off on their bikes searching for more Yankees, I shimmied out a window and ran home.

Later Bobby went down a different road, barely scraping by
in high school and then enlisting and going off to fight in
Afghanistan. By the time he came home a few years later, he'd
changed. He didn't want to talk about his Silver Star, nor the
Purple Heart he'd been awarded. Instead, he joined the Loudoun County Sheriff's Office as a beat cop, surprising a lot of
folks who'd known him before and figured him for being involved with the law—except on the wrong side of the jail cell
bars. It wasn't long before Bobby made detective; last year he
married Kit Eastman, my best friend and the Loudoun County
bureau chief for the *Washington Tribune*.

It wasn't like Bobby to phone at this hour even though he
knew Quinn and I were early risers. But there could be only one
reason for a call just now: it had something to do with the skull
out by the cemetery.

"'Morning, Lucie," he said. "Hope I'm not waking you up
too early."

"No, not at all." I stifled a yawn. I'd finally fallen asleep last
night but not until after I'd heard the grandfather clock downstairs in the foyer chime two and then three. "What's up,
Bobby?"

"I've got good news and bad news about the human remains you found out on your property yesterday," he said. "I
heard from Win Turnbull, the M.E. who caught the case, a few
minutes ago."

Another early bird. "I see. What's the good news?"

"He's pretty sure those bones are so old this is no longer a
criminal investigation that would involve us."

"How old does he think they are?"

"He doesn't know. He says that kind of investigative research is out of his depth. If we want to know anything more he suggests bringing in a forensic anthropologist."

"I see," I said again. Win had mentioned that yesterday. I had a feeling I knew what Bobby's bad news was. "You don't want to do that, do you?"

"Look, Lucie, we've been taking some real hits on our budget this year. Do more with less but don't pay anyone overtime," he said. "I'm sorry but we can't swing the expense of outside expertise on this case. Especially if it's not something the Sheriff's Office can justify investigating because it's too old."

"Right."

"However, there is another possibility." His voice perked up as though he'd just thought of a new idea.

"Are we talking good news or bad news?"

He hesitated. "It depends."

"On what?"

"On whether you would be willing to pay the expense yourself of a forensic anthropologist examining those bones," he said. "Doc Turnbull says he can find someone first-rate. He's got a friend from Iraq who now works for the Natural History Museum at the Smithsonian and owes him a favor. He offered to ask this guy if he'd be willing to come out and take a look at that skull."

Quinn indicated the coffeepot, which had burbled until it was half-full, and held up an empty mug. I nodded and he fixed my coffee, adding milk and sugar, and set it in front of me. It tasted like burned tar. I blew him a kiss and mouthed, *"Thanks."*

"So what do you think?" Bobby asked.

There was no way I wasn't going to do whatever it took to find out more information about the young woman who'd been dumped outside our cemetery, including her identity, and Bobby knew it. I wondered if he'd gambled that I'd agree to pick up the tab and he'd get the answers he needed without denting his budget.

I let out a long breath and made sure he heard it. "Sure. I'll do it. I'll call Win Turnbull today."

"Actually," he said in that same chipper tone of voice, "I figured you'd be good to go, so I already told Doc Turnbull to reach out to his Smithsonian buddy. He said to tell you he'll call you after he hears from him."

Understanding what makes people tick, how they're going to react, and what they will do is part of Bobby's job. It still doesn't mean that, as my friend, he can't be annoying at times by presuming things and taking liberties.

"Maybe his Smithsonian friend should just call you and you can let me know what you both decide."

Bobby's chuckle sounded self-conscious. "Didn't mean to overstep. I'm just trying to help you out here."

I got it then. "Along with the Loudoun County Sheriff's Office as well, right? You want to know what this guy finds out, don't you?"

He sighed. "I'm sorry, Lucie. But I'd really appreciate it. Damn budget cuts. If it gets any worse we'll be buying our own ammunition and bringing our own soap and toilet paper for the bathrooms."

Or asking Loudoun County residents to pay for their own

investigations. He hung up, sounding disgusted, before I could commiserate or say thanks.

So the skull was old. Not too far down the road from us off Route 15 was the small Civil War cemetery commemorating the Battle of Ball's Bluff in Leesburg. Though there were only twenty-five headstones in that little graveyard, which sat in the middle of the former battlefield, there were, in fact, fifty-four Union Army soldiers buried there—or parts of them. According to local legend, at night you could see lights, which were the ghosts of soldiers looking for the rest of their bones so they could have a proper burial. The story had enough truth to it that even deputies from the Sheriff's Office didn't like patrolling the park after dark.

Now that we had uncovered new remains at Montgomery Estate Vineyard, I wondered if this woman would haunt us until we found out who she was and why she was buried outside the cemetery.

It had been less than a day since we discovered her, and though I didn't want to admit it, she was already starting to haunt me.

I DIDN'T TELEPHONE JEAN-CLAUDE de Merignac to ask him about hiring Miguel on Saturday until later that morning when I was by myself. It was already turning into one of those spectacular late summer–early autumn days when the cloudless sky was the kind of brilliant, lacquered shade of blue that hurt your eyes to look at it and the rows of lush grapevines, lit by slanted sunshine, looked pristine and perfect.

I left Quinn and Antonio in the barrel room cleaning the fermentation bins we would need for the Cab Franc while the juice sat on the skins for a few days before we put it in stainless steel tanks. One of them had turned on music that was blasting through the sound system—Journey, with their anthem-like songs and pulsing beat—and the pair of them were belting out the words, loud and off-key, while they worked.

I caught Quinn's eye, held up my phone, and pointed to the door. He nodded and I left for the courtyard, which was far more peaceful and quiet, except for the fading metallic chirping of the cicadas. This late in the summer—only a week before the first official day of autumn—the halved wine barrels we used as planters and the baskets hanging from the colonnade that ringed one side of the courtyard were spilling over with geraniums, fuchsia, impatiens, and ivy. What had started out in spring as a carefully designed color palette chosen by Francesca Merchant, who ran the commercial side of the winery, was now a rioting end-of-summer jumble of tangled flowers and greenery. In a few weeks everything would be gone, replaced by Frankie with pansies in the muted harvest colors of gold, yellow, violet, and rust for autumn and winter.

Truth be told, I was glad Quinn wasn't around to overhear my phone call. What he'd said last night about Jean-Claude—wishing he'd leave Atoka and hinting at a dark past, so troubling that Armand de Merignac was forced to pay someone off, plus exile his son from Bordeaux—had kept me awake for hours. I was over my schoolgirl crush, but our pasts were twined together through family friendships that went back generations. I wondered what had happened, what he had done that was so awful—and whether it was true, as Quinn said, that

Jean-Claude came to La Vigne, not because he was such a gifted winemaker, but because no other doors were open to him anymore.

Jean-Claude answered his phone on the second ring. "Lucie, *mon amour. Comment vas-tu?*"

"*Bien, merci.* How are you?"

"Oh, *ça va, ça va.* You know how it is."

"I hope everything is okay?"

He sidestepped the implied question. "It's good to hear your voice, *chérie.* I haven't seen much of you since I arrived."

"Maybe we can catch up after harvest is finished and things slow down," I said. "And speaking of harvest, I have a favor to ask."

"Ah, and I hoped you were calling just to ask about me." He feigned disappointment and then added, "For you, *ma belle,* anything."

"Could you spare Miguel on Saturday? We're planning to pick our Cab Franc and we're short of help. We'd like to hire him for the day. He really knows what he's doing and we could use someone with his experience. Quinn and I are worried Hurricane Lolita might arrive early Sunday so we want to get everything picked in a day."

"Saturday? Isn't that too early? Are all your grapes ripe? I thought you had problems with millerandage."

Millerandage meant the grapes were ripening unevenly. I wondered how he'd found out about that, although Cab Franc is notorious for millerandage. You can have green pellets next to gorgeous, luscious red grapes and then a few rows away, nothing is ripe or everything is ripe. If unskilled pickers are in the fields at harvest, they pick indiscriminately, which means we have to spend extra time at the sorting table making sure the bitter green grapes are eliminated.

"We do have some trouble with it," I said. "But with all the horror stories about the damage Lolita has done we figure we'd better get the grapes in now. And it's hard to get enough good pickers these days, you know that. We need to get a crew lined up now."

"Miguel is all yours if you can get him to work for you," he said. "Though I'm not as impressed with him as you are."

"Why not?"

"I don't think he's competent. I've come across sloppy mistakes and equipment not properly cleaned or put away. I know it's his fault. He's careless. In fact, last week I told Toby I wanted to let him go. I would have dismissed him, but Toby told me to give him another chance."

"I didn't know about this."

"Robyn wanted him to stay," he said. "She pushed Toby into telling me we needed Miguel. I think it was because his wife is expecting a baby in a few weeks."

"That's right. Isabella. She's Antonio's fiancée's sister."

"In France we wouldn't keep someone like him."

"Oh, come on," I said. "It's a different world in France. Plenty of French vineyards advertise for volunteers during the vendage, you know that. You'll take anybody who'll pick for free in return for room and board and the opportunity to drink as much fresh grape juice or free wine as they like. No previous experience required."

It was true: a lot of small vineyards and even some of the larger ones counted on temporary volunteer labor during the intense few weeks of harvest that was so important to the French economy. In fact, it had become something of an international tourist attraction, appealing to those who conjured an idyllic, carefree romp among the vines or had watched too many reruns of the grape-stomping episode of *I Love Lucy,* or seen *Bottle Shock* or *Sideways.* The reality was that it was hard, backbreaking, physically intense work.

"We don't just take anybody off the street. You know better, or at least you should since your mother's family still owns a vineyard in France." He sounded irked, irritated that I had contradicted him. I'd forgotten how he always had to have the last word. Always had to be right.

"It's a different world in America. In Virginia," I said, ignoring his pique and hoping that would be the end of the discussion.

"I'm surprised you tolerate it," he said, and before I could challenge him, he added, "By the way, I heard someone found a body on your land yesterday."

So the word had gotten out. "It's a skull, not a body. And how do you know about it?"

"I have my spies."

I put two and two together. Or one and one—Antonio must have told Miguel.

"Do you have any idea who she is?" he asked.

He also knew it was a woman. "No, but she's been there a long time."

"Found near your cemetery," he said. "Not far from where your mother is buried, *n'est-ce pas?*"

"Yes." After so many years I could finally talk about my mother without getting emotional or teary, but Jean-Claude caught me off-guard and my voice tightened. I'd almost forgotten he had known her all those years ago when he was younger and she was still living in France before she married Leland.

"What I remember most was how beautiful she was," he said, and his voice suddenly grew soft with memory, his prickliness disappearing. "You're the portrait of her, Lucie. When I saw you that night at Toby and Robyn's party, it was as if I were seeing Chantal again."

Over the lump in my throat I said, "Thank you."

"She had time for everyone," he went on. "Time to listen to your problems or hear you out if you were in trouble."

A warning bell went off in my head. What kind of trouble had he confessed to my mother?

"Yes," I said, "she did."

"Lucie," he said. "I need to talk to someone. I need to talk to you."

"About what?"

He sounded . . . I couldn't tell. Worried? Upset? Uneasy?

"I'd rather not say over the phone. Something that's going on here. I'll tell you when I see you. What if I came by today? Could we meet somewhere private?"

"Yes. Sure. I mean, of course."

He'd gotten me completely flummoxed. Where was *here*? La Vigne? Atoka? And what was "going on"? Something his father would have to deal with? Again? Was he looking for a confidante in me the way my mother had been for him years ago?

"How about three o'clock?" he said.

"Sure. Three o'clock."

"Where could we meet?"

Somewhere private, he'd said. I'd need to figure out an excuse for slipping away from the winery this afternoon without explaining myself. I said the first thing that came into my head. "My family's cemetery. No one will be there. Do you know where it is?"

"I'll find it. *Très bien*. I'll see you at three."

He disconnected and I wondered what was so mysterious and secretive that he wouldn't tell me what it was over the phone.

Although I'd know soon enough. It was just going on noon.

JEAN-CLAUDE ARRIVED AT THE cemetery at three o'clock sharp, driving a white pickup truck with the La Vigne Cellars logo stenciled on the side. I was waiting for him, having arrived early so I could sit on the low redbrick wall facing Sycamore Lane and watch him pull up. Still wondering what this meeting was really about.

He gave me a surprisingly cheery wave as he got out of the truck. He wore faded, stained jeans and a T-shirt with *Festival des Vins du Kefraya* printed on it in French and Arabic. The T-shirt was just tight enough to show off how fit he was, which was something I didn't need to be thinking about or noticing. He was also carrying a bouquet of pale pink roses. A peace offering? Maybe he'd figured out after all that he'd broken my thirteen-year-old heart in pieces, and that he had been my first love, even though I'd never said a word about it.

Earlier I told Quinn I wanted to stop by the cemetery and check on things, but left out mentioning that I was meeting

Jean-Claude. Now I felt vaguely guilty, as if I were doing something wrong or shameful. Maybe this hadn't been such a good idea after all.

"You came," I said as he reached me and leaned in, kissing me on both cheeks. He smelled of alcohol, cigarettes, and sweat. The remark sounded lame, but being alone with him suddenly made me ill at ease.

"I did." He laid the flowers on the wall and slid his arms around my waist. "Let me help you down."

I placed my hands on his chest and gently pushed him away. "You don't need to do that. I can manage fine on my own, thanks."

He dropped his arms instantly. "Sorry."

"It's okay. I just . . . like to do things for myself." I slid down from the wall and reached for my cane.

His eyes traveled to the cane. We had never discussed my accident, but I was sure he knew the story from someone in the family. He picked up the bouquet of flowers.

"I brought these for your mother's grave," he said.

The flowers were for my mother, not me. I should have realized after what he'd said on the phone earlier.

"She loved roses. Especially pink roses."

"I know," he said. "That's why I brought them."

He opened the wrought-iron cemetery gate and held it for me. The yellow crime scene tape that Biggie Mathis had put around the tarp covering what was left of the shed fluttered in the breeze like streamers at a parade, just visible on the other side of the wall now that most of the tulip poplar was gone.

"What a good memory you have," I said.

"Chantal was a truly good person, like an older sister to me.

Always saw the best in people." He gave me a rueful smile. "Even me, when I didn't deserve it."

Which was why she had stuck by my father through the gambling and drinking and the other women. A saint, my mother. Or maybe a martyr. I don't know if I could have done what she did—*for better or worse, richer or poorer*—and right now I didn't want to be thinking about that or any of the past, especially if it included my parents' marriage or the Jean-Claude I remembered from nearly twenty years ago.

As if he guessed my uneasy thoughts, he pointed to the yellow tape, changing the subject. "So that's where they found the skull?"

"Yes."

"It's all covered up."

"To protect it against that storm last night," I said. "Now we're waiting for a forensic anthropologist to come and finish the excavation."

"Any idea who it is?"

"No. Not yet."

"Do you mind if I have a look around your cemetery?"

"Of course not."

I hitched myself back up on the wall and watched him make a pilgrimage through the cemetery, pausing at each headstone until he found my mother's. He went down on one knee, laid the flowers next to her grave, blessed himself, and bowed his head.

Afterward he joined me on the wall. "I know it probably sounds strange, but I like visiting cemeteries and reading what is written on gravestones," he said. "Especially the old ones. It's sort of a hobby. Reading the epitaph chosen by someone who mourned for a person, someone who loved them. Sometimes you find the most beautiful poetry."

I said, surprised, "I know. I do it, too."

"You must miss your mother."

"Every day."

He moved closer and I edged away. He gave me a sidelong look.

"Do you want to talk about what's bothering you?" I asked.

A red-shouldered hawk swooped down out of nowhere and dove for something on the ground just outside the cemetery wall—a mouse or a chipmunk. Jean-Claude and I watched it rise into the air, prey dangling from its beak, as it spread its wings and headed for the woods.

After it disappeared he said in a low voice, "I need to be able to trust you about this."

There was no one here, unless you counted the occupants of the cemetery. This aura of mystery, his secrecy, our off-the-radar meeting, and now these dropped hints felt as if he were piling on the melodrama.

I said, letting my annoyance show, "It seems to me you've already made up your mind that you can, or you wouldn't be sitting here now after telling me on the phone that you wanted to meet me in private to talk about this . . . whatever *this* is."

His smile was pained. "Fair enough."

I waited.

"I know this is going to sound *un peu fou* . . . a little crazy . . . but I promise—no, I *swear*—this is true and not something I'm imagining."

"Jean-Claude, just *tell* me."

"All right," he said. "I will. Someone is trying to kill me."

Five

stared at him, half-waiting for his face to crease into a grin. *Gotcha*.

"You're serious," I said. "Someone really wants to kill you."

"*Je ne plaisante pas*. I'm not joking, Lucie."

"I don't understand. Why? Who?"

"If I knew who it was, believe me, I would do something about it."

I believed him. I also knew he wouldn't call in the law once he knew who he was dealing with. He'd handle it himself.

But he had only answered one of my questions: who. He avoided explaining why and I had the uneasy feeling he deliberately chose not to tell me.

"What makes you think someone wants you dead?" I said.

"I don't think, I *know*." He smacked his fist into the palm of the other hand.

If he was trying to scare or intimidate me, I wasn't going to give him the satisfaction. I said in my blandest voice, "Okay, how do you know?"

He stared at the horizon and the sun-dappled mountains, a brooding, moody look on his deeply tanned face. "Because of things that have been happening at the vineyard. They're meant to look like accidents, but they're not."

"Such as?"

"Such as someone closed the roll-down door to the refrigerator room while I was in there last week and locked it. I pounded on the door until, thank God, Toby opened it. He happened to come by the barrel room to ask me about something and heard the noise. Otherwise God knows how long I would have been in there. The day before yesterday, I put my hand on a counter when I was cleaning around the stainless steel tanks with the power washer. I didn't see that the power cord had a small hole in it, so the bare wire was exposed." He shrugged. "The counter was wet."

"Oh my God."

"The electrical jolt threw me halfway across the room. I could have been killed."

He wasn't kidding. Wineries use a three-phase electrical power supply system, similar to what electrical grids all over the world use because they're so powerful. Being electrocuted by accidentally coming in contact with one of those live wires—especially if water was involved—happened more often than we care to admit in our business.

"Weren't you wearing work boots? Something that could at least have grounded you a little?"

He shook his head. "An old pair of leather sandals."

"That's crazy. You should know better."

"I wasn't expecting the cord to have been tampered with."

"Maybe it was just old and frayed. Why would someone deliberately put a hole in it? And how could they possibly know that you'd be the next person to use the power washer?"

Plenty of accidents happened at vineyards. It was a lot more dangerous—hazardous—than many people realized. We worked around chemicals, pesticides, and heavy machinery. Both of the incidents he described could have been unintentional, the latter the result of equipment that hadn't been well-maintained. He was new to La Vigne Cellars, just learning his way around, so he wouldn't know his equipment as well as Quinn or I knew ours. So what happened could be ruled as careless, definitely. But deliberate?

He gave me a cold stare. "I don't know. But that's not all. I keep finding equipment that's damaged or a part is missing from something. The other day I couldn't get the shaft of the sprayer to work and there was a broken bearing on the wine press. It's more than bad luck. I think someone is sabotaging the equipment. Making it look as if I'm incompetent or careless."

"That's a serious accusation."

"It is. It also happens to be true."

"Who would do something like that?"

"Who do you think?"

"Oh, come on. Not Miguel."

He nodded and pointed a finger at me like he was cocking the trigger of a gun. "Exactly."

My eyes wandered over the graves of my ancestors. For a crazy moment I wished I could ask them if we could discuss this matter among ourselves—just the Montgomery family—maybe take a poll. Believe him? Don't believe him? Was this setting—my family's cemetery—coloring Jean-Claude's accusations so they seemed more sinister? Would I feel as spooked and uneasy if he and I were sitting in a well-lighted Starbucks sipping lattes?

The crime scene tape around the storage shed fluttered again in a sudden gust of wind. Jean-Claude's bouquet of pink roses stood out as a pretty splash of color among the somber greenery and granite headstones of the cemetery. Yesterday Jesús said finding the skull was bad luck and meant there would be another death. Today in almost exactly the same spot, Jean-Claude was insisting someone wanted to kill him.

I tried to make sense out of what he was saying. "So because you wanted to fire Miguel, now he's tampering with equipment and trying to get you killed. Except it's supposed to look like an accident. Is that what you believe?"

"I can't prove it—yet. But it makes sense, don't you think?"

I didn't. What I knew about Miguel Otero, mostly from Antonio, was that he was anything but mean-spirited or vindictive. He was a genuinely good person who appreciated the opportunities he'd received since coming to America, worked hard at learning English, and went out of his way to help other immigrants who were down on their luck—needing a place to stay for a few nights or a couple of dollars for food. He was also proud of the fact that he was studying for his U.S. citizenship test, which he planned to take the week after Antonio and Valeria's wedding. Plus soon he would be a new father. There was no way he would jeopardize his status in the United States, throw away everything he'd worked so hard for by doing something that could get him arrested and thrown in jail. That is, if he wasn't deported first.

"What's really going on, Jean-Claude? There's something you're not telling me."

"And what would that be?" he asked in a cutting voice. "Do you think I am inventing this? Why would I do that?"

Well, as they say, just because you're paranoid doesn't mean they aren't out to get you. I didn't think he was inventing anything that he said had happened. But something must have tripped a switch to persuade him these incidents were all murder attempts disguised as careless accidents—and not the other way around.

"I think you might be making too much out of coincidences and unfortunate accidents. I also think you're wrong to pin this on Miguel, who is a good, decent man."

"Is that so? Tell me, then, who else could it be?"

Maybe no one.

"Why don't you tell me? I've heard rumors . . . they're even going around here, in Atoka . . . that you've got skeletons in your closet. Things you don't ever talk about." I said it in a deliberate way so he couldn't mistake the gauntlet I'd just thrown down. *Something to do with your past. Something your father had to cover up.*

His eyes flashed with anger and he looked at me with contempt. "*Quel dommage,* Lucie. What a pity. I was foolish enough to hope—actually I expected—that you'd believe me, trust me. Our families go back a long way, *ma belle.* You know the de Merignacs, who we are in France. You know me."

He *expected* my unquestioning loyalty and trust. I hate being backed into a corner or bullied.

"I don't know you," I told him. "Not really."

He cocked an eyebrow and gave me a pitying smile. "Oh, come on. Don't think I didn't know you were in love with me that summer when you and your brother came to visit. You were so obvious, *chérie*. Everyone knew it; we were all talking about it. The way you followed me around. Tried to be wherever you thought I would be."

My face turned scarlet. So he had known. And apparently he assumed I still carried a torch for him, that I was still that thirteen-year-old lovestruck girl. Even though it happened nearly twenty years ago, it stung that he would taunt me in such an unkind way, try to strip away my shell and prod me, looking for my vulnerable heart.

"What I know about you," I said, my own anger flashing, "is that you can't go back to France because of something that happened there. So that's part of the reason you've come to Virginia. I don't know what you're running away from, or who, but I do know you've gotten yourself into some serious trouble, something that's still following you, if even half the stories I've heard are true."

He slid off the wall and I instantly regretted letting him bait me. He leaned forward until his face was inches from mine. It was as if I had poked a sleeping rattlesnake.

"You have no idea what you're talking about, what happened in France. So you'd better keep quiet about what you think you know or you'll regret it. My family is powerful, Lucie, especially in the wine business. The de Merignacs could destroy your vineyard and your reputation if we chose to. We could destroy your family's vineyard in France as well and tie

HARVEST OF SECRETS   61

it to you. It was a mistake to tell you any of this. I'm sorry I confided in you."

The threat sounded potent and menacing. *We will destroy you*. How far would his father go to protect his son? I probably didn't want to find out.

I swallowed hard and lifted my chin, still defiant. "I'm sorry you did, too."

He started to turn away. "One more thing," he said, swinging around again. "Get some help with this vineyard. Someone who knows what they're doing. Your winemaker isn't up to the job and with that . . ." He pointed to my cane. "Neither are you."

He had no *right* . . . "Go to hell, Jean-Claude."

He slammed the gate, as I knew he would. The clanging noise reverberated through the old brick so the wall seemed to shudder. I watched him leave, my anger boiling over again.

He really could just go to hell. Frankly I didn't blame anyone at La Vigne who wanted to get rid of him.

Right now I could have killed him myself and felt like I'd done everyone a favor.

BY THE TIME I drove the ATV back to the parking lot, Jean-Claude was long gone. My anger, however, was not, still stoked white-hot. I needed to calm down before I faced Quinn or anyone else and had to explain myself. Why had I let Jean-Claude get to me? Why had he confided in me? To make sure he had a witness to corroborate his stories? Was somebody at La Vigne really trying to kill him? Miguel? Someone in Atoka?

Our little village was everyone's quintessential image of small-town America, as wholesome as *Mister Rogers' Neighborhood* and as all-American as *Happy Days*. Out here time rewinds; we're still old-fashioned in our ways when it comes to small courtesies, simple pleasures, and long-standing traditions. Which is why on weekends Atoka and the nearby village of Middleburg bustle with tourists and folks from Washington, D.C., who drive out here in hopes of rekindling their sepia-tinted memories of a time and place when life was sweeter and more innocent. They find it, too, on our quiet country lanes lined by Civil War–era stacked-stone walls, rolling hills of pastures and farmland, and streets in town named for the signers of the Declaration of Independence who were all friends of the man who founded Middleburg in 1767.

My phone rang while I was still in the parking lot. I had been halfway through composing a text asking Antonio if he'd ask Miguel about working for us on Saturday. The telephone display read *Merchant, Francesca* and I hit the green button.

"Frankie, what's up?"

"Lucie." She sounded distracted. "Can you drop by when you get a chance? I need to talk to you about something that's come up. It has to do with the wedding."

Antonio and Valeria's wedding had started out as a simple affair, but somehow it had ballooned into something that wasn't quite on the planning scale of a royal marriage, but there were days when it certainly seemed like it.

"Sure," I said. "Be right there."

There were no guests in the tasting room when I showed up a moment later, only Frankie and Nikki Young sitting together on one of the leather sofas next to the enormous stone fireplace we used when the weather got cold. They were hunched over a laptop that sat on the heavy oak coffee table, frowning at the display. When I closed the front door the two of them looked up, apparently startled to see me.

"That was fast," Frankie said.

"I told you I'd be right there. I was in the parking lot when you called."

She looked puzzled. "I thought you were somewhere else. I saw a truck from La Vigne speeding down Sycamore Lane as I was pulling into our entrance about fifteen minutes ago. Jean-Claude de Merignac was driving like he was behind the wheel of one of his family's Formula One racecars. He must have been doing fifty. Blew right past the fifteen-miles-per-hour sign, too."

My cheeks turned pink. So much for our private meeting.

"He offered to take a look at the millerandage in the Cab Franc block," I said in my blandest voice. "And he needed to get right back to La Vigne."

Nikki stared at me and I knew she realized I'd just lied. Our eyes met and mine skidded away, but not before I saw the confused, hurt look on her face. Had she heard the rumors about Robyn and Jean-Claude? And now maybe she thought that he and I were—?

Good God.

". . . got a final price from the florist," Frankie was saying. "We're not decorating the White House. It's just a simple wedding."

"Pardon?"

"The florist. I'm talking about the wedding florist and the proposal she just sent. Come take a look at this," Frankie said. "See for yourself."

I went over and sat down across from them. Frankie spun the laptop around so I could see what they had been looking at. Nikki, still silent, watched me, her hands clasped tightly in her lap.

The revised florist's bill was nearly double the original estimate. I closed my eyes, trying to do mental math to figure out just how much this wedding was going to cost. So far.

"The guest list has already crept up to a hundred and twenty-five people," I said, "so the catering bill has gone up. Dominique is going to cut me a break so she makes no profit, but it's still going to be pricey. At least we're providing the wine."

Nikki spoke up. "I'd be happy to do the flowers. I wouldn't charge y'all anything, except the cost of buying what I need. It could be my wedding gift to Antonio and Valeria and, besides, I'd love the experience. There's a flower farm out in Culpeper where you can cut everything you need and it's really inexpensive. A lot of late-summer flowers are still in bloom and the autumn flowers should be starting soon as well." She rattled off a few varieties in her honeyed drawl, ticking them off on her fingers, and it was clear she knew what she was talking about. "I'm sure I can come up with arrangements in Valeria's colors that won't be too expensive."

Valeria's colors were vibrant: red, orange, and yellow. No white anywhere. Even her wedding dress was flame-colored and reminded me of a flamenco dancer's costume.

Frankie gave her a thoughtful look. "You've done some

gorgeous arrangements for the villa," she said. "Are you sure you could handle a whole wedding, though? On your own?"

"Yes, ma'am. Just give me a couple of days off work so I have enough time, but I'd love to do it."

"What do you think, Lucie?" Frankie asked me.

"I think it's a very generous offer. Thanks, Nikki. I'm sure the flowers will be beautiful."

She gave me a small smile, but her eyes were still clouded. "My momma owns a flower shop back home. I used to help her out a lot."

"Well, that problem is solved." Frankie snapped the laptop shut with a brisk click. "Now the only thing left to do is tell the florist we've reconsidered. I'll take care of that."

Nikki stood. "If you don't mind I'll call the cutting farm right now since they're probably closing soon and get a list of what they've got at this time of year. Then I can start putting together some ideas for arrangements."

"Of course," I said. "Take all the time you need."

"Thanks, Lucie. If y'all will excuse me?"

After she left the room Frankie said, "Oh, dear, I shouldn't have put my foot in my mouth about Jean-Claude being here, even if it was just to talk about the grapes. I'm fairly sure he and Nikki split up recently and she's taking it hard. Not that she's letting on that they're no longer seeing each other, of course. I suspect she's hoping whatever happened will blow over."

"I didn't know they split up. She didn't confide in you, tell you anything about it?" I asked.

Frankie had hired Nikki, who was the daughter of a good friend. She had moved to D.C. straight out of college with the intention of finding a job working for a nonprofit and doing her part to save the world. Six months later she was out of money and took the position Frankie offered her as our event planner. She still wanted to save the world, but it would have to wait.

Frankie ran the tasting room and supervised all the events at the winery with the efficiency and strategic planning of a complex military campaign. Delegating didn't come naturally to Superwoman, so I had been pleasantly surprised to see the way she let Nikki handle our event schedule without micromanaging every decision she made. But Frankie also fussed over Nikki as if she were her own daughter. They even looked as if they were related: the same strawberry-blond hair and cornflower-blue eyes. The same open, easygoing manner and warm smile that made the clients feel at ease. Someone to whom you could unload your problems and get compassion and understanding in return. Frankie often joked that she heard more confessions than the priests at St. Michael the Archangel Catholic Church when she was working behind the bar.

"Nikki didn't even tell me Jean-Claude was her new boyfriend when they first started going out," Frankie said. "I think she was worried I'd say something about their age difference. Of course I guessed right away, the way she'd light up every time he dropped by or if someone mentioned his name. You'd have to be blind not to notice. But, honestly, he's old enough to be her father."

"That's what Quinn said. Do you know why they split up? Or who broke it off?"

"He did. Definitely. She's been moping around for the past week like she lost her last friend on earth. And I suspect it was because he is too old for her. He certainly doesn't seem like the type to settle down. I wonder if he's ever been married."

"He hasn't."

"You've known him for years, haven't you?" she asked.

"Our families go way back in France."

I wasn't about to tell Frankie about my own unrequited crush on Jean-Claude. Or the rumors about him and Robyn. It didn't seem as if she knew and there was no point spreading gossip. Plus my latest encounter with Jean-Claude had ended badly, not even an hour ago. *Go to hell*. There were a lot of secrets to keep.

"Well, her heart will mend soon. She's young. And pretty. She'll meet someone else in no time." Frankie sounded confident that Nikki would bounce right back. She glanced over at the window. "Looks like you have a visitor, Lucie. Kit Noland is coming up the walk."

Kit Eastman Noland was Bobby's wife and my best friend since childhood. I'd known her longer than I'd known Bobby. Five years ago she moved home from Washington, D.C., to care for her mother who'd had a mild stroke. She'd left behind a good position as assistant foreign affairs editor in the newsroom of the *Washington Tribune,* managing to get a transfer to the *Trib*'s Loudoun County bureau, which she now ran. The move to Loudoun meant Kit had effectively given up any chance of being noticed for a promotion to an overseas correspondent's job or a senior editor's position. We weren't exactly a backwater out here, but the county was light-years away— in career-killing terms—from Washington. Kit never said a word about lost opportunities or having regrets. Now Faith

Eastman, who had been like a second mother to me after my own mother died, was in an assisted-living home about ten minutes from the vineyard. Kit had probably gone to visit Faith and was dropping by on her way home, as she often did.

The door flew open and Kit blew in, her usual tornado-style of whirling into a room. Her Marilyn Monroe—blond hair was piled into a bun on top of her head and she wore an electric-pink sleeveless minidress with chocolate-brown hand-worked cowboy boots. Her wardrobe was filled with what she called "statement outfits," clothes that made sure no one ever missed her when she raised her hand at a press conference. "I always get called on," she'd said. "I make sure of it."

She gave Frankie and me a breezy wave and said, " 'Evening, all. It's five o'clock somewhere." She paused midstep. "Sorry, am I interrupting a meeting? I was on my way back from seeing Mom at Foxhall Manor and thought I'd stop by . . . but if you're in the middle of something . . ."

"Not at all," Frankie said. "We were just finishing a pre-wedding triage session to fix something that came up. Come on in."

"Is this about Antonio and Valeria's wedding?" Kit asked. "I remember how you fussed over every detail of Bobby's and mine. It was perfect."

Frankie beamed. "Yes and thank you. We try."

"How's your mom doing?" I said. "I was planning to drop by to see her in the next few days and bring her a basket of apples from our orchard. Better yet, maybe I'll ask Persia to make her an apple pie."

"That would be great, Luce. You know how Mom loves Persia's pies."

Kit hadn't answered my question. "She's okay, right?"

"Oh, sure. She's fine. Just . . . fine."

The two of us could finish each other's sentences, practically read each other's thoughts. Faith Eastman wasn't fine.

"Liar, liar, pants on fire."

Kit gave me a worried look. "Maybe I'm imagining it, but lately she seems a little less . . . sharp than usual. A bit forgetful."

"Aren't we all?" Frankie said. "Everyone's doing too much, multitasking all the time. It's hard to keep all the plates spinning, you know? I forget the silliest things, like where my glasses are when they're on top of my head."

Kit's smile was tinged with sadness. "Yeah. Maybe."

"I'll visit her," I said. "I promise. Soon."

"That would be great. Let me know what you think about her, okay?"

"How about a glass of wine? What can I get you gals?" Frankie changed the subject in her best hearty cheer-you-up voice as she walked over to the bar. My artistic mother had designed it and it ran nearly the length of the room, an undulating, graceful S-shape with a stone countertop the color of earthy red-brown jasper and hammered copper trim. Embedded in the façade was a mosaic my mother had tiled herself: twining vines laden with bunches of red and green grapes, lush and full of leaves as if it were just before harvest. She had used brilliantly colored clear glass tiles in shades of red, green, yellow, and gold, and made sure the bar was located in such a way that when the sun streamed through the double French doors as it was doing right now, the light would catch the tiles so they would glow like lit gems.

"A glass of your Sauvignon Blanc for me, please," Kit said, joining Frankie.

"I'll have the same." I pulled out a bar stool and climbed up on it.

Frankie got a bottle of Montgomery Estate Vineyard Sauvignon Blanc out of the wine refrigerator and expertly opened it, pouring two chilled glasses. "Enjoy."

"Lucie? Frankie?" Nikki stood in the doorway between the tasting room and the corridor that led to the offices. "Oh, hi, Kit. I didn't know you were here."

"Hey, Nikki. I was in the neighborhood," Kit said, "so I dropped by."

"What's up?" I asked Nikki.

"I'd like to drive out to Culpeper to the cutting farm tomorrow morning if that's all right and see for myself what they've got. Okay by you?"

Kit looked puzzled so I said, "Nikki offered to do the flowers for Antonio and Valeria's wedding after we got an estimate from a florist in Leesburg that meant we'd practically have to put the vineyard in hoc to pay it off." To Nikki, I added, "Sure, go right ahead."

"Thanks." She disappeared.

Frankie put the bottle of wine back in the fridge. Then she went over and scooped up the laptop from the coffee table. "I'll leave you two to your happy-hour drink. I have to finish up a couple of things in my office."

For years Quinn and I had our offices here in the villa—I took over what had been my mother's office and he occupied the one next door that belonged to his predecessor—but when

Eli, who is an architect, drew up plans for expanding the winery and renovating the tasting room a few years ago, Quinn and I moved to a newly designed suite above the barrel room. Frankie inherited my office and the rest of the space was redesigned to add a larger kitchen and room for four new full-time employees, including Nikki, a bookkeeper, and two motherly women who handled all of our social media, publicity, and off-site sales.

"We'll be out on the terrace," I said.

"Then I'll see you in the morning. I'm taking off after I'm done," Frankie said.

"I'll lock up."

She left and Kit said, "I don't suppose you have anything to munch on, like peanuts or trail mix? I'm famished."

"I think that could be arranged."

"I'm doing the Paleo Diet and it's just not working."

The two of us used to run cross-country in high school. We were good—really good—and we had both been thin as proverbial rails who could eat anything and never gain an ounce. Kit quit running in college, throwing herself into working at the campus newspaper and all-nighter deadlines, and the weight had started to pile on. As for me, after the accident it had been a struggle just to learn to walk again. But I could still eat whatever I wanted with impunity. Eli, who also wrestled with his weight, accused me of having the metabolism of a hummingbird.

Kit and I pushed two deck chairs over to the patio railing and turned them so they faced the vineyard and the Blue Ridge Mountains in the distance. I shoved a small table between them for the bowl of trail mix and our wineglasses and we sat down. Kit propped her feet on the railing, crossing one leg over the other.

"Don't worry too much about your mom," I told her. "She's tough. She'll do fine."

"Thanks." She gave me a guilty look. "Actually, I didn't just happen to drop by."

"Somehow I'm not surprised. You want to know about that skull Antonio and Jesús unearthed for a story for the *Trib*."

"Bobby said it's so old there's no crime involved anymore. But once you find out something I'd absolutely like to know who it was. It is newsworthy."

"If it's not the skull, then . . . what?"

She pulled the bowl of trail mix onto her lap and helped herself to another handful. "I found this out late this afternoon. I wanted to give you a head's up."

I sat up as something zinged down my spine. Kit had started picking out the peanuts in the trail mix so she wasn't looking at me.

"About what?"

She quit her halfhearted search and looked up. "You can't say a word about where you heard this, okay?"

She waited until I said okay and crossed my heart with my finger like we used to do as kids. "One of our reporters happened to be at the Goose Creek Inn the other night having dinner. He was sitting at a table next to Jean-Claude de Merignac who was there with a friend. A woman. Apparently totally, utterly gorgeous. No idea who she was."

I already knew I didn't like where this was going. "And?"

"Well, it seems Jean-Claude complained so much about his meal that his waiter finally called in the big guns and Dominique showed up. The waiter hadn't realized who his guests were and when Dominique saw Jean-Claude, things got ugly."

Oh, brother. Dominique had managed to avoid Jean-Claude as much as possible ever since he moved to Atoka. For all I knew this might have been the first time they'd seen each other in years, after the stormy end to their relationship in France.

"Ugly?"

She sighed and nodded. "They had a pretty sharp exchange of words until your cousin finally told him dinner was on the house, but he had to leave right then and there and never return again."

I set my glass on the table and gave her a dismayed look. "You've got to be kidding. Dominique would never, ever do something like that . . . throw someone out."

Kit wagged an admonishing finger at me. "Oh, but she did. Our reporter wrote the whole conversation down without either of them realizing it. It's, um, going to be in 'Around Town' tomorrow . . . I'm sorry, Luce. I thought I should at least let you know what's coming. Jean-Claude and his friend, uh, were drinking a bottle of your Cabernet Sauvignon."

"Around Town" was a column in the Lifestyle section in which *Tribune* reporters and other reliable sources of gossip reported on sightings of Hollywood actors and actresses who were in town, celebrity weddings, big-ticket charity events, and anything else that happened in the metro Washington region that might be of interest to readers. Truth be told, I read it all the time.

"He trashed my wine, too?"

"I think the only thing he didn't dislike was the silverware and the china. Maybe the carpet."

"What about Dominique? Are you going to tell her about this?"

"The web version of the story goes online this evening," she said. "I, uh, thought maybe you could let her know."

"Me?"

"She's your cousin."

"It's your story," I said. "She'll go nuclear. She and Jean-Claude do *not* get along."

"That was obvious."

Kit finished the last of the trail mix and set the bowl on the table. I was certain she had no idea she'd eaten all of it herself.

The other day when Dominique and I were discussing the catering for Antonio and Valeria's wedding, Dominique had mentioned that Robyn Callahan had also hired her to cater a surprise birthday party she planned to throw for Toby. Robyn had met Dominique at the Inn to discuss the menu and do a sample tasting, but Dominique had also dropped by Toby and Robyn's home a few times when Robyn was sure Toby wouldn't be around.

A few hours ago Jean-Claude insisted someone was trying to kill him and sabotage La Vigne Cellars. And now Kit told me about a nasty public feud between my cousin and Jean-Claude de Merignac. Dominique certainly had a motive to want Jean-Claude to leave Atoka. And since she'd been over at Toby and Robyn's house, she'd also had the opportunity to do something about it. Plus she'd helped out at our family's vineyard in France and mine in Virginia, which gave her the means to pull off any of the incidents Jean-Claude had described to me. But my sweet, wonderful cousin would *never* act on her anger, *never* go so far as to resort to violence, *never* consider murder as an option for getting rid of Jean-Claude. She wasn't capable of killing someone and I was foolish for even letting the thought flit through my mind.

Wasn't I?

Six

When Kit and I walked back into the tasting room after finishing our drinks on the terrace, a man wearing a straw boater had let himself in and was standing at the bar with his back to us, apparently absorbed in something he was writing.

"I'm sorry, sir, we're closed for the day," I said.

"Lucie, my dear." Winston Churchill Turnbull turned around and removed his hat. "My apologies, I didn't realize you were closed. The front door was open so I just walked in. I was returning from a meeting with my forensic anthropologist friend at the Smithsonian. I figured I'd make a detour through Middleburg and take the back road home to Purcellville so I could pass on some news in person."

Win Turnbull looked like the kind of man who didn't text or tweet or even leave messages on answering machines. He seemed old-fashioned, a doctor who would still make house calls to care for his patients and preferred to be speaking directly to you when he had something to say. Particularly if it was bad news.

"Dr. Turnbull," I said. "I'm sorry, I didn't recognize you. Thanks for coming by."

"Please. It's Win."

Kit spoke up. "Dr. Winston Turnbull? You're the new medical examiner. It's nice to finally meet you. I'm Kit Noland. Bobby Noland is my husband. He has only wonderful things to say about you."

Win gave her a warm smile. "It's nice to meet you, too. Bobby is a good man, as I'm sure I don't need to tell you. We've spent some time talking about our experiences in Afghanistan and Iraq. I admire your husband tremendously. Our country could use more men like him. It would be a better place."

Bobby never talked about Afghanistan but it didn't surprise me that, of all people, Win Turnbull would be the one who would manage to draw him out, coax him to talk about horrors he wouldn't share with anyone he knew, not even his wife. Help him purge his demons, if that was even possible.

Win had clearly caught Kit off-guard. Her voice wavered. "Thank you. That means a lot."

"It's the truth." Win smiled at her and walked over to hand me the note he'd been writing. "Why don't I just leave this with you, Lucie? It's some information about what we've been discussing. Feel free to call me when you have a moment."

"This is about the skull," Kit said to me under her breath. "Isn't it?"

I nodded. "Kit's a good friend, Win. Whatever information you have you can discuss it with her here."

"I see," he said. To Kit, he added, "I understand you're a reporter."

Translation: *I'm not divulging anything in front of you.*

Kit corrected him. "Actually I'm the Loudoun bureau chief for the *Washington Tribune*. I also never burn a source, never use something that's said in confidence or off the record. I wouldn't be in the business long if I did. But if you'd rather talk to Lucie alone, I completely understand."

Win caught my eye and I nodded. "If Lucie trusts you, that's good enough for me," he said. "Unfortunately I've got some bad news, but I've got good news, too."

Bobby had said the exact same thing to me this morning. This time I wanted to hear the bad news first and get it out of the way. Hopefully it would make the good news seem so much better.

"In that case," I said, "would you care for a glass of wine before you tell us all about it?"

"Thank you, but no. I'm afraid it would go right to my head and I need to drive home. But I wouldn't mind a glass of water, if it's not too much trouble."

I went behind the bar and got a bottle of water from the refrigerator and a glass. "More wine, Kit?"

She held up a hand. "I'm good. I need to drive, too."

The two of them sat on bar stools and faced me. I leaned forward with my elbows on the bar and said, "What's the bad news?"

"My friend—the one I met in Iraq who works at the Smith-sonian—is busy working with the FBI on one of their cases. So he's not available to help you right now." He sipped his water. "However, I did find someone else who's willing to come

out here and excavate your remains. I don't know her person-
ally, but my friend says she comes highly recommended."

"That's good," I said, heartened. So far the bad news didn't
sound as bad as Win had made it out to be.

"Who is she?" Kit asked.

"Her name is Yasmin Imrie," he said. "She's also a forensic
anthropologist like my friend. His expertise is the medieval
period; her specialty is more modern—colonial America,
specifically colonial Virginia. In fact, she's working on the
Colchester dig right now, so she's nearby. She's also worked at
Jamestown."

Someone who knew Virginia and its early tumultuous
history—many of the Founding Fathers were Virginians—
seemed to me to be a better fit for this project than a medieval
expert.

"What," I said, "is the Colchester dig?"

He grinned. "I didn't know anything about it, either, until
this afternoon. Apparently Colchester was a colonial port
town—a deepwater port, in fact—on the Occoquan River. It
was located on what today is land that belongs to Fairfax
County."

The Occoquan was a tributary of the Potomac River that lay
south of us. It was only about twenty-five miles long and for
years people referred to it as Occoquan Creek until it finally
got upgraded to being called a river. Growing up, Kit and I had
gone canoeing on it with friends during high school summer
vacations. I had memories of lazy afternoons drifting on the
river, our inevitable sunburns, and sneaking an occasional
illicit beer.

Kit met my eyes and I knew she was remembering those

days, too. "The Occoquan isn't a deepwater river," she said to Win.

"It was in the seventeen hundreds," he said. "Until it started silting in. Colchester used to be a tobacco town that competed with Alexandria, it was that important. But in the early eighteen hundreds a fire destroyed almost all of it. The town was never rebuilt and today you'd never know there used to be homes, shops, a tavern—even a vineyard—on that land."

"A vineyard?" I asked.

Win nodded. "That's what I was told. Now it's the site of an historic excavation. Yasmin runs the dig and I understand she really knows Virginia history. I have no idea how old that skull out by your cemetery is, but if Yasmin doesn't have answers for you she'll know someone who does."

"I really appreciate this," I said. "Do you think the skull dates back to the colonial era?"

He gave me a reluctant smile. "I'm sorry, but I'm afraid I couldn't say. Don't worry, my dear, Yasmin will be able to tell you a lot more."

"Of course."

"You seem quite concerned about this woman, Lucie," he said. "You do realize she's someone you couldn't possibly have known, nor anyone from your parents' generation, either, for that matter. I will tell you this: she has been in that grave for quite a while."

"What's bugging you, Luce?" Kit asked. "Is it that you think she might be related to your family?"

"I think the odds are good that she is," I said. "I wish I understood why we found her more or less right next to the cemetery. If she were buried before the cemetery was there, meaning she died in the seventeen hundreds, it would be . . . less upsetting, I guess."

"And if she was buried afterward?" Kit said.

"Then it's like some sort of punishment. As if she were banished from being with the rest of the family because of something she did. Something . . . wrong. I don't know . . . illegal."

Kit's eyes widened, but Win extended his hands, palms down, and patted the air, as if he were trying to slow the gathering momentum of my runaway thoughts before they rocketed out of the gate.

"I know it's difficult," he said, "but I don't think you ought to jump to conclusions like that until we know more."

Win was right. But deep down I was almost certain the anonymous young woman was related to me. Whether she'd done something she deserved to be punished for or not, her story was part of my story.

And any day now, I'd be getting results, learning more about who my ancestors were from the Genome Project. After what had happened yesterday I wasn't sure whether I was dreading it . . . or looking forward to what I was about to find out.

QUINN WAS WAITING AT home when I got there twenty minutes later after Win and Kit had left and I finished locking up.

"Toby Levine just called," he said. "We're invited for cocktails at six-thirty. I hope you don't mind, but I accepted. Afterward I thought we could have dinner at the Inn. I made a reservation for seven forty-five. Eli's joining us. Sasha is in Charlottesville with Zach, visiting her mother. Persia's going to take care of Hope and the two of them—Eli and Hope—plan to spend the night here."

Today my head was so filled with everything that had happened I probably couldn't have boiled an egg without screwing it up. Dinner at the Inn sounded great. And it would be nice to have my sweet niece home again. We could deliberate whether Barbie should wear the glittery princess ball gown or the scuba-diving outfit for the day and rearrange the furniture in Barbie's bubblegum-pink house yet again. Things that mattered when you were four and a half.

I kissed Quinn. "Why would I mind having a drink with Toby and Robyn?"

He put his arms around me and pulled me to him. "You didn't get much sleep last night. I know you're still preoccupied about that skull since you went by this afternoon to check on it. I wasn't sure how tired you'd be when you got home."

"I'm okay," I said, wishing I had told him up-front that the real reason I went to the cemetery was to meet Jean-Claude.

If I told Quinn the truth now he'd wonder why I'd lied, or as Frankie, a devout Catholic would call it, committed a "sin of omission." Maybe he'd figure it had something to do with that long-ago crush on Jean-Claude because I still wasn't over him. And what if I told him about my bruising argument with Jean-Claude over whether someone was out to kill him, as well as his parting shot about Quinn's—and my—competence as winemakers? Jean-Claude had warned me to keep my mouth shut or he'd destroy my vineyard. I had no doubt he'd do it.

Quinn brushed a lock of hair off my forehead and looked

down into my eyes. I saw concern in his, but a shadow of something else, too. Doubt? Curiosity? He was always so good about waiting me out, giving me time to tell him whatever I'd been holding back, which was what he was doing now.

Trust.

I didn't ever want to destroy that, to give him any reason to believe he couldn't trust me. And I always wanted to be able to trust him.

"You don't look okay," he said. "Is anything else wrong?"

"Kit came by for a drink after visiting Faith, and Win Turnbull stopped in with the name of a forensic anthropologist who will take a look at the skull," I said. "That's why I'm late. Give me a few minutes to change and freshen up, okay?"

"Sure," he said. "I'll be watching the news in the parlor. Find out what that bad girl Lolita's up to now."

I changed into a long sundress and found a pashmina shawl. After I ran a brush through my hair and put on pink lip gloss, I stared at myself in the bathroom mirror. Before I told Quinn anything I needed more information about Jean-Claude's accusations. Tonight over cocktails with Toby and Robyn I could discreetly ask about the mishaps taking place at the vineyard, Jean-Claude's so-called nonaccident-accidents.

Maybe learn what was really going on at La Vigne Cellars.

THERE WAS ALMOST NOTHING Toby and Robyn hadn't changed about the nineteenth-century Georgian house they moved into except its name: Wicklow. Mick Dunne, the previous owner, had hired a decorator whose only requirement had been to remain true to the bones and history of the house, and

Mick had spared no expense for historically correct details and fine English and American antiques. The walls had been painted in dark, saturated colors and the art that hung on them looked as if he had raided the Constable and Turner rooms at the National Gallery of Art, along with paintings of fox hunting, hounds, horses, and portraits of his English ancestors in seventeenth- and eighteenth-century finery. Many of them posing with horses and hounds. The house, when Mick lived there, always reminded me of a museum.

Toby and Robyn collected modern art and sculpture; Robyn was a painter whose works paid homage to the early-twentieth-century American modernist movement, but she was also branching out into mixed media, especially textiles, and more avant-garde work. The walls of every room in their home had been painted white, the better to display their impressive collection, which contained originals by Picasso, Matisse, Stuart Davis, Georgia O'Keeffe, and Yayoi Kusama. They also collected art by new up-and-coming artists, especially Rosemarie Forsythe, a local artist who created stunning jewel-like botanicals and intricate geometric paintings incorporating mathematical and scientific formulas. It was as if someone had thrown open all the windows at Wicklow and let in sunshine and fresh air.

Toby himself opened the door when Quinn and I rang the doorbell just after six-thirty. He wore a severely starched blue-and-white pinstriped shirt, navy Dockers, and slip-on boat shoes without socks. A pair of reading glasses hung on a bright red braided cord around his neck. He was short and fit looking, except for a small paunch that hung over his belt. His snow-white hair was thinning and his craggy, lined face showed the consequences of years of sun- and windburn. His most striking feature was his eyes, a piercing electric blue so intense that I occasionally wondered if they could bore right through my skull and read my thoughts.

"Lucie, Quinn, come in. Come in. Nice to see you both." He waved us inside and shook hands with Quinn after kissing me on both cheeks. "Robyn will be down any second now. She spent the afternoon in her studio and she's just showering and changing."

"I heard that." Robyn Callahan ran quickly down the wide staircase and joined us in the spacious foyer, which was dominated by a large bronze-and-granite sculpture that reminded me of an enormous conch shell though I had been told it was called *The Womb*.

The ends of Robyn's long auburn hair were still damp and she was dressed in a pair of flowing, brilliantly colored harem pants, a sleeveless white silk blouse, and gladiator sandals that perfectly suited her slim, willowy figure. She looked fresh and dazzling, smelling faintly of an old-fashioned scent that made me think of lily of the valley.

"Thanks for coming, you two," she said.

She was taller than Toby by a couple of inches and younger by probably twenty or so years, which put her in her late forties or early fifties. Just now, though, she could have passed for Toby's daughter. And she had clearly claimed the spotlight as the center of attention. She gave Quinn and me each a quick hug, before dropping a kiss on Toby's cheek.

"Thanks for inviting us," I said. "We haven't seen you for a while."

"That's because I was up in New York for a meeting of the

Council on Foreign Relations and then a series of discussions and dinners with friends for the opening session of the UN General Assembly," Toby said. "And before that, Robyn was in Morocco."

"Studying their art and textiles," she said. "I spent two weeks with a group of Berber artists in the High Atlas Mountains."

I did not meet Quinn's eyes. According to what he'd told me, Robyn and Jean-Claude had slept together while Toby was in New York at those meetings.

"How was Morocco?" I asked.

"Fabulous, simply fabulous. I adore that country, so much culture and history and color in that part of North Africa. And the food. I'll have to show you the Berber carpet I brought back for Toby's study. And some of the fabrics I got for a new series of projects I'm working on."

"Woven out of twenty-four-karat gold," Toby said in a dry voice, "if the price she paid for my rug is anything to go by."

Robyn grinned and said, "It was worth every dirham. And I did some serious bargaining for it, too."

"How about a drink?" Toby said. "We'll have cocktails in the drawing room."

"I'll ask the maid to bring the hors d'oeuvres," Robyn said and disappeared.

The furniture in the drawing room was mid-twentieth-century modern, sleek lines and blond wood. The colors were straight out of the 1950s: teal, coral, peacock blue, and chartreuse. More art hung on the walls, though the primary focus was a large abstract oil by Robyn in shades of navy, chartreuse, egg-yolk yellow, and turquoise that she had painted when she and Toby were vacationing in the south of France one year. It was the centerpiece of the room and hung over the fireplace. A small plaque at the base of the frame read *Plage du Cap d'Antibes.*

I caught Quinn staring at it, starting to tilt his head to view it from a different angle as if he couldn't make hide nor hair of what he was looking at, and nudged him with my elbow. Modern art was not his thing. He straightened up as Toby urged us to take a seat.

Toby made wickedly strong cosmos for everyone and the maid served Moroccan pastries with savory fillings, tapenade with crusty slices of homemade bread, and spicy Moroccan cookies called *fekkas,* all of which Robyn described for us as we ate.

We talked about their travels, a quilt and textile exhibition Robyn had become involved in with the Loudoun County Museum, and Toby's latest appearance on *Meet the Press* to discuss world politics. They were on their second cosmos—Quinn and I declined—when I asked, "How's harvest coming along?"

Toby glanced sideways at Robyn and said in a neutral voice, "Fine. It's our first, so we don't have anything to compare it to, but it seems to have been a good year."

After an awkward pause, Robyn said, "How about you?"

Quinn glanced at me. "Going good," he said. "Considering."

"Considering what?" Toby asked.

"We're having trouble getting enough men to work in the fields," I said. "They're all scared of ICE and being deported or jailed. By the way, Jean-Claude said it would be okay if we asked Miguel to work for us this Saturday. We're short-handed and we need to get in our Cab Franc."

"If Jean-Claude said it's okay, I'm sure Miguel would be glad to have the extra income," Toby said. "He's a good man."

"Yes," I said. "He is. And everything is going well with Jean-Claude?"

It hadn't exactly been a subtle segue into the subject and Toby raised an eyebrow, regarding me with one of his piercing looks. "What do you mean?"

"Oh you know, new winemaker, new to Virginia," I said in a bland voice.

"There have been a few bumps in the road, but nothing serious." Toby seemed to be choosing his words carefully. "Everyone is getting acclimated. Jean-Claude runs a tight ship."

A knock on the open drawing room door interrupted our conversation. An attractive blonde who looked to be in her late forties stood in the doorway, holding a sheaf of papers in one hand and her eyeglasses in the other, an apologetic look on her face.

"I'm so sorry for intruding, Mr. Secretary. I hate to bother you but I know you need these pages first thing in the morning and I'm having trouble transcribing part of your conversation with the president," she said. "Could I trouble you for a quick second?"

Toby stood up. "Will you excuse me for a moment, please? Lucie Montgomery and Quinn Santori, I'm not sure you've met Colette Barnes, my right-hand woman. I recently managed to persuade her to come back and work for me after she unkindly ditched me for the president of the World Bank when I retired as secretary of state. She knows I can't do anything without her."

Colette smiled, obviously used to the ribbing. "Nice to meet you both."

"He can't do anything without me, either," Robyn said, smiling. "I'm his left-hand woman."

"Of course I can't." Toby kissed the top of her head as he walked by.

Quinn and I both said "Nice to meet you" to Colette, who acknowledged the remark before following Toby out of the room.

"His memoirs," Robyn said after the two of them had left. "He's finally settled down to write them. Of course, a hefty six-figure advance from his publisher and some approaching deadlines provided quite the incentive. That's why he had to have Colette by his side. He's paying her the proverbial fortune."

"I never understood how someone could write a whole book starting from nothing," Quinn said. "I have trouble filling out our monthly reports."

Robyn grinned. "He's in his element. Plus now that he's got Colette, it's smooth sailing. He'd be lost without her. She was with him for years, so she remembers a lot of what he's writing about because she was there, too. Sometimes her memory is better than his."

"How did they meet?" I asked.

Robyn sipped her cosmo and leaned back in her chair, crossing her legs at the ankles. "Way before my time," she said. "Toby was the consul in Bordeaux, just starting his diplomatic career. He was married to his first wife and his kids were young. Colette was a teenager working as a nanny for another American couple and she often babysat for Toby's children."

"Is that when Toby met Jean-Claude?" I asked.

"Yes, although he was closer to Armand, Baron de Merignac, in those days. Jean-Claude was young, in his early twenties. Or mid-twenties. I don't remember."

"So how did Colette end up as Toby's secretary to begin with?" Quinn asked.

"He really took a liking to her. She was hardworking, trying to make her way in the world. I think she'd had a falling-out with her parents so she was truly on her own," Robyn said. "Toby stayed in touch with her—she got married, then divorced soon after—so he eventually hired her as his secretary when he was DCM in Paris. Years later he went back to Paris as the U.S. ambassador, then on to the UN, then he became secretary of state. One of the perks of her working for him on his memoirs is that she lives here in one of the guest cottages."

"By herself?" I asked. "No family?"

"She's very close to a nephew who lives in Boston, but otherwise, there's no one. Except us."

"What's a DCM?" Quinn asked.

"Deputy chief of mission," I said. "The number-two person at an embassy."

"That's right," Robyn said. "Sorry for the alphabet soup. Toby talks in acronyms all the time, so I've finally learned most of them out of necessity. How did you know what it was, Lucie?"

"My grandfather was in the French diplomatic corps. My family in France knows the de Merignacs as well."

"How interesting. So did you know Jean-Claude before he came here?" She sat up straight suddenly and I wondered if I was imagining that she seemed to take a keen interest in my answer.

"I did," I said. "I spent a summer in France when I was thirteen and met him then. We hadn't seen each other in nearly twenty years until he came to La Vigne."

The doorbell rang and Robyn's eyebrows furrowed. "I wonder who that could be. We aren't expecting anyone else this evening."

"I'll get it," Toby, apparently finished helping Colette with her transcription, called out.

"He really should let the maid . . ." Robyn began.

We could hear the front door opening and then Toby, sounding puzzled, "Why . . . hello . . . good evening. What can I do for you?"

A male voice, loud and agitated, spoke in a jumble of English and Spanish.

"Slow down, man. Slow down," Toby said. "I can't understand a word you're saying."

Robyn stood up. "Good Lord, that's Miguel. I wonder what's wrong."

Quinn, whose second language was Spanish, said, "I'll tell you what's wrong. Miguel's been robbed. Right here at the vineyard."

Seven

Quinn and I followed Robyn into the foyer where Miguel Otero, looking distraught and angry, was trying to explain to Toby what had just happened. His English had apparently deserted him and Toby wasn't fluent enough in Spanish to follow Miguel's torrent of words.

Miguel looked up as the three of us walked into the room, registering surprise at seeing Quinn and me. Like Antonio he was good-looking, someone you'd turn your head for, to catch a second glance if he walked by on the street. Tall, slim, with the well-muscled build of an athlete, he had the same straight black hair and soulful brown eyes as Antonio, along with a winning smile when he wanted to flash it, which was not now. He was wearing faded jeans rolled up at the cuffs and a gray La Vigne Cellars T-shirt stained with sweat and dark purplish-red wine spatters that, if you didn't know better, looked as if he'd been shot multiple times.

Antonio told me once that even though Valeria and Isabella

were sisters, no one ever thought they were related. But people did mix up Miguel and him all the time. In fact, the two of them looked so much alike they could have been twins.

"Quinn," Toby said, sounding frustrated, "can you please ask Miguel to explain what happened? I'm a bit at sea here."

Like me, Quinn had grown up in a bilingual household. I learned French from my mother; he learned Spanish from his.

He nodded. *"Miguel, qué pasó? Dígame todo. Y hay que hablar más despacio."*

I understood enough to know he had asked Miguel to slow down and start his story at the beginning. Miguel's English was as good as Antonio's, but he answered Quinn in rapid-fire Spanish. Miguel's gesticulations, however, were universal. He was upset and starting to panic.

"Someone broke into his car and stole everything in his glove compartment," Quinn said finally. "Unfortunately, all his documents were there: green card, driver's license, and his Mexican birth certificate. He has no way to prove who he is without them and he's supposed to take his citizenship test the week after next. Not only that, his license just expired so he was going to the DMV to renew it."

Robyn groaned and I gave Miguel a sympathetic look.

"Miguel," Toby said, "calm down for a minute. I'll make some phone calls tomorrow and we'll get this straightened out. You don't have to worry, okay? I know people who can help with this."

Miguel still looked like a hunted animal that wanted to flee, but Toby's words started to sink in and he seemed to calm down and breathe more normally. "Okay," he said. "Thank you, Secretary Levine. Thank you very much."

"No problem," Toby said, continuing in that reassuring voice. "What I don't understand is how someone knew your documents were in your glove compartment in the first place? Wasn't your car locked?"

I knew Miguel's car. It was an old Honda Civic, silver with one burgundy front fender that he'd had to replace and a few dents in the rear bumper and front passenger door. If you were hunting for something valuable to steal, his car, which looked like it was held together with chewing gum and duct tape, would be just about the last place you'd consider looking.

Miguel shook his head. "I didn't lock it so that's my fault. But my car was parked around back by the door to the barrel room. Only staff goes there. Workers. No customers."

"Do you think one of the workers could have taken your documents?" Robyn asked. "Maybe someone who needed them?"

In other words, someone who was in the country illegally. All vineyards had a don't-ask-don't-tell policy where day laborers were concerned. And we paid in cash. It's just the way it was.

"I don't know who could have taken the papers," Miguel was saying to Robyn. "Jean-Claude knew I wanted to go to the DMV. My license was . . . *vencido*."

"Expired," Quinn said.

"Yes. Expired. Jean-Claude told me he needed me to clean barrels, so I couldn't go today. I had everything in my wallet, so I put all of it in the glove compartment to be safe."

"Someone must have seen you," Toby said.

Robyn folded her arms across her chest. "Well, what are we going to do now? The day workers have gone home. We can't go after them and search them. We don't even know where everyone lives."

"We'll file a report with the sheriff's department that the documents were stolen and Miguel will replace them," Toby said. "Though the Mexican birth certificate is going to take some time."

Miguel's eyes widened. "No. No sheriff. Please, Mr. Secretary. They can't know I don't have any papers. They'll tell ICE and send me back to Mexico. I'll have to leave Isabella. And the baby. Isabella is a U.S. citizen and the baby will be, too. Only me. I'm not American yet. You can't call the *policía*." He was upset all over again, agitated.

"Darling," Robyn said to Toby, "he has a point."

"All right. Let's take this one step at a time, shall we?" Toby had slipped into the authoritative voice I remembered from hearing him on the news when he was about to tell the ambassador or minister of some country that the United States expected it to knock off whatever shenanigans it was engaged in and shape up.

"Miguel," he said, "I think the best thing you can do is go home and get some sleep. Isabella's baby is due any day now and you need to be with her. Let me think about this and make some calls in the morning, okay? You have to trust me."

Miguel nodded. His eyes were still big and dark with worry, though his fears seemed to be subsiding. "Okay. Thank you. Good night, Secretary Levine. Good night, everyone."

He slipped out the front door and sprinted down the driveway, disappearing into the darkness. Toby shut the door and leaned against it, closing his eyes.

After a moment he opened them and said, "Well, that's

certainly enough excitement for one night. I'll make some calls in the morning and get this taken care of. Now, who would like another cosmo?"

Quinn, who had been standing behind me, placed his hands on my shoulders. "Thanks for the offer, but Lucie and I ought to be going," he said. "We're supposed to meet Eli for dinner at the Goose Creek Inn in a few minutes."

"Thank you for your hospitality," I said. "It was nice to see both of you."

"Our pleasure." Robyn still looked rattled. "And our apologies for what just happened."

"There's nothing to apologize for," I said. "We've been lucky enough not to have any theft or vandalism at our place—yet—but it happens. Poor Miguel. His citizenship test coming up and Isabella's baby due momentarily. Plus . . ."

I caught myself. Jean-Claude was the one who had told me that he'd attempted to fire Miguel, but Robyn had put a stop to it when she found out and told Toby not to let it happen. No one else standing here was aware that I knew and I had been about to say something indiscreet about Miguel's relationship with Jean-Claude.

"Yes?" Robyn crossed one foot over the other and gave me an inquiring look.

"Plus Antonio and Valeria's wedding is coming up the week after next. Miguel and Isabella are supposed to be their witnesses."

"I'm sure I can do something about getting his green card replaced," Toby said. "And we'll see about the driver's license. I'm also friendly with the current Mexican ambassador."

"Seems to me you've got enough contacts to get this all squared away pretty quickly," Quinn said.

"Maybe even before Miguel's citizenship test?" I added in a hopeful voice.

"That might be a bit optimistic," Toby said, smiling. "As they say, the difficult takes a little time. The impossible takes a bit longer."

"He's being modest," Robyn said. "Toby's a miracle worker."

"Thank you, darling."

"You're welcome, darling. Though there is one minor thing," she said.

"What's that?" Toby asked.

"Apparently we have a thief in our midst. Miguel said his car was parked by the barrel room and the only people who were around that part of the vineyard work for us."

"Maybe I ought to have a word with Jean-Claude," Toby said.

"I'll handle it," Robyn said, giving him a meaningful look. "I'll speak with him tomorrow morning while you're making your calls."

"As you wish," Toby said in a cool voice. "You talk to Jean-Claude."

"We should go," Quinn said.

ON THE DRIVE OVER to the Goose Creek Inn, I said to Quinn, "What did you make of that?"

He shrugged and put on his signal to turn onto Mosby's

Highway. "It's a good thing Miguel works for Toby and not us. That boy has some serious connections in high places. He'll get everything straightened out."

"Not *that*," I said. "I meant that last exchange between Robyn and Toby about her talking to Jean-Claude. Didn't their conversation seem a little strained to you?"

"Between the darlings? I told you what the gossip is."

"I really don't want to believe it. Toby's a nice man."

"He is."

"Robyn's very attractive."

"She's okay." He concentrated on staring out the windshield at the darkened road. "If you like that type."

I jabbed him in the ribs.

"Ouch. What?"

"Nothing."

"I also told you Jean-Claude's not a very nice guy," he said.

"I have a confession to make," I said. After everything that happened this evening, it was time to 'fess up and tell him the truth.

"You're having an affair with Jean-Claude, too?" he asked in a mild voice.

"Jesus, Quinn. Of course not!"

He waited.

"When I called Jean-Claude this morning to ask about hiring Miguel, he told me he needed to talk to me. In private."

"And?" His voice was still measured, calm. But I saw a muscle move in his jaw and I knew he wasn't going to be happy once he heard what I had to say.

I told him all of it; how Jean-Claude thought someone was trying sabotage him and stage so-called accidents that were potentially fatal. I also said that Jean-Claude thought Miguel was behind it because he'd tried to fire Miguel until Robyn intervened and Toby put a stop to it.

"What are you saying?" Quinn asked. "That Jean-Claude might have stolen the documents to get Miguel in trouble with ICE and the law?"

I threw up my hands in frustration. "I don't know. I can't imagine Jean-Claude rifling through Miguel's glove compartment. It seems so . . . petty. He's the next Baron de Merignac, for God's sake. His father is the tenth wealthiest man in France."

"While his son is working as a winemaker at a small vineyard in Virginia. Look, it does sound like Jean-Claude might have known about the papers. And maybe he saw Miguel put them in the car."

"I know. You could be right."

"So he could have taken them."

"I suppose. Now what do we do? Tell Robyn and Toby?"

"Based on what you told me, they already know about the bad blood between those two. And Robyn is going to talk to Jean-Claude tomorrow."

"That's true."

"Let them handle it, sweetheart," Quinn said. "They're smart. They'll figure it out. You don't want to wade into this. No one will thank you and you'll end up with everyone pissed off at you."

"I've already made a start on that," I said. "My little chat with Jean-Claude ended with the two of us shouting at each other. The last thing I said to him was 'go to hell.'"

"Whoa, hold on. Back up a minute. You said *what*?"

I left out Jean-Claude's remark about Quinn's—and my—competence in running the vineyard, but I told him everything else, including Jean-Claude's threat to destroy our vineyard if I opened my mouth about his past in France and his current suspicions someone was out to get him.

When I was done, Quinn looked like he wanted to punch someone in the face, presumably Jean-Claude. "I told you the guy is trouble," he said. "Let him try to come after us. I'll take care of him."

"Okay, now you hold on. You don't need to be spoiling for a fight."

"What if I am? Do you believe any of what he told you about sabotage and attempted murder?" Quinn sounded scornful. He twirled a finger next to his ear. "Maybe the guy's looney tunes. Maybe that's his problem."

"I just don't understand why he would cry wolf."

"And try to pin it on Miguel. Who, by the way, doesn't seem like the vindictive type," he added. "He's a solid guy. Something's not right about all of this."

"I agree. But, for the sake of argument, let's say there is some truth to Jean-Claude's claims. If Miguel's not behind it, then it has to be someone else, right?"

"*If* there is some truth to it," he said. "But who?"

"I have no clue. Jean-Claude got really upset when I brought up his past in France. Supposedly his father paid off enough people to make whatever he did go away."

"What's your plan? Call Daddy Warbucks in France? Ask him?"

"Nope. But there is someone else we can talk to right now

who might know something about what happened. And who has no love lost for Jean-Claude," I said.

"Who's that?" he asked.

"My cousin. Dominique."

THE GOOSE CREEK INN sits in the bend of a curve on Sam Fred Road on the outskirts of the village of Middleburg, like an island marooned in a vast expanse of ocean. If you happen to come upon the half-timbered building at night bathed in spotlights and surrounded by fairy lights strung through the surrounding trees, it could seem as if you'd taken a detour that brought you to the middle of an enchanted forest. When my godfather opened the place more than thirty years ago, local lore went that everyone told him the location was awful and he'd never be able to compete with the established restaurants in town. No one would drive out to the back of beyond for lunch or dinner.

But my godfather, a maverick, an iconoclast—and a Southern gentleman—firmly told his critics to go to hell, although being a Southerner he'd probably added *please*. He was certain that the wooded estate he'd just bought, with its sprawling, ruined 1920s Tudor manor house on the banks of Goose Creek—another tributary of the Potomac River, although smaller than the Occoquan—could be turned into a romantic country inn that would attract folks who would drive many miles out of their way to dine there. In warm weather guests would eat outside on the flagstone terrace overlooking the creek, surrounded by mature dogwoods, flowering cherry trees, and fragrant wisteria. In cold weather fires would burn cheerfully in the fireplaces of rooms that would eventually be turned into intimate dining rooms on the first and second floors of the old house.

My French mother helped with the decor, which gave the place its Gallic charm and influenced the menu, and before long, the Inn's remote location became one of its best assets as a place for discreet getaways and under-the-radar assignations. It was especially popular with members of Congress, cabinet secretaries, and Supreme Court justices, as well as diplomats and fat-cat Beltway lobbyists. But mostly it gained a reputation as the most sought-after place in the D.C. region to propose marriage or for a romantic evening out.

At 8 P.M. on a Tuesday night in September the Inn's parking lot was still filled with cars, but Quinn angled my Jeep into a spot near the front door that had just been vacated. Inside the place was filled, as usual, with the fragrant aromas of cooking, the pleasant buzz of conversation, and the muted clatter of silverware and china. Dominique's new cookbook, *A Year of Favorites: Best-Loved Recipes from the Goose Creek Inn*, was displayed on a stand in the lobby, opened to her mother's recipe for coq au vin with a whimsical watercolor illustration that had been painted by my younger sister, Mia, an artist who worked in Manhattan. A lighted aquarium filled with brilliantly colored tropical fish took up part of a wall across from the cookbook display and the maître d's stand was occupied by Hassan, who had worked at the Inn ever since he immigrated from Morocco back when my godfather first opened the place.

Hassan kissed me on both cheeks and shook Quinn's hand.

"I've put you in the green room so you can have some privacy. Eli's already there."

The green room was the Inn's smallest, most intimate dining room. Dominique often saved it for high-ranking guests, among them a former president and First Lady, who welcomed the privacy and the possibility of not disrupting the meals of other guests with their security details. The room was also conveniently located near a back door to the parking lot.

"Thanks, Hassan," I said. "Could I ask a favor? Would you mind asking Dominique if she'd join us for a few minutes?"

"But of course." He handed two menus to a waiter who walked us through the crowded restaurant to a small green-and-gold jewel of a room where my brother sat at a table, nursing a beer and checking his phone.

Eli looked up when he saw us. "Hey," he said. "I was about to text you."

"We're not that late." I gave him a defensive look. "Ten minutes. It's only seven fifty-five."

He held up his phone, which showed the time on the display. "Seven fifty-six."

Eli was punctual to a fault, which could drive me nuts, especially if I was involved in his plans. I will concede, however, that his obsession with numbers and accuracy was one of the attributes that made him such a good architect, in addition to his gift for visualizing and designing a client's concept of what kind of home or building they wanted—or thought they wanted—and turning it into reality. But his pickiness over my occasional tardiness—I'm really not that bad—did get on my nerves.

Quinn and I sat down across from Eli and gave our drink

orders to our waiter. One of the reasons we were ten—okay, eleven—minutes late was that the two of us had sat in the Jeep in the parking lot discussing how we were going to ask Dominique about Jean-Claude's past in France without revealing anything he'd said to me at the cemetery.

"I'll tell you how," I'd said. "With everything that happened today I nearly forgot. The reason Kit came by tonight was to give me a heads-up that 'Around Town' has something in tomorrow's *Trib* about Dominique throwing Jean-Claude out of the Inn last week because he pitched a fit saying how awful his dinner was."

"Are you kidding me?" Quinn pounded his fist on the steering wheel, sounding gleeful. "Damn. She should have sold tickets. I would have paid to see that. How did the *Trib* find out?"

"One of their reporters was sitting at the next table and took notes. The waiter didn't recognize Jean-Claude so he fetched Dominique. It went downhill from there. And he was drinking a bottle of our Cab Sauv."

Quinn groaned. "Oh, God. That's all we need," he'd said and then we had gone inside to meet Eli.

Our waiter returned to our table with our drinks—a beer for Quinn and a glass of Argentinian Malbec for me—and the three of us ordered dinner.

"I stopped by the cemetery today," Eli said, slabbing Dominique's garlic-and-herb butter on a thick piece of homemade *miche*. "What's left of the fieldstone shed is covered with a tarp so I couldn't see anything. Did Antonio and Jesús only find a skull? What happened to the rest of . . . everything?"

"The rest of *her*," I said. "Yes, just the skull. The new

county M.E. found a forensic anthropologist who is coming over tomorrow morning to finish excavating the site and see if there's . . . more."

"I wonder who she was," he said, licking butter off his finger. "Let's hope we don't find any more skeletons when we break ground for the new house. We're getting to be like a body farm."

Quinn suppressed a smile, but I said in a severe tone, "Don't even joke about that. It's only the second time we've found a body on our property. It's not like it's a regular occurrence."

"Speaking of your house, what's happening?" Quinn asked, steering the subject away from a potential sibling poking match. "You haven't said anything about it for a while."

Two years ago after Eli went through a bitter, messy divorce and lost his job, he and his now four-and-a-half-year-old daughter, Hope, moved back into Highland House. Though we had our share of moments of brother-sister friction, it worked out surprisingly well to have him back home, plus I absolutely adored my niece.

Then Quinn moved in last spring after we got engaged, and soon Eli and Hope were spending more time at the home of his new fiancée and her son. Partly to be with Sasha and Zach, but I think the real reason was to give Quinn and me some space and time alone. Still, Eli was at the house nearly every day since he had converted our old carriage house into an architectural studio and gone into business for himself. A month ago I finally persuaded him that it made sense for him to design and build a home for himself, Hope, Sasha, and Zach at Highland Farm. We had walked the land together one weekend and he and Sasha picked out a site that was less than a quarter mile from Highland House. We'd need to put in a new road, but that was easily taken care of.

There was a part of me that had always fantasized about all of us living together at the farm again, including Dominique and Mia. It was my own version of a Hallmark happy family movie, where everyone gets along and everything always works out perfectly. Already, thanks to Eli, we had converted one of our barns into apartments for Jesús and his wife and Benny and his girlfriend. Antonio and Valeria lived in the property manager's cottage near the winery. And for now, the winemaker's house where Quinn used to live sat empty.

"I haven't had time for the house plans or even another visit to the site. I've been too busy with a husband and wife who are slowly driving me crazy," Eli said to Quinn. "She wants a McMansion. He wants Fallingwater."

"Do they agree on anything?" I asked.

"It has to have walls and a roof."

"Good luck with that," Quinn said.

Eli made a grimace. "If they don't kill each other, the fee will easily pay half a year's income."

"I forgot to tell you that when Quinn and I arrived I asked Hassan if Dominique could drop by for a minute," I said to him. "Kit came by tonight for a drink to let me know about a story that's appearing in 'Around Town' in tomorrow's paper."

Bringing up Kit Noland was another series of landmines for Eli and me. Years ago Kit and Eli had dated and it had been serious. Then Eli met his future wife and the breakup with Kit had been acrimonious. To this day they still didn't get along.

"The gossip page?" he said. "Well, it figures that now she's writing gossip."

"Don't be mean. And she didn't write the story." I told him about Dominique throwing Jean-Claude out of the Inn and caught the knowing look that passed between him and Quinn.

"I saw that smirk, you two," I said. "What's going on?"

Eli shrugged. "Jean-Claude had been spending a lot of time here, mostly in the bar chatting up women. At least it explains why he hasn't been around lately."

"How do you know how much time he spends in the bar chatting up women?"

"I hear things."

"Truce, you two," Quinn said. "Here comes Dominique."

"Maybe we should have this conversation in a room with padded walls," Eli said in a warning voice. "She's going to explode when she finds out."

The family story about my petite, auburn-haired, and boyishly slim cousin was that she was Saturday's child from the Mother Goose nursery rhyme: she worked hard for a living. Or as we also said, Dominique was born without an off switch. A few months ago, to no one's surprise, she had been offered the job as executive chef at the White House, which had recently become vacant. Then, to everyone's surprise, she turned it down, though she did agree to help out occasionally for state dinners or other big events. The reason, she told me, was that she realized the price she'd pay for that kind of celebrity status would be to forfeit a personal life for the next few years. I'd wondered if it had something to do with moving into her mid-forties, on her way to fifty and half a century. Either way, she still worked hard for a living, but it was all for the Goose Creek Inn and its catering business, which were her life and her passion.

She exchanged kisses with everyone before she sat down and our waiter returned to take orders for coffee and dessert. Four espressos. A double for Eli. A shared piece of Double-Chocolate-Died-and-Gone-to-Heaven layer cake and four forks.

"Hassan said you wanted to see me," Dominique said to me. "What's going on, *chérie*? You look like the cat that ate the canary's tongue."

In spite of the fact that my French cousin had lived in the U.S. for a dozen years and was now a citizen, American idioms still baffled her. Get her upset and the English could go completely out the window.

Eli nudged my foot with his under the table and I resisted the urge to nudge him back.

"A reporter from the *Washington Tribune* was here the night you threw Jean-Claude de Merignac out of the Inn," I said. "There's going to be something about it in tomorrow's paper in 'Around Town.' Kit Noland told me earlier this evening."

For a moment Dominique didn't say anything. Instead she stared down at her coffee cup, stirring her espresso with a tiny spoon. I knew her well enough to know that she was angry. Actually, she was furious, as Eli had foretold.

"He was insufferable that evening," she finally said in a tight, clipped voice. "Nothing suited him. He sent back every dish, two bottles of wine, and had my waiter and sommelier practically in tears. No one should insult another person the way he treated the two of them. They were doing their best to please him and there was nothing wrong with his meal. Or his wine. I think he was just determined to be . . . the way he can be. Arrogant. Rude. I'm not sorry I did what I did."

"Good for you," Quinn said. "I think the guy's a jerk, too."

"Had you seen him before that evening? Since he became the winemaker at La Vigne Cellars?" I asked.

She shook her head. "I found out that he was there by accident. Robyn Callahan is organizing a surprise party for Toby's seventy-fifth birthday, so she called two months ago and asked us to cater it. You can't repeat any of this, but it's going to be a big affair, with friends flying in from all over the country and even overseas. Everyone they know in Washington is coming as well, it seems. Robyn told me Jean-Claude would be handling the wine. Of course I didn't tell her I already knew him. She's been to the Inn to choose the menu and I've gone over to Wicklow when Toby was out of town to discuss how we're going to stage it. Fortunately I never ran into Jean-Claude."

"He came here a lot." Eli picked up a fork and started to attack the extra-large slice of cake the waiter had brought. "He spent plenty of time in the bar."

"I'll take his money," she said. "As long as he pays his tab and behaves himself. But I won't let him treat my staff the way he did that night at dinner."

"Do you remember much about him when he was still living in France?" I asked. "Do you know why he had to leave Bordeaux or who his father paid off to keep quiet about it?"

"You mean, aside from sleeping with every woman he laid eyes on?"

"Well . . . yes."

Dominique folded her hands on the table and leaned in closer to the three of us. "I heard rumors—that were never proven, of course—that Jean-Claude got caught trying to sell de Merignac *grand cru* vintages that had been cut with Algerian wine," she said. "One of the dirty secrets about Bordeaux is that more wine is bottled every year than could possibly be produced from the actual tonnage of grapes grown. It's robbing Peter to pay the piper."

"I've heard about that practice," Quinn said. "So that's why he can't go back to Bordeaux."

Years ago the winemaker at the California winery where Quinn had worked had been caught in exactly the same scandal, selling adulterated wine in Eastern Europe. The result had been jail time for the winemaker and the owner was forced to shut the vineyard doors. Quinn had been tarred with that brush ever since, though he'd known nothing about the illicit wine. We almost never talked about his past, but it was the chief reason he'd left California for Virginia.

Dominique finished her espresso. "I suspect that's why he can't return, but, as I said, nothing was ever proven. A journalist who tried to write about it was sued. His newspaper defended him but Armand de Merignac won. When you have as much money as that family has, you can make anything happen. Make any scandal go away."

"Any scandal?" I said, puzzled. "Was there something else?"

"I think you were too besotted with Jean-Claude to realize what was going on the summer you stayed with us," Dominique said with unaccustomed harshness. "He hurt a lot of people. Used them and then discarded them."

She meant *women*.

"Including you," I said. "I did know, Dominique, and I'm sorry about what he did to you."

The bitterness in her laugh surprised me. "You didn't know all of it, Lucie. Nor you, Eli. Jean-Claude's father cleaned up his son's messy affairs," she said. "Paying for abortions, putting up the girls at clinics. Paying them off to say nothing."

"Jesus," Eli said. "How many were there?"

"At least two that I knew of."

For a long moment no one said a word. It seemed as if time had stopped and everything and everyone around us went sharply out of focus. I tried thinking back nearly twenty years ago to that summer, wracking my brain to try to remember . . . something.

Why no one explained Dominique's abrupt departure for a "little vacation" in the countryside. How she returned a week later, unaccountably sad and withdrawn.

My cousin lifted her chin and stared at all three of us, her eyes blazing and her expression fierce and unforgiving. "That's right," she said. "One of them was me."

Eight

We left the Inn soon after that.

"I wish you had told me," I whispered to Dominique as we said good-bye. "Why did you have to bear it alone all these years?"

"My parents knew," she said. "That was hard enough. I didn't want to talk about it to anyone. You were only thirteen, Lucie. I would never have told you." She took a deep breath. "And, to be honest, Jean-Claude never knew, either. It was just one time—isn't that crazy?—but once was enough for me to get pregnant. I paid for the abortion out of my savings. I wasn't about to be bought off by Baron de Merignac like the other one, whoever she was. To this day the de Merignacs have no idea. Certainly not Jean-Claude. I never told another soul until this evening . . . I'm not even sure why I told the three of you."

"Because it was time. I'm glad you did. Though you must still be so angry, even after all these years. How could you forget something like that?"

She gave me a lopsided smile. "Oh, I wanted to kill him for a long time. Then I wanted to kill myself," she said with a candor that stunned me. "Finally I had to make peace with what happened, learn to live with it. So when I threw him out of my restaurant the other day after he gave me the perfect excuse, it felt good."

I wanted to kill myself. All these years Dominique had never said one word about any of this. Maybe that was why she had thrown herself into her work, made it her life.

"What happened that night will be in tomorrow's newspaper," I said.

She shrugged, the earlier anger now gone as if she were too weary to sustain the energy required to keep it stoked. "You know, you can only sweep the rug under the carpet for so long. Sooner or later, people are going to find out who the real Jean-Claude de Merignac is. He'll get what's coming to him. I guarantee it will happen."

QUINN AND I SAID almost nothing on the drive home, each of us lost in our own thoughts. His, I was sure, had to do with Armand de Merignac saving his son's precious hide after Jean-Claude tried to pass off adulterated bottles of his family's coveted world-class wine as the real thing. As for me I couldn't stop thinking about what Dominique had gone through that summer and for years afterward—her abortion and then the blame and self-recrimination after that. How deep her despair had been.

Eli followed behind us, driving a little too close, his headlights flashing in the rearview mirror like strobe lights as both cars drove down the dark, deserted country roads back to the vineyard. After Persia told us what a perfect little lamb Hope had been and left for her apartment above Eli's studio in the carriage house, the three of us split up. Eli claimed he needed to work on some drawings in his studio, Quinn wanted a cigar and a cognac at the summerhouse, and I said I needed to catch up on email and a few business items, so I'd be in the library. The truth was, none of us could face going to bed just yet.

Quinn poured me a drink from the bottle on the dining room sideboard before taking the cognac bottle and a glass for himself outside for his own drink. I wondered how empty it would be when he finally put it back.

Before he left he gave me a kiss and said, "Meet you in bed, okay? I won't be long."

I nodded. "Me, neither. I just need to clear my head. And I do need to catch up on email."

I closed the library door and drew the curtains, lighting only the lamp on the antique partners desk that had belonged to Leland. Everything else seemed to soften and colors faded in the dim light, turning the room into a warm, sheltering cocoon. The gilded pages of the Montgomery family Bible, which lay open on one of the bookshelves, gleamed faintly.

Earlier this evening Win Turnbull had told Kit and me about the forensic anthropologist who would be coming by in the morning to begin excavating the grave where the skull had been found. In addition to my father's genealogical records, our Bible contained a detailed family record of births, deaths, and marriages inserted between the Old and New Testaments. It was a family tree, some of it in spidery handwriting and faded ink, which dated back to the early 1800s. Maybe figuring out who the mystery woman was could be as simple as checking those pages as Quinn had suggested, once I knew more about how long she had been in that grave.

The computer squawked when I booted it up. I sipped my cognac, waiting for the login screen to appear.

The first thing I did was search for Jean-Claude's name, which gave me thousands of hits, mostly relating to other vineyards where he worked before joining La Vigne, along with photos and links to charity fund-raisers and social events, many on behalf of his family's Formula One racing team where he'd usually appeared with some breathtakingly stunning woman who cast an adoring glance at him as she hung on his arm. I plowed through those for a while before giving up. Then I searched for "de Merignac" plus "Algerian wine." All I found was a small article in an arcane French wine blog that mentioned the possibility that fifteen years ago Château de Merignac's Bordeaux and Pauillac wines had been adulterated with Algerian wine but, as Dominique had said, nothing had been proven. Armand de Merignac had shut down the rumor mill entirely. Wasn't it amazing what money and influence could do?

I abandoned that search and clicked on my email, listening to the ding-ding-ding of a flurry of incoming messages landing in my inbox. Thirty-seven new emails. I scrolled through them, deleting almost everything. No, I didn't want to meet married men looking for adventurous women, consult a psychic, or try sexual performance—enhancing drugs. Then my eyes fell on an email that was fifteen hours old; in fact, based on the time stamp, it had come in while I was at the cemetery talking to Jean-Claude. The subject line said *Your Reports Are Ready.*

The sender was the Genome Project.

Did I really want to do this right now? Maybe it would be better to wait until morning to learn the results they'd gleaned from my vial of spit. What if I *was* related to a serial killer or a notorious criminal? Hadn't I learned enough devastating secrets for one night?

I'd had more alcohol in the last eight hours than I usually did in two days, beginning with that glass of wine with Kit on the terrace at the villa, followed by a cosmo with Toby and Robyn, more wine at the Inn, and now a potent glass of cognac. What the hell.

I clicked on the email. A cheery one-line message said, *Welcome to You! We're thrilled to let you know your results are available,* above a green button that said *View Reports.* My computer key chain signed me in to the website once I clicked on the link.

I don't know what I'd been expecting, but it came as a surprise when I realized that I'd been holding my breath. My ancestry report showed—quite sensibly—that I was mostly of northern European heritage; heavily Scottish and English, which would be on Leland's side, and French on my mother's. At the bottom of the page was another link. *Connect With Your DNA Relatives* and a warning that I should be aware I could potentially discover the identity of individuals I didn't know were related to me or allow individuals I might not want to hear from to find me as well. I was in this for the whole ride. It took a few seconds to set up a profile.

I hit Enter and another screen appeared. I stared at it for

the longest time. Not a serial killer who was a previously un-known relative, but something else just as shocking. It felt like a bomb had exploded under me.

We have found a very high probability of a brother-sister relationship between you and David Phelps through your father Leland Montgomery.

Who the hell was David Phelps? My father had another child, another family that none of us knew about? When? Where? Before he married my mother? *After?*

I scrolled some more but there was no additional informa-tion on David Phelps. Then a moment later, as if it were pre-ordained, my email dinged again. The subject line read: *From your half brother.*

The sender was David Phelps.

The door to the library opened and I nearly jumped out of my skin. Quinn poked his head around the corner as my hands flew to my chest and I tried not to look as if I'd just learned news that had knocked my world completely off-kilter.

I said, half-breathless, "Oh, God. Sorry, but you scared me to death. Next time please knock, okay? I thought you were going straight to bed."

"Sorry, sweetheart. I didn't mean to scare you. Are you ready to go upstairs?" He gave me a puzzled look. "Are you all right?"

"Yes, fine. Perfectly fine. I'm not quite ready for bed. I have one more email to take care of and then I'll be up," I said. "It won't take long. I'll join you soon."

"Are you sure nothing's wrong?"

"Positive." I couldn't tell him about what I'd just learned. Not yet. Still, he knew I was upset and I had to say something.

"Actually, it's Dominique. I can't get over what she told us. It just breaks my heart."

It was the truth.

"I know. Me, too."

He glanced over at Leland's gun cabinet. It was a beautiful piece of furniture, custom-made by Amish carpenters who had designed the hand-etched glass doors and carved molding on the solid cherry cabinets to my father's exacting specifications. Inside his substantial collection of weapons and ammunition were secured by heavy-duty steel bars and an internal steel safe. Tiny spotlights inside the glass cabinets made it look as if you were viewing a museum display.

Quinn's gaze shifted from the guns back to me. I knew without checking that the cognac bottle was a lot less full than it had been earlier and that he was a bit drunk, too. The anger in his eyes unnerved me. If what happened to Dominique had happened to me and Quinn found out about it, he wouldn't let it go. Even after twenty years. He'd do something about it.

He'd make Jean-Claude pay.

Thank God the guns were locked up and Jean-Claude was nowhere nearby.

"You ought to get some sleep," I said. "We're all too emotional about this right now, plus harvest has been exhausting."

He nodded. "You really never know about people, do you?" he said in a soft voice.

"No. You don't. Go to bed, love. I'll try not to wake you."

He closed the door, leaving me by myself again and momentarily regretting that I hadn't decided to go upstairs and join him in bed. David Phelps had just written to me, only minutes ago, from somewhere in cyberspace. It hadn't taken him long—practically the wink of an eye, mere seconds after I set up my profile and clicked on that green button—to realize I'd joined the universe of people who agreed to share DNA information, searching for long-lost relatives or seeking more information about who they really were.

To find me.

How long had he been waiting? A week? A month? Years? What if I went to bed right now without reading his letter and waited until morning when the curtains were open and sunlight streamed in through the mullioned window, lighting all the dark corners of the room? When nothing seemed as spooky or eerie as it did at this moment.

Except I knew I wouldn't sleep if I didn't know.

I pressed Enter and David Phelps' email appeared in a separate window. No clues about his identity—a job or a location—from his address, which was a plain vanilla Gmail address.

His letter was short and succinct.

Dear Lucie,

I saw that you recently submitted your DNA to the Genome Project database and indicated that you were willing to let individuals who are related to you contact you. I do not know if this will come as a surprise or a shock, but through a distant relative of your family who was in the database I was able to learn that your father, Leland Montgomery, was also my father. He had a brief relationship with a woman who I was able to determine is my biological mother and the result was me. That woman gave me up at birth and I was adopted and raised by

Margaret and Joe Phelps, my wonderful "real" parents, who loved me and cherished me as if I were their own son.

Sadly, both of them passed away—my mother two years ago from breast cancer and my father three years before that from a heart attack. I miss them every day. Neither one ever told me anything about my biological parents; either they didn't know themselves or they were trying to protect me. Though I always wanted to know who my biological mother and father were and possibly understand why they gave me up, I did not seek any information out of respect and love for my mom and dad. However, after my mother passed away, I began searching for my biological parents in earnest.

I am aware that Leland Montgomery died a couple of years ago; however the woman with whom he had the affair is still very much alive. She occupies a position of considerable influence and power and, unfortunately, does not want to hear from me. Which leaves you, if you're willing to be in touch.

There are several pieces of information that I think might be important for you to know—some of which, I suspect, might be difficult for you to learn—but first and most important, I would like to know if you would be interested in being in contact with me. Either by email or by phone, and perhaps eventually, in person.

I hope to hear from you and I apologize if this email causes you any pain or unhappiness, as it certainly is not my intention.

Sincerely,

David Phelps

I don't know how long I sat there trying to take in the information that I had a half brother out there somewhere who had known about me for nearly two years. Too late to meet Leland, but I wondered if my father would have wanted to meet or even acknowledge that he had a son with a woman he hadn't married. Had he known about the child? Dominique never told Jean-Claude she was pregnant, but then again she'd also had an abortion.

And who was this woman, David Phelps' birth mother? He'd said she had an important and influential job, but apparently didn't want to acknowledge him as her son. Whoever she was, she was the only one still alive who could answer his questions.

Who could answer *my* questions.

Because, by now, there was a lot I was wondering about, too. All the blanks David Phelps hadn't filled in: how old was he, where did he live, what kind of life did he have? For all I knew he could have been writing from the White House. Or a prison cell.

Mostly I wondered how this woman had met my father and what kind of relationship they'd had. Other than the obvious one.

I went back to Google and began a new search. At least his last name wasn't Smith or Jones, but there were still a lot of David Phelpses, many more than I would have imagined.

Did he live in Virginia? Presumably Leland had the affair here—though it could have been a one-night stand on a trip to Las Vegas for all I knew. Leland had been a hell of a gambler. Vegas had been a favorite place. There were three possibilities who had Virginia addresses, but I cross-checked with the address finder and discarded two because they were clearly too old and the third who was a married father with two children. My David Phelps hadn't said anything about a wife and kids.

I fared no better on Facebook and gave up counting when I reached one hundred people named David Phelps. Their avatars were no help, either. Some had no photos, others had pictures of (probably) their kids or a pet or a motorcycle. Some were just the wrong ethnicity: Asian-American, African-American, from the Indian subcontinent. All I had to go on was a name; David Phelps had been cagey about supplying any information I could use to find out more about him.

I turned off the computer and went into the dining room. There was no way I was going to answer that email tonight. Right now I didn't know if I would ever answer it.

I'd played with fire and now I'd gotten burned. I knew something I couldn't un-know. Ever.

The nearly empty bottle of cognac sat on the sideboard. I didn't need any more alcohol tonight, but I poured myself another glass anyway. Then I went back to the library, sat on the sofa in the shadowy darkness, and drank. Had my mother known about Leland's other child? Love child? A child born of a one-night stand? David Phelps didn't sound bitter or resentful; he sounded curious.

It should have come as no surprise—my father was a bon vivant, a gambler, a reckless and restless man. He also had a wandering eye. I wondered how my mother had stayed with him, but in truth, I knew. She loved him with all her heart and all her soul and she forgave his transgressions every time because he always promised her it was "the last time." Plus there were Eli, Mia, and me. My French mother had met my father when he made a whirlwind trip to France; my dashing, handsome, charismatic father had swept her off her feet. She'd left her family and their vineyard, returning to America with Leland, certain that everything he'd told her about his five-hundred-acre estate in Virginia's horse-and-hunt country was God's truth.

What she found was rundown and dilapidated, nothing like what he'd described. Instead of complaining or going back to France, my mother slowly set to work restoring the house to its former glory, researching the style and architecture, painting it the proper colors. She also scouted antiques stores and yard sales for furniture, which she restored as well. Next she tackled the garden, deciding that *Thomas Jefferson's Garden Book* would be her Bible and completely renovating the gardens around our house. Finally, she told Leland that she wanted to plant grapes and establish a winery as Virginia began its foray back into grape growing and winemaking in the 1980s after decades of recovering from the Civil War and Prohibition. And so, almost singlehandedly, my French mother restored her Scottish-American husband's ancestral home to something that resembled what she'd envisioned when he first described it to her in France.

And somehow they'd stayed together. That summer after Eli and I came back from France and Mia returned from Charlottesville, they seemed to have reached a detente or truce in their marriage and there was no talk of divorce. For the next year things were better and we were almost a normal family. Until Leland went back to his old ways.

I finished my cognac and went upstairs, my alcohol-fogged

mind still reeling with what I'd just learned. Maybe . . . maybe my father never knew that the affair resulted in a child. Maybe he never knew about his son or that the child had been given up for adoption. You hear stories like that all the time where the mother kept the pregnancy a secret from the father for reasons of her own. She didn't want him in her life anymore. Maybe she was already married . . . David hadn't mentioned one way or the other.

Or maybe I just wanted it to be that way. Absolving my father of any responsibility. Leland just *didn't know*. Like the proverb says, what the eye doesn't see, the heart can't grieve over.

I opened the bedroom door and slipped into our room. Quinn stirred, but he didn't wake up until I slid under the covers. He turned over on his side and pulled me toward him, giving me a sleepy kiss. Downstairs I heard the front door open and close, followed by the beeping of the alarm system being set. Eli had just come in from his studio.

David Phelps was his half brother, too. And Mia's.

I had no idea what I was going to do about what I'd just learned. A moment later Quinn was snoring lightly, his arm flung across my chest. I lay there, staring at the ceiling and wishing I had thought to brush my teeth or swish mouthwash before I got back into bed, to get rid of my cognac breath.

For the second night in a row, I didn't sleep.

Nine

Quinn was in the kitchen when I came downstairs at 7 A.M. still wearing my nightgown. He leaned over and gave me a kiss as he poured me a cup of coffee.

"Morning, sleepyhead. You were out like a light when I woke up. I didn't have the heart to rouse you. Figured we'd just get a late start today."

"I'm sorry. You should have said something. I didn't hear you get up."

"I don't think you would have heard a bomb go off." He picked up his coffee mug. "I made us an omelet. Kind of used up everything I found in the refrigerator."

"Great." There had been leftover spaghetti sauce, a container of yogurt, and some arugula in the refrigerator, along with condiments and a six-pack of beer. Maybe better not to ask what he'd put in the omelet.

I got plates out of the cupboard.

He took them from me and divided the omelet neatly in two. We sat down at the kitchen table in silence.

I took a bite of his omelet. "This is delicious. What's in it?"

"You sound surprised. Cheese, arugula, and a tomato." He paused and added, "Are you going to tell me what's going on?"

Eli's footsteps pounded down the back staircase and a moment later the door to the kitchen flew open. My brother burst into the room in Virginia Tech sweats and a faded Tech T-shirt, with his customary wild-man morning hair, and headed straight for the coffeepot.

"Morning, all."

I caught Quinn's eye, a silent acknowledgment between us that anything we'd been about to discuss was done with for now.

"Good morning," Quinn said. "If I'd known you were going to be down so early I would have made a bigger omelet. There are still half a dozen eggs and more leftovers in the fridge you can use."

Eli opened the refrigerator door. "There's beer, spaghetti sauce, and yogurt in here," he said. "I think I'll stick to toast and coffee."

He pulled bread out of the breadbox and put two pieces in the toaster.

"Did anybody get the paper?" he asked.

I'd nearly forgotten. The gossipy story about the feud between Jean-Claude and Dominique was supposed to be in today's *Washington Tribune*.

"No," I said. "Not yet."

Eli disappeared and returned a moment later brandishing

a folded copy of the *Trib*. One of our workers kindly picked it up from our mailbox on Atoka Road and drove it to our doorstep every morning. My brother thumbed through the pages until he found the Lifestyle section and laid the paper in the middle of the kitchen table open to "Around Town."

"Might as well get this over with," he said.

"Maybe it won't be as bad as we thought," I said.

He cast a sideways glance at me. "Don't hold your breath."

The paragraph on Dominique and Jean-Claude's dust-up at the Goose Creek Inn was short and succinct. There were individual photos of both of them and the cheesy caption "*Oo La La*" above the article.

> *A nasty—and surprising—altercation occurred at* le trés chic *Goose Creek Inn in Middleburg recently when owner Dominique Gosselin gave the boot to fellow countryman and noted winemaker Jean-Claude de Merignac, currently the winemaker at La Vigne Cellars and scion of Baron Armand de Merignac, one of France's wealthiest men, after the younger de Merignac, who was accompanied by a strikingly gorgeous redhead, complained repeatedly about his meal. According to diners who overheard de Merignac's exchanges with his waiter, his* saumon au papillote *was cold, undercooked, and tasteless. He had similar complaints about the appetizer, side dishes, and dessert as well as the wine he chose, a Cabernet Sauvignon from local winery Montgomery Estate Vineyard. Gosselin reportedly told de Merignac that his meal was compliments of the house on the condition that he never return to the Goose*

Creek Inn again. The multi-award-winning establishment, a perennial regional favorite, is reportedly under consideration to receive a rare, coveted third star in the new issue of the prestigious Washington, D.C., Michelin Guide, *making it the only restaurant in the region to be so honored. Will the negative review by de Merignac, an influential gourmand, have an impact on the outcome for the Goose Creek Inn? Stay tuned. As for the feud between Gosselin and de Merignac,* c'est la guerre *in the otherwise peaceful, charming hamlet of horsey Middleburg.*

"'The peaceful, charming hamlet of horsey Middleburg'? Who writes that crap?" Eli said in disgust. He eyed me. "I hope you're going to say something to Kit about this, complain about it."

"No. I am not."

"Why not? De Merignac dissed our wine. It's not just the Inn that he trashed."

"Because, Eli." I planted my flag: we were *not* getting into this, especially after what happened between Jean-Claude and me yesterday. It would be like pouring gasoline on a fire.

"He said what he said and someone overheard him and Dominique. It was newsworthy because of who they both are. The best thing we can do is to let it die and go away. Everything will be forgotten by the next news cycle, as Kit always says," I went on. "If we make something of it, the story will only get bigger and uglier."

Eli walked over to the toaster and removed two slightly burned slices of toast. I thought I overheard him say, "Chickening out."

Someone's phone rang. Eli glanced at the kitchen counter where both Quinn and I had left our phones.

"Yours, Luce. Winston Turnbull." He picked it up and tossed it to me.

I caught the phone before it hit the floor and answered it.

"Good morning, Win."

"Good morning, Lucie." He sounded wide-awake and cheery. "I just wanted to let you know that Yasmin Imrie will be at your grave site this morning. She said she'd probably get there around eight-thirty. I didn't know if you wanted to stop by and say hi."

"I do," I said. "Thanks for telling me. What about you? When are you coming by?"

"Not sure. I have patients to see this morning and a body to examine at the morgue. Someone who was fished out of the Potomac last night over by Ball's Bluff. Looks like a drowning. Young kid, maybe thirteen or fourteen." He clicked his tongue against his teeth, an expression of regret or dismay. "No I.D. yet. And no one reported someone fitting his description as missing."

I caught my breath. How could a mother or father not report that their child hadn't come home yesterday at the usual time? "I hope you find out who he is."

He sighed. "We'll do a match through the dental records. Whoever he is, he's seen a dentist."

After he hung up I said to Quinn and Eli, "I'd like to stop by the cemetery and meet Win's forensic anthropologist before I go to the winery. Do either of you want to come?"

"Thanks, but I'll pass," Eli said. "I've got to take Hopie to preschool and then work on the drawings for the Couple from

Hell. I'd better go upstairs and get my daughter out of bed and dressed. I'll see you two later."

He left and I looked at Quinn.

"Would you mind if I didn't go, either?" he asked.

"Of course not. Why not?"

"It's the guys," he said. "Antonio and Jesús. They're kind of weirded out about finding that skull. Before they dug her up, each of them accidentally walked over the spot where she was buried. They both believe that if you step on someone's grave, you summon their spirit and that person will haunt you."

"Oh, God. They think she's haunting them?"

"I haven't exactly asked."

"We don't need to have either of them spooked in the middle of harvest. Don't worry; I'll talk to this woman myself. The sooner we wrap this up, the better."

Quinn got up and brought our plates over to the sink. "You and I still have an unfinished conversation to continue."

I gave him a guilty look. "I know. Later. I promise."

Then I fled.

On my way out I grabbed my car keys from the Portmeirion bowl on the demilune table in the foyer, a depot for mail, messages, and keys. Leland's marble bust of Thomas Jefferson watched me from an alcove across the room, as he always did. Persia hadn't arrived yet so the door to the library was still closed and the curtains would be drawn as I left them last night.

Later I would think about David Phelps' email and what to do about it, whether I wanted to answer it. And what I was going to tell Quinn when we finally finished our conversation.

I WAS EXPECTING YASMIN Imrie to be a sturdy, slightly professorial-looking middle-aged woman with her hair sensibly tied up under a bandanna, a sunburned, ruddy face, denim work shirt over a T-shirt with a logo on it, and a pair of dusty boots worn with either shorts or blue jeans. I couldn't have been more wrong. She was a slender, doe-eyed beauty, probably my age, her curly jet-black hair pulled back in a flattering French braid, skin the color of dark caramel, and perfect toothpaste-commercial teeth. She did wear boots with white socks and a blue-jean shirt over a T-shirt and khaki shorts that showed off slim, runner's legs.

A large clear plastic bin filled with what presumably were the tools of her trade sat a few yards from the storage shed. A flat shovel and a mesh screen leaned against the bin. She had removed a camera from an olive-green backpack and was already taking photos of the site. A stenographer's notebook, open to a page filled with handwritten notes, lay on top of the backpack next to a couple of pencils.

"Good morning." She came over to me, holding out her right hand and shifting the camera to her left. "I'm Yasmin. You must be Lucie. Nice to meet you."

We shook hands. "Win said you come highly recommended. Thanks for taking on this . . . project."

She nodded. "My pleasure. We're on a break from the Colchester dig right now, so I had some time."

"Win told me about Colchester. I'd never heard of it before."

"Fascinating, isn't it?" Her smile was dazzling. "Our very own lost city of Atlantis, right here in Fairfax County, Virginia. It's been a gold mine of information on the colonial period and the Civil War years."

"What about this?" I gestured vaguely at the place where the skull still lay in the ground. "Do you have any idea how old it . . . she . . . is? How long she's been here?"

"Not yet," she said. "First I want to see if the rest of the skeleton is here. Most graveyards are laid out east to west—like yours is—and the bodies are buried with their heads facing east so the beloved dead can see the sunrise every day from their graves."

"I didn't know that."

"Yup. The thing is, based on the direction of your skull, it looks like she was buried facing northwest."

"Which means?"

"Possibly that she was dumped here in a hurry." Yasmin pointed a finger at the skull and traced a trajectory that went in a straight line, like an arrow. "If the body is intact, I should find more bones where you'd think they'd be. That's how I'm going to dig and see what I find. But if something disturbed the body after she was buried, they might be scattered."

"You mean, by an animal?"

"Most likely," she said. "Tell me, how do you want to do this? Do you want regular updates, or should I just proceed and let you know what I've done or found at the end of the day?"

The truth was, I wouldn't have minded remaining right

here watching her do her work, step by step. I just wanted to *know*: who was she?

"An update at the end of the day is fine."

"Great. It will probably be more efficient if I can just keep doing what I do and you don't need to weigh in on every part of the process."

"Sure. You just . . . go right ahead." I paused and she gave me a questioning look.

"What?" she asked.

"I don't understand how you can do this. Every day. You don't seem like someone who would choose to spend her time . . ." I broke off. "Sorry. I'm not saying this very well."

"Why do I choose to spend my time digging up dead people?" She grinned. "Don't worry, you're not the first person to ask."

"I couldn't do it."

"It's not a profession for everyone." She put the lens cap back on her camera and stared out at the distant Blue Ridge as if she were trying to decide how to frame her answer. "To me every person I examine—the remains of that person—is someone's missing loved one. A father, a mother, a child, a husband, a wife. Someone grieved for them and, if that person is still alive, they are wondering with every day that passes what happened. They just want to know."

She turned her gaze on me. "Every single set of remains I come across is different. I search for clues in those differences that help me learn someone's identity, figure out who they are. Or were. How they died. If I'm lucky—really lucky—sometimes I can come up with a name. It doesn't usually happen when I'm doing research at a site like Colchester—it's too long ago—but sometimes if the records were good, I can come fairly close to figuring out who an individual was. But in instances like a plane crash or a mass grave in a war zone where there's very little left to identify, it can be more difficult."

I shuddered.

"I know," she said with a kind smile. "I spent some time working for the International Commission on Missing Persons in Sarajevo after I got my doctoral degree. Their mandate is to search for individuals who have been the victims of armed conflict, human rights violations, or natural disasters. The things I saw in Bosnia were just . . . brutal. Horrific. The commission's headquarters is in The Hague, but the best forensic lab in the world is in Sarajevo."

I thought of Win Turnbull and his work in Iraq. Both he and Yasmin had witnessed unspeakable horrors in war zones. Yet they seemed so centered and confident. I wondered how they coped, how they managed to remain so normal.

"I didn't know that about the lab in Sarajevo."

She nodded. "Someone has to do this work, as distressing and difficult as it is. I'm good at it. I'm not going to be able to wave a magic wand and bring that person back to life. But at least I can help find closure for the family. That's important. It's worth doing."

"So what will you do now? Start digging?"

She set her camera on top of the backpack. "Not right away, but yes, eventually. First I need to take measurements, photographs, make sketches and notes so everything is documented before I do any digging. Then I'll probably do what's called shovel skimming with that flat shovel you see over there."

"You take off the top layer of dirt?"

"That's right. I'll be looking for what's called the grave cut. No matter how old a grave is, the soil is always different there from what surrounds it." She ticked items off on her fingers. "It's less compacted, it's a different color since topsoil was mixed in with deeper soil as the grave was filled in, and either it's still mounded from adding all that earth back on top of a body or, if there has been significant decomposition, there will be an indentation where the remains are."

"You can really find the actual grave, even without a coffin?"

She nodded. "The odds are good that it won't be that deep, either, because there isn't a coffin. People always dig graves that are way too shallow—usually no farther down than two meters, or about six feet—and they make them too short. So you often find the pointed bones sticking up out of the earth. Specifically the knees and the feet."

In spite of the subject matter, I found what she was saying mesmerizing. "I didn't know any of that."

Yasmin pulled out her phone. "I probably ought to get started. Let's swap contact information, so I can let you know if I find anything," she said. "Then I'd better get to work."

"Of course," I said, and reached for my own phone.

After we exchanged cell phone numbers and email addresses, I said, one more time, "I really want to know who she is."

"The lab will be able to tell a lot from the DNA in her teeth," she said. "I ought to swab you, too, and get a sample of your DNA to send along to the lab. If there's enough of a match, you're related."

"Win said something about a database that you can check."

She smiled. "At that point I suspect Win thought this might possibly be a criminal investigation. If that were true, then yes, I'd have access to the law enforcement database. But since it's not, I can't use any of the DFS labs in Virginia. I've got to send your samples to a private lab. The one I like to use specializes in working with bones and teeth, and they're the best."

"What's DFS?"

"Sorry. Department of Forensic Science. And, just so you know, it's going to take the lab some time to process everything. It will be weeks, more likely a couple of months."

I should have expected that, but I was still disappointed. "So definitely not like on television."

She grinned. "'Fraid not."

"I'm already in the DNA database," I said. "I did one of those ancestry tests."

She gave me a tolerant smile. "Actually this lab works with its own database," she said. "There's more than one, unfortunately. As for those discover-your-ancestry tests, they're all well and good for what they tell you—which is mostly anthropological information—but in the profession we call that 'recreational genomics.' At the other end of the spectrum is CODIS, the law enforcement database."

"What does CODIS stand for?"

"It's short for Combined DNA Index System. It's a software program run by the FBI," she said. "It uses a combination of forensic science and computer technology to link violent crimes to each other and connect to known offenders. When I help out with criminal cases, those DNA samples go through CODIS to assist the National Missing Persons DNA Database in identifying missing and unidentified individuals."

"Does that mean that what I found out through the tests the Genome Project ran on my vial of spit could be wrong?" I asked. *That David Phelps might not really be my half brother?*

Yasmin laughed. "Not at all," she said. "But it's a completely different system, for a completely different purpose. The companies that sell those test kits use an algorithm to determine someone's ancestry composition by comparing their DNA to public and private reference data. People 'find' relatives by connecting with someone who is also in that specific database and who has shared DNA segments. The more segments you share with someone else, the closer the familial relationship."

"I see."

She gave me a curious look. "You seem to have a lot of fairly specific questions about this. I don't want to pry but sometimes these companies, as well-intentioned as they are, don't do enough to prepare people for the reality that they might discover information that could be life changing. It happens often enough in cases of adoption. An adult child wants to find their birth parents and then they're devastated once they discover that a birth mother or father doesn't want to have anything to do with them. Especially if it's someone who had every expectation that their identity would always and forever be protected by privacy laws and a contract they signed with the adoption agency. They've moved on, they have a new life and a family that knows nothing about this child. It can leave some terrible emotional scars. On everyone involved."

"Oh, no, it's nothing like that." I waved my hand like I was banishing a pesky fly. "I just thought everyone used the same database so you could already access my DNA."

"'Fraid not," she said again, and I wondered if she believed me or was just pretending she did. "Don't worry, Lucie. Like I said, once I get a little further along in this excavation, I'll do a buccal swab on you . . . swab your cheek, that is. I won't be telling you the likelihood of whether you and your DNA relatives are more or less likely to have sweaty feet or drink green tea compared to the rest of the population like those ancestry tests do." She flashed that smile again. "But I will let you know if you and this woman share DNA."

"Thank you," I said. "Now I'd better get back to work and leave you to get started. Call me or text me if you need anything."

"I will. With that hurricane coming, I'd like to be finished as quickly as possible now that the structure that protected the skull all these years is gone." She smiled again and turned back toward the grave site.

I walked down the hill to my car and wondered if the skull in the old storage shed would reveal yet another secret that would catch me as off-guard as the one I learned last night.

I really hoped not. But the way things were going, I wouldn't bet my life on it.

Ten

climbed into the Jeep after I left Yasmin Imrie and phoned Quinn. "I'm finished at the grave site," I said. "I'll see you in a few minutes."

"I'm checking Brix in the Cab Franc block again. The grapes won't be ready by Saturday, but we don't have a choice about when to pick," he said. "The latest weather report I heard says Lolita will be here Sunday morning. We've got to get everything done Saturday." He paused. "Or else."

He didn't have to say or else what.

Hurricane Lolita. My thoughts shifted from the unknown past outside my family's cemetery to the nerve-wracking present and the looming, ominous threat of things we couldn't control. The wind. The rain. The damage Lolita could inflict.

No power. No water. No lights. No phones. Goose Creek overflowing and flooding Sycamore Lane. We couldn't afford the expense of a generator big enough to keep the equipment running in the winery. We could survive a couple of days, but after that things would start going downhill.

A knot formed in my stomach. "We'll just get it done then."

"Yup. Hey, did Miguel ever tell you that he would work for us on Saturday?"

Miguel. My mind went blank for a moment. "Damn. No, he didn't. I texted Antonio yesterday and asked him to speak to Miguel, but neither of them got back to me. After what happened last night, Miguel might have forgotten all about it."

"We'd better get an extra person to help in the field. You were right about that." I didn't like the sense of urgency in his voice.

"Why don't I just drive over to La Vigne and talk to Miguel myself?" I said. "If he can't do it because he's tied up sorting out his legal problems, I'll ask someone else."

"Let me know how it goes."

I disconnected, opened my text messages, and groaned. The text I thought I'd sent to Antonio was still on my display from yesterday. I'd never sent it. No wonder neither of them had replied.

I backed the Jeep onto Sycamore Lane and drove to La Vigne Cellars. It seemed impossible to imagine that by the end of the week, the sky would be black and menacing and it would be raining as if it were time to build an ark. Today was gorgeous; a perfect mid-September morning of sparkling sunshine, clouds as white and fluffy as sheep, and a cerulean sky. It wouldn't be long before the first hard overnight freeze when the trees would turn the vivid colors of autumn, the summer sound of the cicadas would go silent, and the sunlight would slant cooler and lower, lengthening the shadows. Our work, after the frenzy of harvest, would slow down as the vineyard went dormant for winter.

After everything that had happened in the last few days, this year I would be glad when those quieter months finally arrived. Right now it felt as if my life was moving so fast I had to run just to keep up.

I put on my signal and turned left onto the private road that led to Wicklow. At the top of the hill I took the fork leading away from the house, and drove toward the stables and the vineyard. Showing up unannounced like this meant there was a good chance I'd bump into Jean-Claude. But it was better to get that meeting over with sooner rather than later and let him know he hadn't intimidated me. That I didn't give a damn about his threats. Especially now, after the story in today's *Trib* with him trashing the Goose Creek Inn and our wine. Gloves off. I didn't plan to pick a fight with him, but I did mean to let him know I was angry.

I stopped in front of the entrance to the tasting room. Unlike us, La Vigne Cellars didn't open their winery every day. There was a CLOSED sign on the front door so I drove around to the back of the building where the winery was located.

The place was Sunday quiet—almost eerily so—as if no one was around. I parked next to Miguel's Honda Civic, reached for my cane, and climbed out of the Jeep. The crush pad door leading to the barrel room was open, which was odd. At this time of year, you only raised that roll-up hangar door when you needed to move grapes into the cellar. Jean-Claude still had some reds on the skins in fermenting bins in the barrel room.

The sweetness of the juice-changing-into-wine would attract bugs like a magnet. One of our dirty little secrets was that no winemaker could avoid having dead bugs floating in those thousand-gallon bins however hard we tried, but the last thing anyone wanted to do was put up a neon sign with an arrow that said, THIS WAY TO FOOD: DIVE RIGHT IN. So much of our job revolved around cleanliness and sterilization, eliminating anything that could contaminate the wine. That included bugs. Especially bugs.

I walked inside the barrel room and yelled, "Hello?" No one answered above the whirring noise of the fans that were running full blast to disperse the potentially fatal buildup of carbon dioxide released by the fermenting grapes. Why would Jean-Claude—or anyone else—leave the crush pad door open and walk away? You were just asking for trouble.

It was a good thing La Vigne Cellars was closed to the public today. Otherwise there was always a chance some visitor might wander in and decide to explore the place, like a kid let loose in a candy store. Every vineyard owner had stories of the curious guest who removed the bung—the stopper—from a wine barrel when no one was looking, "just to see" what was inside and then didn't replace it. By the time someone discovered the open barrel, the entire contents—say, anywhere from six to ten thousand dollars' worth of wine—had been ruined. And occasionally there was the bright light that thought it would be fun to drink directly from the spigot of a stainless steel tank like it was a public water fountain.

La Vigne's barrel room was L-shaped, with a closed-off room at the long end of the L: a narrow dark cave extending underneath the tasting room where most of their red wine fermented in cool darkness in row upon row of barrels stacked on racks from floor to ceiling. I turned the corner. In the dim light of a single exposed lightbulb at the far end of the room, there was a sliver of darkness as if the door to the wine cellar was ajar.

I continued calling "Is anybody here?" and "Hello?" and hearing my voice echo in the silent, deserted room. Even before I got to the cellar I knew for sure the door was open. There would be hell to pay when Jean-Claude found out.

I reached for the handle, unsure whether to close it or pull it open and see if anyone was inside. Except no one had answered my calls. So who did I think would be there, someone who would jump out from behind a wine barrel, scare the hell out of me, and yell "Boo"?

I opened the door and gripped my cane tighter, raising it in the air like a club. I'd only taken a couple of steps into the room when the odor hit me. Mingled with the overpowering tangy scent of fermenting wine was an unpleasant metallic smell that made me think of iron or copper.

Or blood.

I pulled my phone out of my pocket, turned on the flashlight, and bit back a scream. Lying on his back, arms outstretched, a dark red-black pool of blood seeping from underneath him, was Jean-Claude de Merignac.

The day before yesterday Antonio and Jesús warned me that unearthing that skull by the cemetery meant someone would die soon. I'd dismissed their fears as an old wives' tale, a baseless superstition. Then yesterday Jean-Claude swore he was sure someone was trying to kill him here at La Vigne and make it look like an accident.

The three of them had been right—almost. Jean-Claude's eyes were partially open as if he were staring at something. But he was most definitely dead. The only premonition that hadn't come to pass was that no one would ever consider his death to be an accident.

He'd been murdered.

I backed out of the room, hoping I wouldn't be sick. My phone showed no bars so I had to get out of here before I could call 911. Something felt sticky under my work boots, which made a squishing sound on the concrete floor as I walked. I stopped and turned around. A trail of bloody footprints led from the wine cellar.

Mine. I must have stepped in Jean-Claude's blood before I turned on the flashlight. Now I really wanted to throw up.

I tried to run, but ever since my accident the best I can manage is to walk faster. At times—like right now—it terrifies me because I am vulnerable and powerless. If I am being pursued, I'm at someone's mercy. What if Jean-Claude's killer was still here, watching me from some hidden place? No one knew where I was except Quinn. How long would it take him to realize something must have happened to me if I didn't show up for a while?

Probably a long damn time.

Wait. Just calm down.

With the hangar door wide open the temperature in the barrel room had warmed up to the ambient temperature outside. But in the cave where I'd discovered Jean-Claude it had been sharply cooler, probably between forty-five and fifty degrees Fahrenheit. Chilly enough to slow the decomposition of a body. Maybe Jean-Claude had been dead longer than I thought. And if I were the killer, I wouldn't hang around after I finished what I came to do. I'd take off. My heart, which had been rabbiting against my rib cage, slowed to a more normal rate.

As soon as enough bars showed up on my phone I called 911. For the second time in three days I told the dispatcher what she needed to know and said I'd stick around until someone got here. Then I called Toby's mobile and got his voice mail. I left a message and tried Robyn. Same thing.

It was just going on ten-thirty. Last night Robyn said she planned to talk to Jean-Claude first thing this morning about Miguel's papers being stolen. If she had been here, she might have been the last person to see Jean-Claude before the killer showed up.

Maybe if I called Wicklow, Colette Barnes or the maid would know how to reach Toby or Robyn. The maid answered on the fifth ring and I told her Jean-Claude was badly injured. Did she know where anyone was? In heavily accented Spanish she asked me to hold while she found Colette.

I heard Colette's voice before she came on the line. "No, Marta, I'll handle this. I'll tell Secretary Levine and Ms. Callahan myself."

Marta murmured something that sounded like disagreement and Colette snapped back at her. "I said, I'll take care of it."

A moment later, she was on the phone with me. Her voice was still sharp. "Lucie? What's wrong? Marta said something about an emergency, that Jean-Claude was injured. Are you sure?"

"I'm so sorry, Colette. Jean-Claude is dead. I didn't want to tell Marta before I had a chance to speak to Toby or Robyn. I just called nine-one-one and someone from the Sheriff's Office is on the way. Do you have any idea where either of them are?"

"Oh my God, *dead*? How awful. Where did you . . . *how* did you find him? What happened?"

"I'm not entirely sure what happened, but he's lying in a pool of blood. I stopped by because I needed to speak to Miguel about something. The crush pad door was open and so was the door to the cave in the back of the barrel room," I said. "Look, I really think we need to find Toby and Robyn and let them know about this. Do you have any idea where either of them are?"

"They're out for the morning hack," she said. "Together. The secretary met a friend for breakfast in Leesburg—he left the house around seven. Robyn had an eight-thirty appointment here with your cousin. I overheard Secretary Levine planning to meet Robyn at the stables after he got back from Leesburg so they could ride together. I'll drive over there right now and give them the news myself. They should be back."

"I left messages on both of their phones. If they've returned from their hack then they might already know."

She gasped. "I'd better get over to the stables just in case," she said. "Are you going to stay there until someone from the Sheriff's Office shows up?"

"I'm not going anywhere," I said and then she hung up.

I sat down on a bench and took a look at the soles of my work boots. Jean-Claude's blood had seeped into the grooves, where it had now congealed.

I threw up in a nearby clump of bushes.

• • •

IT SEEMED LIKE AN eternity before two Loudoun County Sheriff's Office cruisers pulled up in front of the crush pad, their light bars pulsing red and blue and jangling my already stretched-thin nerves. At least they hadn't turned on their sirens. Biggie Mathis climbed out of one of the cruisers.

"Ms. Montgomery," he said. "We have to stop meeting like this. I understand you phoned in a homicide?"

I nodded. "Jean-Claude de Merignac. He's the winemaker here. Was. The winemaker here."

"Where is he?"

"Inside," I said. "There's a separate wine cellar at the back of the barrel room. In there."

The deputy from the other cruiser said, "I'll check it out."

Biggie nodded and his colleague disappeared inside the winery. I wondered if he, too, would accidentally step in the widening pool of Jean-Claude's blood and then decided he would not make that kind of rookie mistake. Especially after he saw my footprints.

Toby's black Mercedes came roaring down the hill, stopping behind the two cruisers with a spray of gravel. Car doors slammed, three quick pops like gunfire, as Toby, Robyn, and Colette flew out and ran toward Biggie and me.

I watched Biggie size up the three of them: Toby and Robyn, windblown and sunburned in riding clothes, and Colette, immaculate in white jeans and a red T-shirt. Robyn looked as if she had been crying and Toby's face was the color of ashes. Only Colette seemed in control of her emotions.

"Good morning. Are you folks the owners?" Biggie asked.

He focused on Toby, as if he were trying to figure out why he looked familiar.

Toby took charge, answering for everyone. "I'm Tobias Levine and I own this winery, Deputy. This is my partner, Robyn Callahan, and my assistant, Colette Barnes. I got a call from Lucie—Ms. Montgomery—that she found my winemaker, Jean-Claude de Merignac, a short while ago . . . apparently there's been some kind of accident. I'd like to see him at once, please."

"I'm Deputy Mathis," Biggie said. "I'm sorry to tell you this, Mr. Levine, but your winemaker is apparently deceased. We've just started our investigation so right now this place"— Biggie gestured to the entire barrel room—"is off-limits to everyone, including you, sir."

"For how long?" Toby asked, his voice tightening.

The other deputy emerged from the barrel room. "He's dead, all right, Big. I called the M.E. and the crime scene guys and reported a homicide," he said to Biggie.

"Homicide?" Toby sounded stunned. "Someone killed Jean-Claude? Who would do something like that?"

"That's what we intend to find out," Biggie said. "Now, until I finish interviewing Ms. Montgomery I need you people to wait over there." He pointed to Toby's car. "I'll be speaking with each of you individually in short order."

"But . . ."

"Sir." Biggie took a step toward Toby. "It's not a request. Please wait where I asked you to."

"Mr. Secretary," Colette said, slipping an arm through Toby's, "we should let the man do his job."

"Come on, Toby," Robyn said. "Colette is right. We'll sort all of this out later."

Toby didn't look pleased, but he let Colette and Robyn walk him over to the Mercedes. Biggie turned to me. "Okay," he said. "What happened? What were you doing here and how did you happen to find Mr. . . ." He consulted his notes. "De Marinero."

"It's 'de Merignac.'"

"Right."

I told him, including the fact that he would find my footprints near Jean-Claude's body and my fingerprints on the door handle.

When I was done he said, "I need you to stick around. You're not in the database so we need to take your fingerprints since you were there. And an imprint of your boots, after what you just told me. Sit tight while I talk to your friends. I'll be back."

Biggie was still speaking with Toby when another car pulled up and parked behind Toby's Mercedes. Win Turnbull got out of his now-familiar mint-green paneled station wagon. How in the world could he have gotten here so quickly? The deputy had called him less than five minutes ago.

When he saw me, he looked as surprised as I was. "Lucie. What in heaven's name are you doing here? I was with Yasmin when I got a call that I was needed for a homicide at La Vigne Cellars."

Win had only been next door at my vineyard. At least that explained his speediness arriving on the scene.

"It's Jean-Claude de Merignac," I said. "He . . . was . . . the winemaker here. I found him and—"

"Doc?" Biggie's partner joined us. "This way, please."

Win placed a comforting hand on my shoulder and said, "Excuse me."

I still hadn't been dismissed by Biggie when Bobby Noland drove up in an unmarked car. By now the crime scene van had arrived along with a white van that eventually would be taking Jean-Claude's body to the morgue once Win finished with his examination. When Bobby didn't look surprised to see me I knew Biggie had filled him in that I'd be here. Bobby gave me a cursory nod and disappeared inside the barrel room.

When he emerged fifteen minutes later, he came straight over to me.

"I know Biggie took your statement," he said, "but I need to ask if you have an alibi for this morning."

"I was at our cemetery with Yasmin Imrie," I said. "The forensic anthropologist Win Turnbull found for me."

Bobby's eyes narrowed as though he were trying to figure out who I was talking about. Then his face cleared. "Right. Until what time?"

"Ten . . . maybe nine-thirty."

"Then what?"

"I came here."

"Why?"

I told him about wanting to speak to Miguel, but left out the part about his papers being stolen from his car.

"Did you see anybody when you got here?"

"No."

"Any idea who might have wanted Jean-Claude dead?"

You didn't beat around the bush with Bobby or try to pull

a fast one. Sooner or later it would come out that the last time I spoke with Jean-Claude he'd threatened me and we'd argued. Plus there was the fact that I knew that Jean-Claude believed someone at La Vigne was trying to kill him and make it look like an accident.

So I told him. His eyes grew dark and his face became an inscrutable mask. Bobby was my childhood friend and my best friend's husband, but he was also a Sheriff's Office detective. I knew how it went. His job trumped our friendship plus it also made it harder for him to deal objectively with me.

"Nobody saw you drive in here?" he asked.

"No. The place was deserted."

"Can you be more specific about what time you arrived?"

"I think it was around ten. I don't know."

"A few minutes ago you said maybe nine thirty. Which is it?"

He was really drilling down on me, lobbing questions like one of those machines that spits out tennis balls for practice.

"Oh, come on," I said. "Surely you don't think I killed Jean-Claude. I'm the one who found him. I'm the one who called nine-one-one."

"You also argued with him the last time you spoke. By your own account it was pretty nasty. And I, uh, saw 'Around Town' in the *Tribune* this morning. You can't have been too happy with that story, Jean-Claude trashing your wine and your cousin's restaurant. Maybe you came over here to set the record straight?"

My mouth fell open. "*No.* Of course not. I came over here to talk to Miguel Otero. I told you that."

"Okay," he said. "Calm down. You know I needed to ask."

I calmed down. "I know."

"What about what Jean-Claude told you? Did he have any idea who might be trying to kill him?"

I hesitated and he said, "Answer the question, please."

He was going to find out sooner or later and I knew better than to stonewall him.

"He said he'd had an argument with one of the workers."

"Which one?"

I took a deep breath. "Miguel Otero. He thought maybe Miguel was trying to sabotage equipment and cause trouble to make him—Jean-Claude, that is—look bad to Toby and Robyn."

"Detective?" For such a large man, Biggie Mathis knew how to move stealthily. Neither of us had heard him come up behind us.

Bobby turned around. "Yes?"

"I think you'd better come with me. We found something."

"Be right there."

Bobby followed Biggie over to where a crime scene technician in a blue jumpsuit held a sealed plastic bag by the edge so Toby, Robyn, and Colette could examine the contents. I was right behind him.

A pair of secateurs, the standard clippers we used out in the field for cutting grape clusters at harvest or pruning vines in the spring, was in the bag. Something that looked a lot like blood coated the blades.

"Where did you find these?" Bobby asked the technician.

"In the room where the body was located," she said. "All

the way in the back behind a row of wine barrels. They could be the murder weapon. We'll check to see if the blood matches the deceased."

"Get that taken care of immediately," Bobby said.

"Copy that."

Bobby turned to Robyn, Toby, and Colette. "Do you have any idea who these might belong to?"

"Miguel Otero." Robyn's voice sounded strangled. "Those are his initials scratched into the handle. M.O."

Bobby turned to Toby. "I understand he's one of your employees."

"My foreman. He's a good man, Detective, not a murderer."

Bobby nodded, but I knew it wasn't because he agreed with Toby. Thanks to me, he already knew about the trouble between Jean-Claude and Miguel, but he still didn't know that Jean-Claude had tried to fire him. Nor was he aware that yesterday Miguel's legal documents had been stolen from his car and Miguel suspected Jean-Claude. As soon as Bobby filled in the rest of that picture, it was going to look even worse for Miguel than it did right now.

Win Turnbull emerged from the barrel room and joined our group. "We might have found the murder weapon, Doc," Bobby said. "Have a look."

Win examined the secateurs and nodded. "Mr. de Merignac was stabbed repeatedly in the back with a knife-like object and bled to death." He pointed to the sealed bag. "Those secateurs could have made wounds like the ones I found."

"Where is Miguel Otero?" Bobby asked Toby.

"I spoke to him right here this morning," Toby said. "He said he was going out into the field to do some work."

"Do you know where?"

"He wasn't specific."

Bobby turned to Biggie. "Find him," he said. "Take someone with you and bring him in."

Eleven

The first thing I did when I got back to my vineyard was go home and get my old work boots. Luckily I'd kept them as a spare pair. I used a garden hose to rinse the blood off my other boots, but somehow I didn't think I'd ever be able to wear them again.

It was mid-afternoon when Bobby's car showed up in the winery parking lot. Maybe he had more questions for me, though I couldn't imagine what he wanted to know that he hadn't asked already.

I met him in the courtyard. "Hey," I said. "What brings you here?"

"I'd like to talk to Antonio Ramirez."

That was a surprise. "About what?"

He gave me a look that said don't-make-this-difficult. "About Jean-Claude de Merignac."

"Don't tell me you suspect Antonio. No way, Bobby. He was out in the field with the men all day. He just got back."

"I just need to talk to him," he said. "Do I need a warrant to be here, Lucie?"

He'd never asked me something like that before and for a moment, I couldn't speak. "No," I said, finally. "No, of course not."

"Good. So where's Antonio?"

"I think he's in the barrel room with Quinn."

"Could you call and find out, please?"

"Why?"

"I don't want to scare him off and I don't feel like running."

"Bobby . . ."

"He's not under arrest, Lucie. I just want to ask him a couple of questions."

I phoned Quinn. "Hey," he said. "What's up?"

"Is Antonio with you?"

"Yeah. Why didn't you call him yourself if you wanted to know where he was?"

"Give me a minute." I disconnected and said to Bobby, "Please don't ever ask me to do something like that again."

It will be a while before I forget the look of betrayal in Antonio's eyes when Bobby and I walked into the barrel room a few minutes later.

"Afternoon, guys," Bobby said. "Antonio, how's it going?"

Antonio wiped his hands on a shop towel and set it on top of a wine barrel. His eyes darted from Bobby to me. "All right." He gave Bobby a wary look.

"Do you know why I'm here?" Bobby asked.

"No."

"You probably have an idea, though."

"Then why did you ask me?"

"Bobby, I told you Antonio was here all day . . ." I began.

"I need to hear this from Antonio, Lucie. Let him talk," Bobby said. "Antonio, we're looking for Miguel Otero. Do you have any idea where he is?"

Antonio didn't flinch. He looked directly at Bobby and said, "No. Why are you looking for him?"

"We have a few questions for him concerning the murder of Jean-Claude de Merignac," Bobby said, and this time Antonio did react.

His eyes grew dark. "Miguel didn't kill anyone."

"I didn't say he did. I'd like to hear that directly from him, but unfortunately he's gone," Bobby said and my heart sank. "We just want to talk to him as a person of interest in the murder of Jean-Claude de Merignac, is all. It would help if he would come in voluntarily. Do you think you could persuade him to do that?"

"I don't know where he is," Antonio said.

"You didn't answer the question."

"I don't know if I could persuade him."

"Your fiancée and his wife are sisters. He's practically a member of your family."

"It doesn't matter."

"Why not?"

"Because all his papers, his legal documents, were stolen from his car yesterday. He's scared. He's got nothing to prove who he is."

Bobby's face didn't give away whether he had learned this piece of information since I spoke to him earlier or if it was the first he'd heard of Miguel's papers being stolen.

"We could help him with that if he comes in," he said.

"Unless you arrest him. Or deport him."

"If he didn't kill Jean-Claude de Merignac, he has nothing to worry about. I'm giving you my word," Bobby said in an even voice. "You have a phone. You could call him. Say, maybe right now?"

"You think Miguel killed Jean-Claude because his pruning shears were found covered with blood. Am I right?"

Bobby looked unfazed that Antonio already knew this. No doubt the word had gone around the vineyard workers like wildfire. This conversation between the two of them had been nothing but a game of cat and mouse.

"I don't know who killed Jean-Claude," Bobby said, still in that matter-of-fact tone. "I just want to talk to Miguel, that's all. The longer he stays out, the worse it's going to be if we have to find him. His car is still at La Vigne Cellars so we believe he left on foot, meaning he can't have gotten very far . . . yet. You'd be helping him if you make that call . . . so will you? Please?"

Antonio pulled his phone out of his back pocket and thumbed through it. Then he tapped a number and put the phone to his ear.

"Could you put it on speaker, please?" Bobby asked.

Antonio obeyed and I held my breath. The phone went to voice mail and a disembodied voice said, "The person at this number has not set up a mailbox. Please try again later."

Antonio clicked off his phone and looked at Bobby. "He's not answering," he said.

"All right," Bobby said. "Look, Antonio, in times like these, we know people on the run often turn to family for help. If he comes to you, you need to let me know. Understand? Otherwise, you could be charged with hampering a murder investigation."

Antonio turned pale. "I understand."

Bobby looked around the room at all of us. "I think I'm done here," he said. "I'll see myself out."

"I'll walk you to your car," I said.

We left the barrel room, Bobby's heavy shoes and my work boots crunching on the courtyard gravel. "Miguel's really gone?" I asked.

"In the wind," he said.

"That doesn't make him guilty of murder."

"I know that. But running isn't helping him."

"He's scared and he has no papers. Maybe someone's trying to frame him, make it look like he did it."

"Who and why?"

"I don't know."

We reached Bobby's car. He rested his hands on my shoulders, but it felt less like a comforting gesture than his own need for support. He knew what he was doing, what he had to do, but he also knew how divisive this was going to be in his own backyard.

"I'm not any happier about this than you are, Lucie, but I need to find out who killed Jean-Claude. And my guess is it's someone who knew him, not a stranger who wandered in. He hasn't been the winemaker at La Vigne that long so the odds are good it's someone we all know around here."

"Am I on your list?" I said half-jokingly. "Do you think I did it?"

"Lucie." He gave me a world-weary look. "There, but for the grace of God, go any of us. You. Me. Anyone. You don't know what you're capable of doing in a moment of extreme anger, when you're really provoked and you just totally lose it. If you did, it might surprise and scare you. How many times have I heard someone say 'I didn't mean it' or 'I never meant it to go this far' or 'I don't know what happened' just before they confess that it was an accident. They still believe they shouldn't be punished because they're a good person who got trapped in a bad situation."

He opened the car door. "I'd better get going. I've still got a bunch of paperwork to take care of back at the office." He climbed in and started the engine, powering down his window. "And, no, you're not on my suspect list. But I will be looking for anyone with a motive. So if you know anything or think of anything, give me a holler. Okay?"

"I will," I said. "Be seeing you."

He drove off and I watched him go. If he was right—and I knew he was—the murder of Jean-Claude could have been a crime of passion that anyone who worked at La Vigne Cellars could have committed. And being the international celebrity that he was, with his family's name known worldwide, his sensational death at a small Virginia vineyard was going to attract a lot of soap opera media attention.

It wouldn't take long before the press would show up. I was already dreading that.

ANOTHER SET OF FOOTSTEPS crunched on the gravel behind me. I turned around. Antonio, his eyes flashing with anger, strode up to me.

"Miguel didn't do it."

"How do you know?"

"Because I know him."

"Antonio, Bobby questioned me as well. Even though I'm the one who found Jean-Claude's body and called nine-one-one. It's part of the normal routine in a murder investigation. They need to ask questions, find out who saw what. Who had a motive for wanting the victim dead."

"Come on, Lucita, Bobby never thought you did it for a moment." He folded his arms across his chest and gave me a challenging look. "Miguel, he's another story. Right? He's not American. He's not one of you. That's already one big strike against him."

Antonio was an American citizen, just like I was, but he didn't say *one of us*. I didn't want to have this conversation with him, but in my heart I knew he was right.

My cheeks felt hot. "You're not being fair. Look at this from Bobby's perspective. Miguel's bloody secateurs look like the murder weapon and now he's gone. What's Bobby supposed to think? What would *you* think?"

Antonio shook his head, his eyes locked on mine. "Valeria is home crying her eyes out. We're supposed to get married in ten days and Miguel is supposed to be my best man. Isabella's baby is due any day now and she's scared what might happen to Miguel with no papers and, like you said, his clippers looking like what killed Jean-Claude. What if her baby has to grow up with a father who goes to jail? Or what if he gets deported?"

"I'm so sorry. I mean it, Antonio. I'm really, really sorry. I don't know what to say."

"Say you're gonna help."

"Of course . . . we'll figure out something for the wedding—"

"Not that," he said. "I'm not talking about the wedding. The wedding is off until this is over."

"You can't be serious. You can't cancel—"

He steamrolled on. "I want you to find out who really killed Jean-Claude. Because, I'm telling you, it wasn't Miguel."

I held up both hands like I was trying to push back, to stop him from saying anything else, though it seemed pointless against his gale-force insistence. "Whoa. Wait right there. The Sheriff's Office is doing that. They're going to find out who killed Jean-Claude."

"You think they're going to keep trying to find someone else when they've already got Miguel's secateurs with blood on them? They've got their suspect. Your family and Jean-Claude's family go way back," he said. "You two talk in French all the time . . . talked in French. Miguel heard some stories about Jean-Claude, things that happened in France that got him in trouble. He told me about it a few weeks ago."

"What things? Heard about them from whom?"

"I don't know . . . something he did. But I bet you could find out. Maybe it has something to do with why he was killed."

"Antonio . . ."

"I'm telling you this, Lucie. The guys are all scared. You think you had trouble getting pickers to come before this happened? Wait until you see who shows up when you want the Cab Franc picked. *Nadie.* No one. Somebody has to stick up for the immigrant community. If you have faith in me, if you trust me, I'm telling you to believe me that Miguel is innocent. I just need you to help prove it." He still stood there, arms folded, still that implacable force of nature. "Then the others will trust you if you stand up for one of us."

He had just thrown down a gauntlet that he expected me to pick up without asking any questions. The audaciousness of his demand nearly took my breath away. He hadn't said it, but I knew this was true as well: *I'll trust you, too.*

I hated ultimatums. I hated being backed into a corner. Usually I said no, just on general principle even if it meant doing something I already knew I'd regret later. Quinn said it was my Scottish stubbornness.

"I can't interfere with a police investigation, Antonio. And if you know where Miguel is, Bobby wasn't kidding. You'll be in trouble."

"I'm not asking you to interfere. I'm asking you to ask some questions, find out things Bobby Noland probably isn't interested in finding out right now because he's too busy looking for Miguel."

"That's a cheap shot. Bobby's a good detective."

"Miguel is an innocent man."

He waited me out.

"Okay," I said, finally. "I'll do what I can. But I'm not getting in trouble with the Loudoun County Sheriff's Office, not getting in their way. Are we clear on that?"

"Yup."

"Do you know where Miguel is right now?"

He laid a hand over his heart. "*Palabra de Díos.* Word of God. I do not. Trust me, Lucita."

We locked eyes again and Antonio gazed into mine without flinching. *He knows something.* Maybe he didn't know exactly where Miguel was at this second, but he had some idea where he might be. And Antonio certainly knew where he wasn't. If I pressed any further, we were both going down the slippery slope.

"Okay," I said. "I trust you."

But we both knew I didn't.

Twelve

Antonio left for the barrel room after our stormy conversation, leaving me to my roiling thoughts. Now what? How was I going to find out who killed Jean-Claude?

And on a purely practical level, Antonio had just called off his wedding until Miguel was cleared of a murder charge. I needed to tell Frankie so she and Nikki could put the brakes on all their carefully made plans. I was on my way to the villa when my phone rang. Perfect timing. My caller ID showed Frankie's name.

When I answered she said, "Stay where you are."

"Pardon?"

"I can see you out my office window," she said. "There's a reporter in the tasting room. She just showed up with a cameraman and she's looking for you because the word is apparently out that you were the one who found Jean-Claude this morning at La Vigne. I told her you weren't here and made up a story about a meeting you had in Delaplane. She still hasn't left. You need to disappear before she sees you."

The last thing I wanted was some reporter asking me to describe my emotions when I discovered Jean-Claude lying in a pool of blood this morning. What do they think you're going to say, anyway?

I said, with fervent gratitude, "Thanks for covering for me."

"No problem. It's the reporter who gave you so much trouble when Jamie Vaughn's car crashed into the front gate last spring. The one who kept bugging you about holding back information."

"Pippa O'Hara?"

"Yup. In person."

"I'd rather face a Rottweiler than that woman."

"I remember. Look, maybe you should just take the rest of the afternoon off. You've had a hell of a day."

Some days I wondered if Frankie remembered I owned the place. "There's something I need to tell you," I said. "Why don't you ask Nikki to close up this afternoon and you can meet me at the house for a drink?"

"Nikki didn't come in today, remember? She went out to that flower farm in Culpeper to start looking into prices and what's available for the wedding flowers. Are you okay? You don't sound so good."

I had a feeling Frankie didn't know about any of the developments surrounding Jean-Claude's murder, including Miguel's secateurs being found at the scene covered in blood and that Miguel was now on the run. She certainly didn't know Antonio had just called off the wedding until his future brother-in-law was cleared of murder. Until *I* figured out who killed Jean-Claude or somehow exonerated Miguel.

"It's about the wedding," I said "It's off."

"*What?* You can't be serious. It's in ten days. Everything's all planned, all ordered. Don't tell me Antonio chickened out."

"It's a lot more complicated than that," I said.

"This better be good. He can't leave Valeria standing at the altar, you know. They have a little girl to think of."

And then I told her.

ON THE WAY HOME my phone rang again. This time it was Kit, calling from her office in Leesburg. This would be a business call, not personal.

"I'm so sorry you were the one who found Jean-Claude, Luce. How are you doing?"

I could tell by her tone of voice that she was circling around to asking me to tell her what happened.

"I don't know. I guess I'm still in shock."

"Could you tell me about it?"

"You mean, for the *Trib*?"

"Well . . . yes. Your story is the only piece of the puzzle that's missing."

"There's nothing to tell that you probably don't already know from your husband."

"Can't you take me through it?" she asked. "Please?"

"I don't want to be quoted and have my name in the news, Kit. I just got rid of Pippa O'Hara . . . actually Frankie did."

"That woman wouldn't waste her time asking you to turn

around so she could stab you in the back if you were in her way. She'd just stab you in the chest and step over you. Did you talk to her?"

"Of course not." I pulled into the driveway and shut off the engine.

"What if I don't quote you? You could just be an informed source. No names."

"All right. But that's it."

"Great. So tell me."

"There's not much to tell. I went over to La Vigne looking for Miguel Otero this morning. When I got there, the crush pad door was wide open and the place was deserted. I found Jean-Claude in the cave in the back of the winery where they keep their reds in barrels."

"You mean you didn't find him in the barrel room itself?"

Damn. She hadn't known that fact. "No. Remember my name is out of this."

"Sure, sure. So how did you find him? I mean, how did you come across his body?"

"The door to the cave was ajar. He was lying right there, just inside the door."

"Right." I could hear the faint click of her computer keys and her lightning-fast typing. "Then what?"

"Then I called Toby and Robyn and left messages on their voice mail. Finally I reached Colette Barnes, Toby's secretary, at the house and she said they'd gone out for their morning hack. All three of them showed up in Toby's car right after Deputy Mathis arrived."

"How did they seem?"

I thought for a moment. "Shocked. As you'd expect. Colette

seemed a little more in control, but she'd just started working for Toby recently so she wouldn't have known Jean-Claude that well."

"Right." More typing. "Why were you looking for Miguel?"

"We're short-handed and I wanted to ask him if he could work for us this weekend."

"Guess that's not going to happen with him disappearing."

"Nope. My turn to ask. Does Bobby think Miguel killed Jean-Claude?"

"I'd be the last person he'd tell. You know that. Bobby bends over backward to make sure I have to work harder for any information I get than anyone else, so it doesn't look like favoritism."

I did know that. "You've been putting the puzzle pieces together, as you said. What do you think? Did Miguel do it?"

She didn't answer right away, which I took as a good sign. Finally she said in a thoughtful voice, "I don't know. It seems he had means, motive, and opportunity, which doesn't rule him out. What about you? Do you think he's guilty?"

I said immediately, "No."

"Well, that's certainly emphatic. Why not?"

"Gut feeling."

"Right." She sounded dubious. "Okay, I guess that's about it unless there's anything else you can tell me. Anything more about the crime scene?"

There was no way I was going to say that I'd stepped in Jean-Claude's blood and I didn't think I'd ever wear those work boots again.

"I don't think so."

"Thanks, kiddo," she said. "I owe you."

"I know." I got out of the Jeep. "Don't worry, I plan to collect."

PERSIA HAD LEFT A note in the kitchen explaining how to reheat the dinner she had prepared for Quinn and me as if we were a couple of inexperienced teenagers. Eli phoned as I was preheating the oven.

"Change of plans, Luce. Hope and I are staying at Sasha's for the night," he said. "I saw a Channel 3 news van in the winery parking lot when I got back to the studio a while ago and didn't want Hopie asking any questions. Word must be out that you're the one who found Jean-Claude."

"It is. I just hung up from a call with Kit."

"Are you going to be okay? It must have been pretty gruesome."

Eli was squeamish when it came to seeing blood or even talking about it, so I kept my answer as sanitized as possible.

"I can't get the image out of my head of seeing him lying there and realizing he was dead. And then the crime scene technician finding Miguel Otero's secateurs a few feet away in the wine cellar."

"It was the lead story on the news a little while ago. Even ahead of Lolita. I heard it as we were driving over to Sasha's. I turned it off since Hope was in the car, though I caught enough to know they're looking for Miguel."

"Antonio swears he's innocent."

"Yeah, but it doesn't look so good for Miguel if he's on the run," Eli said. "Occam's razor, Luce. The simplest answer is usually the right one. Miguel and Jean-Claude didn't get along and Miguel's secateurs look like they were the murder weapon. Now Miguel's gone."

I told him about Antonio's ultimatum. "Antonio also told me Miguel knew Jean-Claude was in trouble for something that happened in France. After what Dominique said last night I searched the internet looking for information about an Algerian wine scandal and the de Merignac wines."

"And found nothing, I bet."

"Nothing worthwhile."

"The old man—Baron de Merignac—can pay off anyone he needs to in order to keep family secrets from getting out. Besides, that Algerian wine scandal happened years ago." My brother sounded dismissive. "I can't believe something so far in the past would be a motive for murdering Jean-Claude now. I mean, why wait so long? I'm sorry, but my money is on Miguel. He just . . . lost his temper and did something in a moment of rage. Killed someone in a fit of anger."

I didn't want to believe Eli or Bobby or anyone else who thought Miguel was guilty, in part for Antonio's sake, but also partly—and somewhat selfishly—for mine. I couldn't afford to have our crew boycott us and refuse to work during harvest. But Eli was right: it didn't look so good for Miguel.

Before he hung up, Eli told me he wanted to walk the land where he planned to build his new home first thing tomorrow morning. "I've been thinking about moving the site," he said. "Don't worry, it's in the same area we've been talking about."

"I thought you were happy with the site you picked. Your drawings are finally finished and you were ready to sign a contract with a builder. What happened?"

"I just want to be one hundred percent sure before anyone brings a Bobcat in and starts digging the foundation."

"Weren't you one hundred percent sure last week?"

"I tweaked the design last night so the back of the house gets full western sunlight like Highland House. I might need to shift the location."

When Eli went into perfectionist mode, I'd learned my lesson years ago. Just say okay.

"Okay," I said. "But please let me know what you decide."

I hung up as Quinn texted me.

Home in 20 minutes. Ready for a drink. What's for dinner?

I wrote back. *More than ready for a drink. Persia's eggplant parmigiana & homemade garlic bread. Just talked to Eli.*

He texted a smiling emoji, presumably because of the meal and not my talk with Eli. I put the eggplant parmigiana in the oven along with the foil-wrapped garlic bread, and went into the library. David Phelps' email was still sitting in my in-box waiting for my answer. I booted up the computer. Did I want to meet him?

Who was he, anyway? He'd been cagey and fairly opaque in giving out any details about himself except for mentioning a few things about his adoptive parents and the highly personal fact that he and I shared DNA, thanks to my father having sex with his biological mother. Once? More than once? *When?*

I sat down and reread his email. He wanted to know about his father—*our* father—but now he'd aroused my curiosity as well. I wanted to know about his mother. Who was the woman with whom Leland had had an affair? David Phelps at least owed me that information after detonating a bomb in the middle of my life and leaving me feeling like I was holding pieces of Humpty Dumpty. I would never, ever be able to put everything back together again.

I heard Quinn's truck pull into the circular driveway. I glanced at the clock on the fireplace mantel. He was five minutes early. I clicked on the icon for a new email before I changed my mind, and wrote quickly.

Dear David,

You are correct that your letter has come as a huge surprise, and I do think it would be a good idea for us to meet. I have no idea where you live—you have dropped into my life out of nowhere—but perhaps we could meet some place in the Middleburg area? First, though, please tell me about yourself as I am totally in the dark about you while you have the advantage of apparently knowing quite a lot about me.

The front door opened and closed. I heard Quinn call my name and the dull thud of his keys landing on the telephone table in the foyer.

I didn't know how to sign David's email. *Your half-sister Lucie? Sincerely? Hope to hear from you? Cheers?*

Finally I just typed my name.

"In here," I called and hit Send. By the time Quinn poked his head around the door, I had turned off the computer screen.

"Are you okay?" he asked.

"Just checking email."

"Jean-Claude's murder is going to be on the six o'clock news. I didn't know if you wanted to watch it, see what they're saying. I'll pour us drinks."

Eli was right: the death of Jean-Claude de Merignac was the lead story on the news, even ahead of Hurricane Lolita. As soon as the announcers said "Good evening," a *Breaking News* banner flashed across the bottom of the screen and the camera switched to Pippa, who was standing in front of the La Vigne Cellars sign. It was a live report. Frankie had already told her I wasn't around and I wondered if she would make any comment about my unavailability.

She did. ". . . body was discovered this morning by Lucie Montgomery, owner of Montgomery Estate Vineyard in Atoka, and next-door neighbor of former secretary of state Tobias Levine and his partner, Robyn Callahan. Ms. Montgomery was—apparently—not available for an interview, but News Channel 3 has learned that the murder weapon was a pair of pruning shears owned by Miguel Otero, an employee at La Vigne Cellars. The Loudoun County Sheriff's Office is looking for Otero, who disappeared shortly after de Merignac's body was discovered. The Sheriff's Office says Otero should be considered armed and dangerous. Anyone with information . . ."

"*Apparently* not available?" Quinn asked. "That was a dig."

"Well, I was available. Just not for her. But 'armed and dangerous'? Miguel?" I said. "Is she kidding?"

Quinn pointed the remote at the television and hit the Mute button. "Antonio's really upset. I finally sent him home to Valeria."

I drank some wine. "I know Antonio's upset. He says Miguel's innocent and wants me to prove it or no one will show up to pick the Cab Franc on Saturday. Or do anything else around here. He says all the guys are scared of ICE. Even the legal ones."

Quinn eyed me. "You? Why is it your responsibility?"

"Because my family and the de Merignacs go way back in France, which apparently is supposed to give me an in with finding out who really killed Jean-Claude. Oh, yes, he also called off the wedding until this is all sorted out."

Quinn got up off the sofa and held out a hand to me. "Come on," he said, pulling me up. "Let's eat. I'm starved. We can finish talking about this over dinner."

"What about Lolita?" I said. "Don't you want to see the latest?"

He gave me a weary look. "I think we've both had enough bad news for one day, don't you?"

But even after dinner we were still talking about Jean-Claude's murder. We both heard the rumble of a helicopter crisscrossing the sky overhead while we were eating. The Loudoun County Sheriff's Office didn't own a search-and-rescue helicopter, but next-door Fairfax did. The Fairfax County Police Department must have sent it to help Loudoun in the search for Miguel. I wondered how long they would continue looking for him before quitting for the night.

"Someone must have seen Miguel in the area," Quinn said as the sound of blades whirred overhead one more time. "Those helicopters have huge searchlights."

"They're flying over us. Highland Farm."

"I know."

"Do you think he's hiding here?"

"He left on foot. Maybe he's still in the area. I can't imagine he'd want to be very far away from Isabella, especially in her condition."

"He must be terrified."

We had gone outside on the veranda and were sitting on the glider finishing the last of the dinner wine. The weather had cooled off and a fresh, clean breeze rustled the trees. The faded chirping of the cicadas and a dog barking in the distance were the only sounds now. The noise of the helicopter's twilight search had receded, which I hoped meant it had gone back to Fairfax.

"If Miguel didn't kill Jean-Claude," Quinn said, "then who did? There's a murderer out there somewhere."

I set my wineglass on the floor and shifted so I was lying with my head on Quinn's lap, staring up at the pale blue veranda ceiling, a color we called *haint* blue. It had been painted that soft blue-green as long as I could remember because of an old Southern superstition that the color warded off haints, the restless spirits of the dead who still hadn't moved on from the physical world. Tonight I didn't want any spirits—specifically Jean-Claude de Merignac—lurking here, or anywhere in my thoughts for that matter.

"I know," I said and shuddered as one of our phones, which were lying on the coffee table, rang.

"Yours," Quinn said and handed it to me.

"It's Yasmin Imrie." I swung my feet around so they hit the floor and sat up. "I completely forgot about her with everything that's happened. We were supposed to talk at the end of the day."

When I answered she apologized for calling so late.

"I was at the grave site until it was too dark to see anything," she said. "I hope I'm not bothering you at this hour. Win Turnbull stopped by after he finished over at La Vigne Cellars, so I heard that you were the one who discovered the winemaker who was murdered. What an awful experience for you. I'm so sorry."

"Thanks. It was a shock. Actually, it still is."

"You know, maybe it wasn't such a good idea to call you tonight. Why don't we talk in the morning?" she said. "I can tell you my news then. It's nothing that can't wait."

My pulse quickened. Yasmin had spent the entire day at the gravesite. She must have found something to keep her there so long.

"You have news?"

"I do, but I'm fairly certain it won't be what you're expecting. It's a bit grim. After everything you've been through today . . ."

I didn't need any more grim news, but there was no way I was going to let her go without finding out what she'd discovered.

"It's okay. Maybe you should just tell me what it is. Quinn Santori, my fiancé, is listening now, too." I put the phone on speaker.

"Hi, there," Quinn said.

"Hello." She blew out a long breath that sounded like air being let out of a tire. "If you're sure, Lucie."

"I am."

"All right. First the good news, relatively speaking. The rest of the skeleton was in that grave. Not only was it completely intact, it was quite well-preserved. The shed did a good job protecting it from the elements and keeping out predators.

Otherwise the bones would have been scattered to the four winds."

I waited for her to go on.

"Also, it looks as if the body was placed in the grave, not dumped in the ground. It was wrapped in a quilt." It sounded as if she paused to take a sip of a drink before continuing. "Now for the bad news. Unfortunately after I removed the skull from where you discovered it, I found signs of blunt force trauma to the back of the head. It had nothing to do with something that might have happened in the grave. Someone hit her with something. Hard."

I envisioned the skull as Yasmin described it, what it must look like after a massive blow. And then wondered about the flesh-and-blood woman who'd been the victim. "Hard enough to kill her?"

"There was evidence of multiple blows, so yes, I'd say so."

The coppery smell of Jean-Claude's blood came back to me as sharp and pungent as if I were standing next to him again in the wine cellar.

I sucked in my breath. "Wow."

"We don't have to go on, Lucie. I know this is not pleasant."

"It's okay. Do you think the quilt was used to transport her to where she was buried?" I asked.

"It's possible. I didn't see any traces of blood on the fabric where it came in contact with the wound. So maybe she was already dead when she was wrapped in it," Yasmin said. "Still, it's hard to say after all this time."

She paused and I had the feeling she was holding some information back.

"Is there anything else?"

"As a matter of fact, yes," she said. "I found a man's cuff-link in the grave. It was engraved with the initials CM."

"What would a cufflink be doing in her grave?" I asked.

"My guess would be that it belonged to whoever dug that hole. It's not uncommon for a button or a cufflink to come off a jacket, or a pair of glasses to fall out of a shirt pocket and disappear in the soil without the individual realizing it at the time."

I closed my eyes. "CM," I said. "The *M* might stand for Montgomery."

There was no point stating the obvious. If that were true, one of my ancestors had buried this woman in an unmarked grave. Maybe the woman wasn't related to me. Maybe whoever killed her was. Maybe CM was the murderer.

I felt as if I couldn't catch my breath. "If I'm right, it changes everything," I said. "Someone in my family was trying to hide this woman's body. Possibly the person who killed her."

Quinn covered my hand with his. "You don't know that. A lot of people have last names that begin with *M*."

"It's too much of a coincidence," I said. "What do you think, Yasmin?"

"I don't know," she said in a thoughtful voice. "If I were a member of your family and I'd killed someone—let's say the owner of the cufflink was the murderer—I'd put her body in a field in the middle of nowhere or dump her in a lake. I wouldn't bury her a few feet from the family cemetery."

"And if she's a Montgomery—the victim, that is," Quinn said, "why wasn't she buried in the cemetery?"

My head was starting to ache. "None of this makes sense," I said. "Yasmin, do you have any idea how old this grave is?"

"Eighteen hundreds," she said right away. "Probably mid-eighteen hundreds; say around eighteen fifties or eighteen sixties."

"So either immediately before or during the Civil War," Quinn said.

"That's right," she said.

"If CM is related to me," I said, "every Montgomery since the early eighteen hundreds is listed in the record section in our family Bible. Including the name and birthdate of spouses, along with names and birthdates of all their children. Now that I know roughly when she died, maybe I can figure out who he was, which would solve one of the mysteries."

"You might be able to find out something about her as well," Yasmin said, "in that family Bible."

"Meaning one of my relatives killed another member of the family?" Now we were really moving into uncharted territory, something out of a Greek tragedy or a bad reality television show, a place I had no desire to explore.

"It happens, Lucie." Yasmin's voice was gentle. "It might explain the rationale for the grave being so near your family's cemetery."

"What about the quilt?" Quinn seemed to want to change the grisly subject. "Did you find anything wrapped in it? Besides her, I mean."

"Unfortunately no," Yasmin said. "I had to remove it in order to get at the rest of the remains. I'm afraid I'm no expert on quilts, so I can't really tell you anything about it. I'll give it to you when I see you, Lucie. It's quite fragile, but perhaps you can have what's salvageable restored. I imagine it would be of historic interest."

"I know a textile expert I can ask about that," I said. "Now what happens next?"

"It's up to you," she said. "I don't know if you want to see her in situ, or if, under the circumstances, you'd prefer for me to remove the samples I need and bring them to the lab so I can conduct some tests. I could cover the site until you're ready to make any arrangements. And don't worry, I'll make sure it will be as watertight as possible so there won't be any damage from the hurricane. In the meantime, perhaps you want to contact a funeral home that would be able to help you with properly interring the remains."

"I plan to have her reburied in our cemetery," I said. "And before you take your samples I'd like to see her just as you found her."

"Are you sure?"

"I am."

"All right, then, why don't I do that buccal swab when you come by? That way the lab can compare your DNA with hers. How about tomorrow morning, say nine o'clock?"

"Tomorrow at nine is fine," I said.

"We'll both be there," Quinn said.

After she disconnected, I said to Quinn, "You don't have to come. There's so much going on at the winery . . . so much work to do."

"The place will survive without us for half an hour. I'm coming," he said. "No arguments."

I gave him a wan smile. "Thanks."

"Are you going to be okay?"

I knew what he was asking. "Quinn, she was buried in a storage shed. No coffin and someone apparently murdered her. Maybe someone related to me."

"You might never know what really happened, sweetheart. How she died. How she ended up where she did."

"I have to at least do my best to find out."

He pulled me into his arms and whispered into my hair. "Let's take this one step at a time. It's also possible someone didn't have time for a proper burial and she was put in that shed to protect her remains. Maybe she was hidden there on purpose."

I sat back and stared at him. "You could be right. Maybe whoever buried her there didn't want anyone to know she was dead, so it could appear she just vanished, or ran away."

He reached for my hand and pulled me up from the glider. "Look, it's been a hell of a day. What about taking out the telescope and doing some stargazing?"

Getting lost in the stars and planets and all the other phenomena in the night sky was Quinn's escape when things became too intense right here on earth. "You're reduced to your proper size in the universe," he'd said to me once. "Even the biggest problems don't seem that important once you can actually see how small our galaxy—and Earth—really is in the vastness of outer space."

I disentangled my hand from his. "Would you mind if I don't join you? I'd like to take a look at the Bible and maybe some of Leland's genealogical records. I really do want to find out who CM is."

"Do you have to do that tonight?"

When I didn't answer he said, "All right, I know when

you've already made up your mind. I'll be at the summerhouse all by my lonesome self, if you decide to join me."

I kissed him. "I love you."

He kissed me back. "I love you more."

I left him on the veranda and went inside, waiting until I heard his footsteps and then the treads creaking on the stairs. Through the window I watched his dark silhouette moving through the garden. When it disappeared I walked into the library, flipped on the lights, and hit the space bar on the computer. The screen flickered to life and the mail icon indicated eight new emails. I sat down and opened my inbox. The very first email that had come in was from David Phelps. He had wasted no time in replying.

I opened it and read.

Dear Lucie,

I apologize for being so mysterious in my first email and sharing so little information about myself. So here is my story: I grew up in Washington, D.C., and lived here all my life, so I'm a local boy. I had what can only be described as an idyllic childhood and never doubted that Joe and Margaret Phelps loved me as if I were their own son, so I was blessed. I was fortunate to be educated in private schools in D.C. and went on to study theology and history at Harvard. After that I got a master's in history at Princeton. For the last five years I have been working as a photographer for *National Geographic* since I have never been without a camera in my hands my whole life. My parents gave me my first one when I was ten and it has been a love affair ever since. I also freelance on the side—mostly pro bono work for charity—but I am a restless soul, a travel junkie, and constantly seek out new places and the next adventure. Photography gives me a good way to express what is important to me, to show my worldview. More on that another time. I have been told by friends that I am never far from a soapbox.

There is one other thing you should know that you may not be prepared for: I am biracial. My biological mother is African-American. It wasn't until I learned about Leland that I realized I was half-white. Or "only" half-black, depending on how you look at it. It was a huge shock to me and, in retrospect, I'm glad I didn't know growing up because it was very simple to check the "African-American" box whenever the question of race came up on medical forms or college application papers. Otherwise I might have felt forced to choose since you're only supposed to check one box.

If, after learning all this, you're still willing to meet me, I'd be happy to drive out to Middleburg or Atoka so we could talk and get to know each other. For obvious reasons it might be best if it were somewhere private. I'll leave it up to you to suggest the time and place; if I do not hear back from you, I'll understand that after learning more about me, you might prefer to leave things as they are.

Hopefully,

David

I sat there for a moment, trying to catch my breath. A half brother who was biracial.

I hit Reply.

Dear David,

I would very much like to meet you. We would have privacy to talk at the old Goose Creek Bridge on Mosby's Highway, just outside the town of Middleburg. I'm at the vineyard every day since we're in the middle of harvest, but I can get away for an hour, so why don't you pick the date and time? Perhaps we could meet before Lolita arrives?

—Lucie

Then I hit Send, shut off the computer, and went and found the cognac bottle on the dining room sideboard. I poured myself a glass and brought it back to the library.

I'd sent my saliva sample to the Genome Project because I wanted to learn more about my family and our heritage. Now I knew things I'd never bargained on, family secrets I was certain no one expected would ever be uncovered. I went over to the bookshelves and picked up the Montgomery Bible.

For my own piece of mind I needed to see if I could figure out who CM was. And hope I didn't get burned. Again.

Though I wasn't very optimistic about that happening.

Thirteen

The enormous gilt-edged Bible with its weathered brown leather cover, gilded tool work, faded gold cross, and the barely decipherable embossed names of Thomas and Mary Montgomery probably weighed at least six or seven pounds. Two worn grosgrain ribbons, white and black, marked pages in the Old and New Testaments, placed there by whomever had last been reading it. I found them in Psalms, on the page containing the twenty-third psalm, and in the Gospel of John at the story of the wedding at Cana, Jesus' first miracle. A third burgundy ribbon was placed at the beginning of the section called *Family Record*. I turned to the last page and ran my finger over my mother's elegant handwriting with which she had recorded her marriage to Leland and the birth dates of Eli, Mia, and me. Leland had written in the date of her death. I had filled in my father's death date. Eli's first marriage wasn't listed, nor was Hope's birth. Eventually there would be my marriage to Quinn and Eli's to Sasha.

We had some catching up to do.

I found the page listing the births and deaths in the mid-1800s and skimmed them. The only names beginning with the letter *C* belonged to women, but Yasmin had been very clear that she'd found a man's cufflink. I started over, checking entries from the late 1700s until the beginning of the twentieth century. Nothing. No man whose first name began with *C*. In a way, that was probably good news and perhaps CM wasn't related to me.

Maybe it was the victim in the grave who was a relative, after all. Susanna Montgomery, the youngest child of Hugh, who had ridden with Mosby's Rangers, had only a birthdate listed next to her name: October 5, 1843. The skeleton had been in her late teens or early twenties when she died, according to Win Turnbull. If it were Susanna, it would fit with Yasmin's assessment of the grave dating from the 1850s or 1860s. There was also the fact that there was no marriage date or date of death—not even a question mark as if acknowledging that no one knew when she died. Had her death been covered up from her own family? *By* her own family?

Years ago Leland had hired an archivist from the Thomas Balch Library, the history and genealogy library in Leesburg, to assist him with cataloguing our family documents and putting them in chronological order. The archival boxes that had survived the fire a few years ago were stored in a barrister's bookcase next to my father's antique partners desk.

I slid open one of the glass-and-wood-fretted pocket doors, and checked the labels on the boxes. I found nothing in the boxes from the 1850s, but when I got to the 1860s I got lucky, especially because several years were missing, having been destroyed in the fire. Tucked among the newspaper clippings about Mosby's Rangers and the success of their raids thwarting the Yankees between 1863 and 1865 was a letter from Abigail Montgomery, Hugh's wife and Susanna's mother, dated August 8, 1862. Somehow it had been misplaced. It took me a while to decipher the crabbed, cramped handwriting, but eventually I figured out that it was a letter to someone named Cousin Simon telling him about the engagement of "our beloved Susanna" to Captain Charles Montgomery. The wedding between Susanna and Cousin Charles, as she also called him, would be a simple affair and would take place when he was home on leave from the war, probably in the autumn.

Reading between the lines, it seemed as if Abigail was not entirely pleased with her future son-in-law's financial situation, as the owner of the Goose Creek Ordinary, a tavern located halfway between Middleburg and Upperville, in addition to the Rectortown General Store. She also seemed to imply that Susanna, whose marital prospects had not been good, had been lucky to have Cousin Charles take such an affectionate interest in her, asking her to be his wife.

I set the letter on the desk and sat back in Leland's creaky chair, trying to make sense of what I'd just read and everything I knew after what Yasmin had told Quinn and me this evening. Or what I thought I knew. According to the family Bible, Susanna had never married and supposedly no one knew when she died. Had "Cousin Charles" murdered his bride-to-be when he came home from some bloody battlefield and then tried to cover it up? Had the rest of the family gone along with it for some reason and deliberately left her death date blank? Not because they didn't know when she died, but because they didn't want it known that Charles, who was fighting bravely for our cause, had killed her?

The Rectortown General Store, which sat on the corner of Atoka and Rectortown Roads, was now known simply as the General Store. Thelma Johnson had owned the place ever since God was a boy. As far as I knew, Thelma had inherited it from her mother and father who inherited it from her grandparents, and so on. But Abigail had written that Charles Montgomery owned it, along with the Goose Creek Ordinary.

Tomorrow as soon as Quinn and I finished our meeting with Yasmin, I intended to pay a visit to Thelma. We needed to stock up on water, batteries, and candles anyway before Lolita arrived. But I also had some questions about Charles Montgomery that I hoped she'd be able to answer.

I put the boxes and their files back where I'd found them—including Abigail's letter—turned out the lights, and went upstairs to bed. Quinn was already asleep, his breathing quiet and regular. I undressed and slid under the covers. The night had turned chilly and I moved closer, pressing myself against him and feeling the heat of his body warm me up. He rolled over so he faced me, now wide-awake.

"Hey, you," he said in a drowsy voice, "come closer. You're freezing. Why'd you stay downstairs so long? Did you spend all that time trying to find out who that woman might be? Or CM?"

"I did," I said. "I'll tell you in the morning."

"Mmm," he said. "Tell me everything."

Everything. "Of course I will."

When was I going to tell him about the Genome Project and the discovery of a half brother who had sought me out? That Leland once had an affair with a now-prominent African-American woman who apparently wouldn't want her life disrupted by meeting the adult son she'd given up? When was I going to tell Eli? And Mia? The longer I kept this secret, the harder it was going to be.

Mia would be devastated. Eli would be hurt, but I knew he'd also be angry. At Leland, for sure, and maybe at me for opening Pandora's box. For pulling both of them into a maelstrom of my own making. Eli avoided confrontation like the plague and Mia was a fragile soul.

As for Quinn, I wanted to meet David before I said anything to him. His own father had walked out on his mother before he was born and he never, ever wanted to talk about it. David's situation would hit too close to home, except this time it was *my* father—who had hired Quinn while I was still living in France—who had walked out on his son.

"You okay?" he asked now, still sleepy.

I snuggled deeper into his arms and pushed my own confused feelings about what my father had done to the far recesses of my mind. "Now I am."

"Lucie," he said, no longer sounding drowsy. "I want to take care of you, you know that."

"I know. Though you know I can take care of myself."

"You're tough," he said. "That's why I love you."

"You're pretty tough yourself. And I love you, too."

He rolled over onto his back and pulled me on top of him. "Prove it," he said.

So I did.

. . .

I FELL ASLEEP SHORTLY after our second round of lovemak-ing, exhausted from the events of the day and lack of sleep the night before, my mind totally distracted by the things Quinn's hands and tongue had done to me. Once again he was up be-fore I was and the smell of freshly brewed coffee woke me. I got up and within ten minutes had showered, dressed, and scraped my hair back into a ponytail.

Quinn poured my coffee and handed it to me with a kiss as soon as I walked into the kitchen. "Feel better today?" he asked.

I leaned against him and nodded. "I think so."

"I'll get the newspaper," he said. "Be right back."

He left the room and I pulled out my phone, quickly scroll-ing through my mail. David Phelps had replied last night. In fact, according to the time stamp, he'd written back practically the moment he'd received my email.

How about tomorrow afternoon, Thursday? 2 p.m.?

Thursday. That was today. Quinn would be back any sec-ond. I hit Reply.

See you today at 2.

The swooshing sound of my email being sent coincided with the kitchen door swinging open. I set my phone on the counter.

"Anything new this morning?" Quinn asked. "I haven't checked my mail yet."

"Just the usual stuff. I suppose the *Trib* did a big story on Jean-Claude's murder?"

"You could say that."

He unfolded the paper and laid it on the kitchen table, open to the front page. I took one look and my heart sank. A banner headline dominated the page and it wasn't about Hurricane Lolita.

DEATH AMONG THE VINES: INTERNATIONAL CELEBRITY WINEMAKER FOUND MURDERED AT HOME OF FORMER SECRETARY OF STATE TOBIAS LEVINE.

Two articles took up the top half of page one. The other half was devoted to Lolita and the tax bill churning through Congress.

The most prominent story about Jean-Claude's murder was an account of what had happened; the other—with an especially dashing picture of Jean-Claude at the Cannes Film Festival last year—was an extensive biography of his career and his famous family. There was also a grainy picture of Miguel with a photo credit that belonged to someone with a Hispanic surname I didn't recognize. I wondered how the paper had gotten hold of it and who had given it to them. The article about what Toby had done professionally since leaving diplomatic life and buying La Vigne Cellars—TOP EX-DIPLOMAT REAPS BITTER HARVEST—was on the front page of the Lifestyle section. My name was left out of any of the articles—Kit had kept her word—but she did put in the details I gave her about where Jean-Claude was found, mentioning me only as "a neighbor" who had discovered the body.

Quinn and I leaned over the table, shoulders touching, and read in silence. When we finished, he refolded the newspaper and placed it on the counter next to yesterday's paper, his mouth set in a grim line. Had it only been a day ago that we were reading about Jean-Claude and Dominique feuding at the Goose Creek Inn in "Around Town"?

"It doesn't look good for Miguel," Quinn said.

"I know."

"What if he really did it?"

"He wouldn't screw up his chance for citizenship, nor would he leave Isabella all alone with a new baby. I don't think he's guilty."

"Then who killed Jean-Claude, if it wasn't Miguel?"

"A lot of people around here didn't like Jean-Claude," I said.

"Including me," Quinn said in an even voice. "Come on. If we're supposed to meet Yasmin at nine o'clock, we'd better get going."

As we left the kitchen I glanced at the two newspapers side-by-side where Quinn had left them on the counter. Someone had drawn devil's horns coming out of Jean-Claude's head and given him a sinister-looking goatee in yesterday's photograph. Who would do something . . . never mind. It was probably Quinn.

He'd admitted yet again that he didn't like Jean-Claude. But he'd never, ever consider murder to get rid of someone he didn't like.

I was sure of it.

ON THE DRIVE OVER to the cemetery I told Quinn that I suspected the woman buried in the shed was Susanna Montgomery, Hugh Montgomery's youngest child and only daughter.

"Except for her date of birth—which was 1843—there's nothing else listed in the Bible next to her name," I said. "No marriage date, no date of death. I also found out she was engaged to someone named Charles Montgomery."

"As in CM, owner of a missing cufflink?"

"Possibly. Maybe very possibly."

But Quinn was focusing on something else. "Was she going to marry . . . a relative? Like a cousin, maybe?"

"I don't think he was a first cousin, but yes, Abigail's letter referred to him as 'Cousin Charles.' He was also Captain Charles Montgomery. He served in one of the Virginia infantry brigades."

"You do that a lot in the South, don't you? Marry your own family." Quinn looked as if I'd told him we also ate our young after boiling them in oil here in the sultry South.

"It's not just a Southern practice," I said, feeling defensive. "In many cultures marriage among cousins is quite common. Especially second cousins marrying each other. Look at the history of European royal marriages. They married among themselves all the time, since there was a limited pool of available candidates."

"It just seems weird to me."

"You're from California. You guys invented weird."

He grinned and parked the green ATV next to the cemetery wall. "So if you're right, Susanna married her cousin Charles and then he killed her. Doesn't sound like happily-ever-after."

"You're not funny. What if they didn't get married? What if they argued about the marriage and he got upset and killed her because she didn't really want to marry him?"

"Or maybe he didn't want to marry her, so he got rid of her. We could speculate forever, you know," he said. "Let's go see this grave site."

Yasmin Imrie was waiting for us, somehow managing to look chic and stylish in faded jeans and a worn denim jacket over a Hungry Heart Springsteen T-shirt. The items that had been in her storage container yesterday were now fanned out around her—a whisk broom, a trowel, a couple of paintbrushes with big mop-like bristles. Even a pair of chopsticks. The shovel and screen were off to one side next to a mound of dirt heaped on a blue tarp and the entire area around the grave had been marked off by a grid system of red nylon twine that had been tied to a spike protruding from the cemetery wall. Yasmin was sitting cross-legged on another blue tarp making notes in a well-used notebook, engrossed in her work.

I introduced her to Quinn and caught the flicker of appreciative interest in her eyes as she got up and they shook hands. An unwelcome prick of jealousy stabbed me as he smiled back at her. I tried to push it away.

Quinn and I hadn't set a wedding date yet, though we'd talked about it a couple of times. For now we were content to get used to living together and neither of us felt in a rush to change the status quo. Quinn had been married before; his divorce after discovering his wife's affair with his former boss had been bitter. As for me, I didn't want a marriage as rocky and tempestuous as my parents' had been. In spite of everything I still wanted the fairy tale with the happily-ever-after ending. I *wanted* to believe it was possible. What I'd just learned about my father—his betrayal of all of us, but especially my mother—and now my overly possessive or, maybe even insecure, reaction to Yasmin's friendly smile when she met Quinn made me wonder if I'd ever be ready.

But now she was turning that smile on me, standing up, brushing dirt off her jeans, and asking if we wanted to see the excavation site. I said yes.

The skeleton lay at the bottom of a two-foot-deep rectangle. I was surprised at how quickly she'd worked. The skull had been placed in its correct location in relation to the rest of the body, meaning we couldn't see the consequences of the blows she had described last night. I knew it had been a deliberate decision and I was grateful for Yasmin's consideration and compassion.

"I removed what was left of her clothes, as you can see. Each item is sitting on a paper bag over there." She waved her hand in the direction of the shovel and mound of dirt. "We'll take a look at everything after we're through here and then I'll bag it to protect it. The quilt is there as well. It must have been quite beautiful. You can still see some of the original colors of the fabrics in places where it was folded over the body and not exposed to the elements."

Quinn and I glanced at the area she pointed to, but she was already moving on.

"There are a several items of interest that I found when I uncovered the grave cut," she said. "I did what's called a single context excavation."

She saw our blank looks and smiled. "Don't worry. I'll explain everything."

"Such as 'single context excavation,'" Quinn said.

"Exactly. What that means is that I removed layers of dirt in increments of five millimeters, beginning in the first half of the grave. It's a British technique not often used in America, but it allows great certainty that whatever is uncovered will relate to the examination site itself. In other words, everything that belonged exclusively to this grave. It would be clear that, say, a coin or bottle cap that was also uncovered would not be relevant to this excavation."

I glanced at Quinn. "I think we get that," I said.

"Whoever dug this grave used a shovel that had a nick in one side. You can see the shovel marks right here." She pointed to scrapes in the compacted dirt and we could see the consistent indentation on the left side. "He also used a pickax—I'm presuming it was a man since I doubt a woman would have done this. Here, let me show you."

She dropped gracefully into the hole she'd dug. Quinn and I knelt and I felt as though I were at a church altar rail, about to take part in something holy and sacred. Susanna Montgomery, if that's who she was, had died nearly a century and a half ago. There was no scent, no whispering voice in the wind, no telltale sign that any trace of who she was still remained.

"After all this time you can still see shovel marks?" Quinn sounded dubious. "The *original* shovel marks?"

"I can assure you that they're not mine, if that's what you're implying," Yasmin said in a dry voice. "Nothing had disturbed this grave. No animals, no insects. *Nothing*. She must have been buried late in the year, perhaps just before the ground froze for winter. That would also help slow down decomposition."

That fit in with Abigail's letter and the wedding time-line. *Sometime in the autumn.* When Charles came home from the war.

"Right." Quinn looked chastened. "Sorry about the question."

She gave him a brisk nod. "No worries. What about you, Lucie? Something's on your mind."

"It's what you said about the shovel. When my parents first started the vineyard, my mother, who was an artist, wanted to decorate everything—including the old dairy barn where we keep our equipment," I said. "So she got a lot of old tools and shovels and things that had been lying around, cleaned them up, and hung them on the wall. I wonder . . ."

Quinn finished my sentence. "If there might be a shovel with a nick in it hanging on that wall? Are those tools that old?"

"They might be."

"Let's check them out as soon as we're done here."

"I should take a look at anything you've got as well," Yasmin said. "I can confirm whether it's a match with what I found here."

"Did you find anything else besides the cufflink you told us about last night?" I asked.

"Sorry. That was it. Everything else belonged to the victim."

"I did some research looking through family papers after we spoke," I said and filled her in on what I'd found and what I suspected.

Yasmin started to hoist herself out of the grave. Quinn held out his hand and she let him pull her up.

She nodded thanks and said to me, "It sounds like you might have a good start on figuring out who this woman is. I can definitely confirm whether you're related once I compare your DNA. That should give you something concrete so you'll know for sure."

"Though it won't explain why Charles buried her here after someone killed her," I said. "Unless he did it and hid her here so no one would find her. If CM is Charles Montgomery, that is."

Yasmin and Quinn remained silent.

I threw up my hands. "I wish she could talk."

"Let's see what the lab turns up," Yasmin said. "In the meantime, you still have what's left of her clothes, the quilt, and the cufflink. That's quite a lot to go on."

I could sense Quinn's weight shifting from one foot to the other next to me. He was growing impatient. We had work to do and he wanted to get back to the winery. Lolita would be here in three days.

"Is there anything else you can tell us?" he asked Yasmin.

"I think that's about it," Yasmin said. "The rest might be up to the two of you, looking through newspapers and genea-logical records at the library or documents at the courthouse in Leesburg . . . that sort of thing."

"What happens now?" I asked.

"I'm going to remove one of her teeth and a femur . . . I'll take care of that later and of course I'll return them once the lab is finished so she can be properly reburied," Yasmin said and I was grateful once again that she would spare us seeing this woman being dismembered, even if it was essential to identifying her. "I'll also be removing all of her bones from the site so they can be properly interred."

"You mean, like putting them in a box?" I tried to wrap my

head around the idea of a box of human bones. Though it probably wasn't much different from an urn of ashes. Except for the size.

"That's exactly right," she said. "Of course you realize there's nothing to hold them together anymore—no cartilage and obviously no flesh. It's part of the natural evolution of all living creatures, Lucie."

"Right," I said. "Ashes to ashes, dust to dust."

"Seen enough, sweetheart?" Quinn asked me.

I nodded.

"All right," Yasmin said. "Lucie, if you're ready to be swabbed, we can do this now and then you're done."

"I'm ready."

Unlike my vial of spit for the Genome Project, Yasmin's buccal swab of the inside of my cheek took seconds. When she was finished, she put the sample inside a test tube, which she then sealed and placed in a plastic envelope, which she also sealed.

"Let me give you all of the personal effects," she said. "Unless you want me to keep them with the bones?"

"No," I said. "I'll take them, thanks."

The clothes were tattered and had disintegrated so much that they were almost unrecognizable as garments. The quilt was faded and fragile-looking, and it didn't look like any quilt I'd ever seen. Each block consisted of narrow strips of fabric plainwoven as if they had been on a loom and then stitched along the perimeter to keep the weaving locked in place. The intricate quilting—what remained of the tiny, precise stitches—made the ribbony weaving even more secure, plus it seemed as though there were some kind of backing that helped stabilize the quilt. I didn't recognize the pattern, an elaborate geometric design that reminded me of a tessellation or three-dimensional motif—a design within a design—that must have been maddeningly complicated to keep track of in order to make it turn out so perfectly. Whoever made this quilt had been remarkably skillful.

Yasmin put the cufflink in a tiny cardboard envelope after letting Quinn and me examine it. I slipped the envelope into my left jeans pocket so I wouldn't lose it, just as my right pocket buzzed.

I pulled out my phone. Eli. I nearly hit the button to mute his call and then decided to take it.

"It's my brother," I said to Quinn and Yasmin. "Excuse me for a moment."

I answered and said, "What's up, Eli?"

"I think you'd better get over here." There was a warning note in his voice that made the hairs on the back of my neck prickle. "Now."

I moved away from Yasmin and Quinn. "Here, where? Are you at the site for your house?"

"Yup."

The clearing where he wanted to build was bounded by woods on two sides. What had he found? Why did I have to get over there right away?

"What is it?" I asked, but I already knew what he was going to say.

"I might know where Miguel is. Or where he *was*."

My heart sank. Miguel was hiding out on our land. Possibly in plain sight. He had managed to make his way across the border from Mexico to the U.S. and evade being caught years ago. He knew how to take care of himself, move under cover of darkness, and survive in hostile territory.

"We'll be right there."

I disconnected and said to Quinn, "That was Eli. Something has come up. He's at the site for his new house. It's kind of important. He'd like us to see something."

I hoped he could read between the lines because I wasn't about to say anything about Miguel in front of Yasmin.

"This is about his house?" Quinn frowned, a look of annoyance crossing his face. "Look, why don't you go check it out? After Yasmin takes her samples, she needs to cover up the grave. It has to be well-protected so nothing happens when Lolita shows up. I said I'd stick around and help her. You can take the ATV and she'll drop me at the winery when we're through. I'll bring the quilt and all the clothes in her car so nothing happens to them."

I wanted to tell him that I really needed him to come with me, that he had it wrong about Eli. Instead I said, "Sure. I'll catch up with you later. And, Yasmin, thanks for everything."

"I'm glad to have been able to help," she said. "I hope you get the answers you were looking for."

I walked over to the ATV and glanced over my shoulder. Quinn was saying something to Yasmin, who was laughing as he pointed at her T-shirt.

I wondered what answers I'd get when this was said and done, after Yasmin finished extracting DNA from a tooth and femur of a young woman who'd been beaten to death and wrapped in a quilt, someone I was presuming was Susanna Montgomery, and therefore related to me.

And if they'd be the ones I wanted to hear.

• • •

MULTIPLE VEHICLES MAKING MULTIPLE trips over many weeks had more or less cut a path through the fields to where Eli planned to build his new house. Eventually we would hire someone to put a proper road in, but for now it was serviceable unless it had rained really hard, which turned it into a mud-rutted, teeth-jarring adventure. After Lolita, it would probably be a swamp.

I parked next to Eli's car, a four-wheel-drive SUV that he'd left in a clearing surrounded by woods. Good thing I'd seen the car because this place didn't look familiar at all. I thought he only wanted to move the site a few feet from his original choice.

My brother was nowhere to be seen so I pulled out my phone and called him. If he was close by, I should have heard his phone ring. I didn't.

"Where are you?" I asked when he answered.

"Do you see a grove of tulip poplars where the woods begin? Four or five trees? One has a weird forty-five-degree elbow bend."

I saw the unusual tree. "I do."

"Start walking toward them. I'll meet you."

I tucked my jeans into my work boots and zipped up my windbreaker. Though spring and summer are the peak seasons for deer ticks, which spread Lyme disease here in Virginia faster than gossip travels in a small town, they were still around since it had been an unusually warm fall. The ticks attach themselves to you when you walk through tall grass. Miss finding and removing them at your peril. Lyme disease was no joke.

Eli met me on the other side of the trees. The look of fore-boding on his face told me I wasn't going to like what he wanted to show me.

"It's a bit of a hike," he said, glancing at my cane. "You going to be okay?"

I hate being treated like an invalid or a cripple. Eli, of all people, knew that better than almost anyone except Quinn. I said through gritted teeth, "I'll be just fine. I can do anything you can do. It just takes me longer."

He raised both hands in the air, a sign of surrender. "Sorry. Just asking. You don't need to be so tetchy."

The ramshackle stone cottage was nearly invisible behind a breakfront of trees, pines, and wild hollies until we stood in front of it. The little house blended into the woods so artfully I wondered if whoever decided to put it there had done so intentionally, ensuring it wouldn't be discovered. I had never seen it before and by the look on his face, neither had Eli.

I turned to my brother. "What the . . . ?"

"Hey, don't look at me. I had no idea there was a cottage here, either."

It looked as battered and storm-tossed as if it had twirled down from Kansas with Dorothy and Toto during the tornado. The wooden front door hung on a single hinge and there was so much greenery twining over the façade it looked as if the house had grown a beard and sported bushy eyebrows above the windows.

"Maybe it was another hiding place for Mosby and his Rangers like the Ruins used to be until the Yankees burned it down," I said. "Although this place is really hidden away. A secret hideout."

"I went inside," Eli said. "It's just a big room with two windows, a dirt floor, and a fireplace. And a ladder that leads to a crawl space. I didn't check it out since the ladder was in bad shape."

"What makes you think Miguel was here?" I asked.

"Someone was here. Recently."

"How do you know?"

"The floor was swept too clean," he said. "Like someone was trying to cover their footprints. Plus I found matches and a couple of candles behind a stone in the fireplace that was sticking out a little too much."

"Our old trick. Like we used to do at the Ruins when we were growing up."

In the days when the Ruins were still actual ruins, before Eli renovated the burned-out tenant house and turned it into a stage where we hosted concerts and plays during the warm-weather months, he and I had used it at various times to secretly drink and make out with our latest hot dates. We'd hidden candles, matches, and booze behind loose bricks.

"I'd like to see inside for myself," I added. "Are the front steps okay?"

"No. They're rotted, too. I'll have to give you a boost."

Eli's boost was more like a space launch. I managed to catch myself in time so I landed in a crouch rather than on my hands and knees. He hoisted himself inside and pulled me up so I was standing beside him.

A gust of wind blew through the room, rustling the leaves on the vines that twined around and through the house. The whispery scratching sounded like fingers moving the foliage out of the way in order for someone to watch us from a hidden vantage point outside. I spun around and blinked, certain I would catch a flash of movement through one of the windows, like a curtain closing or a winking eye as the leaves and branches settled back into place.

"What's the matter?" Eli asked. "You look like you saw a ghost."

"I'm fine. It just feels like we're being watched."

Eli glanced over his shoulder. "Now you're getting me spooked."

"You really think Miguel stayed here?"

"I don't know. But, like I said, someone did. Not that long ago."

"Yesterday?"

"Possibly." He shrugged. "I wonder if he's coming back."

"If it *was* Miguel, maybe he just stayed here last night and moved on. I wouldn't come back, if it was me," I said.

We looked at each other. "Who's going to tell Bobby?" he asked. "Me or you?"

"Tell him what? All this is just speculation. We don't know anything for sure," I said. "Besides, do you really believe Miguel would leave his secateurs in that wine cellar where they'd be sure to be found right away? Covered in Jean-Claude's blood? That's like having a neon sign saying MURDER WEAPON with an arrow pointing directly at them. How obvious could you be?"

"What are you saying?"

"I think it's possible Miguel was set up. More than possible."

"And you don't think Bobby's smart enough to draw that conclusion as well?"

I flushed. "Of course I do. But right now Miguel has already been tried in the press and found guilty. I think he's innocent."

"Okay, then, who didn't like Miguel besides Jean-Claude?" Eli asked. "Enough to frame him."

"You're asking the wrong question," I said. "You should be asking who didn't like Jean-Claude. Enough to kill him. And that list is a mile long."

My phone dinged in my pocket and I pulled it out. A text from Quinn.

Where are you?

"I've got to get going," I said to Eli. "It's Quinn."

I texted back.

Still with Eli. On my way soon. Where are you?

"I'm coming with you," Eli said. "So what do we do about Bobby? Say nothing?"

Another ding. *Barrel room. Showing Yasmin around.*

"Luce?"

"What?"

"I just asked you about Bobby."

"Oh. Right." I shoved my phone back in my pocket. "I'll let him know. I'll call him when I get back to the winery. Miguel's long gone anyway."

He held out a hand. "Come on. Let's get out of here. I'll help you down."

I looked around one more time. "How old do you think this house is? How long has it been here?"

"Pretty old," he said. "It's been here a long time."

"Thanks for that insight, Captain Obvious. You're the architect. Can you be any more specific?"

"Maybe mid–eighteen hundreds," he said. "I did poke at

some rotted plaster and lathe and saw what looked like news-papers tacked to the wood. They would have been used as insulation. I'll come back and take a closer look when I've got more time. Maybe there's a date on one of them."

I looked at the hole in the wall he was pointing to. "Maybe."

"Let's go," he said, lowering himself through the door. He turned and reached out to me. "Come on. Jump and I'll catch you."

We had to walk single file through the dense undergrowth back to his car and the ATV. He led the way. Over his shoulder he said, "I'd really like to restore that little cottage. Maybe move it so it's near my new place. Okay by you?"

I grabbed a branch he'd held on to so it wouldn't snap back and whip me across the face. "I'd like to know more about its history before you move it. How it got there and who built it. And why nobody in the family ever mentioned it before. It's not on any plat of our land that I've ever seen."

"I'll do some checking. Maybe we missed it."

The phone in my pocket had dinged twice more as we were walking.

"Everything okay between you and Quinn?" Eli asked.

"Fine. Why?"

"You've been ignoring his texts. At least I'm assuming he's texting you."

"Nothing's wrong. I left him at the grave site with the fo-rensic anthropologist. They were going to cover it up after she took her bone samples so when Lolita arrives, it will be weather-tight and hopefully nothing will get damaged."

He gave me a suspicious look. "If you say so."

"I do. Yasmin Imrie, the anthropologist, found a cufflink

with the initials CM on it. I did some checking. It's possible
CM was a distant cousin named Charles Montgomery and she
was Susanna Montgomery, Hugh's youngest daughter. I also
found a letter about their engagement among Leland's papers.
Unfortunately Yasmin found evidence that the woman in the
grave was probably bludgeoned to death. As for Susanna,
there's no record of her marriage or when she died. So it could
be Susanna's body we found."

Eli didn't speak for a few moments. Then he said, "That's
horrible. What do you think happened?"

"I don't know. Maybe Charles killed her. Or someone else
killed her and he buried her. Who knows?" I said. "Yasmin is
sending her DNA to a lab and she swabbed me, so we'll start
by finding out if we're related. Though I'd bet the farm she's
Susanna Montgomery."

We had reached our vehicles. Eli walked me over to the
ATV and I climbed into the driver's seat.

"What are you going to do now?" he asked.

"Go back to the winery and get ready for Lolita. We're
picking Cab Franc on Saturday. Could you spare some time?
We're really shorthanded."

"Sure. I can help out. Let me know if you find out anything
more about that grave," he said. "Or the body."

My phone dinged one more time.

I WAITED UNTIL HE got into his car and drove off before
checking my phone.

*Leaving barrel room with Yasmin, heading over to the equip-
ment barn.*

She enjoyed the winery tour. He'd added a thumbs-up emoji.

Hey, are you okay?

Lucie???

There was a long break until his next-to-last text, which he'd just sent a moment ago.

We found a shovel. Yasmin says there's a nick in the right place so it's the one used to dig that grave.

Then one more text. *Found a pickax, too.*

I texted back. *On my way.*

I clicked off the phone and drove back to the winery. Somehow I had known the shovel with a nick in it would be there, that it was one of ours.

But like so many times in the past few days, I wished with all my heart that I hadn't been right.

Fourteen

found Quinn cleaning one of the stainless steel tanks when I arrived back at the barrel room. He turned off the hose when he saw me.

"I said it was okay for Yasmin to take the shovel and pickax to the site to confirm that they were the ones used to dig the grave," he said, drying his hands on a towel. "I hope you don't mind."

"Of course not."

"What was so urgent you had to go rushing off to see Eli?"

"He found an old stone house that neither of us knew was on our land. Eli thinks it was probably built in the eighteen hundreds, so I wonder if it could have been another Mosby hideout."

"That couldn't wait with everything else that's going on?" Quinn sounded a bit irked. "I wish you'd been here when we found that shovel. And the pickax."

"I know, but Eli thinks someone was in that house recently. Maybe last night."

"Miguel?"

I nodded. "It would make sense. That helicopter was searching for him here last night."

He looked stunned. "What are you going to do?"

"I'm not happy about it, but Eli and I agreed I'd call Bobby and let him know. Under the circumstances, I don't think I have a choice."

"Under the circumstances, I don't think you do, either. By the way, I left the quilt and the bags with the clothing in them at the house. They're in the library. I wasn't sure where to put them."

"Maybe I'll drive back to the house and take a look at everything. I can call Bobby when I'm there. Then I thought I'd stop by the General Store and stock up on water, batteries, and a few other things in case we lose power when Lolita shows up. Hopefully Thelma hasn't already been cleaned out by everyone else in town."

"Let me know when you get back," he said. "I'll wait for you for lunch."

I still needed to explain my absence while I met David Phelps at the Goose Creek Bridge. "I'm sorry. I promised Kit I'd meet her for lunch in town. I should have told you."

"You don't need my permission to have lunch with Kit." He scrutinized me. "What's going on, Lucie?"

"Nothing."

"It doesn't seem like nothing. Never mind. You'll tell me when you want to." He turned on his heel and walked back to the tank he'd been cleaning. When he turned the hose on again, the spray came on with full force, a violent hissing sound like an angry snake.

I left without saying a word. But just now I couldn't bring myself to tell him about David, about Leland's son with another woman and how hurt I felt after discovering that my father had betrayed my mother, Eli, Mia, and me. Plus I was still reeling from the possibility that Charles Montgomery, one of my cousins, might have murdered his fiancée. And gotten away with it.

I needed to get my complicated, bruised feelings about my family straightened out before Quinn and I got married. Quinn was hurt and mad that I shut him out and I knew it. How could I tell him that it was because I loved him? That I needed to make peace with my family's complicated past once and for all.

It was the only way I knew to go forward.

I REACHED BOBBY NOLAND on his private number when I got back to Highland House a short time later. He sounded distracted, which was a sure sign he was driving, meaning he was focusing on the road, whatever incident he was headed to, and more or less what I was telling him. So I didn't have his undivided attention.

He didn't exactly have mine, either. I was in the library kneeling next to the coffee table, sliding each of the garments Quinn had brought back from the grave out of its protective paper bag so I could examine them more closely. If I had thought I would get any sense of the woman who'd worn these clothes nearly a century and a half ago, it didn't take long to realize that they were now just pieces of fabric, tatters of what had once been a dress or an undergarment.

"I'll send a cruiser by to check out that cottage," Bobby was saying. "But like I told you yesterday, we just want to talk to Miguel. He's a person of interest at the moment. Not a suspect."

"So who do you consider a suspect?" I wasn't going to get an answer fishing like that and I knew it.

"Someone with a motive."

"Such as?"

"You tell me. I know Jean-Claude and Miguel had a beef, but I've got a list as long as your arm of women who had a relationship with him. That boy got around. Do you know anything about his lover-boy reputation?"

I sure did. I'd fallen for him nearly twenty years ago myself. So had Dominique. As for now, Nikki was the latest conquest that I knew about. And the rumors about Robyn. Did Bobby believe either of them had motives for murder?

"The de Merignacs and my family have known each other for years, Bobby. Generations. Jean-Claude has had a reputation as a playboy for as long as I can remember."

"What about recently? Since he arrived at La Vigne Cellars?"

When I didn't reply right away, he said, "Lucie?"

He expected an answer. An honest one.

"Apparently he was seeing Nikki Young," I said. "You remember her, don't you? She started working for us in June."

"Sure, I do," he said in a neutral voice, which meant he already knew about Nikki. "Anyone else?"

The paper bags were making a rustling sound that I was

sure he could hear so I slipped the last of the items back in its place and sat down on the sofa.

"No one I have firsthand knowledge of."

"But you do have secondhand knowledge of someone." A statement, not a question.

"Not really." I can't lie. I never get away with it.

"So far I know of two women who talked to Jean-Claude the morning he was killed," Bobby said in his best no-nonsense cop voice. "Nikki Young and your cousin."

"Dominique?" I said, startled. "Are you sure?"

"I hope that was a rhetorical question," he said. "Of course I'm sure. Dominique had a meeting with Robyn at the house first thing in the morning about some party for Toby. Apparently after that she drove down to the winery to have a talk with Jean-Claude over that article in the *Trib*. According to Robyn your cousin was pretty angry."

I could hardly catch my breath. "Dominique wouldn't kill Jean-Claude."

"Why not?"

"I don't know. She just wouldn't."

Her abortion happened nearly twenty years ago. If she hadn't said anything to Jean-Claude in all these years, she wouldn't bring it up now.

Would she?

I'd gone fishing and Bobby had unspooled enough baited line to hook me with that comment about Dominique. Now he was reeling me in and I wasn't supposed to realize what was happening.

"Uh-huh," he said. "What about Nikki?"

What about her? It was news to me that she'd gone to visit

Jean-Claude the morning he was killed instead of driving out to Culpeper to visit the flower farm for ideas and prices for Antonio and Valeria's wedding like she'd said she was going to do.

I hesitated. "I don't know. She's a sweet kid whose ambition is to make the world a better place. We're just a temporary stop for her until she finds a real job. She carries moths and crickets outside and sets them free if she finds them in the villa because she can't stand to kill one of God's creatures. I don't think she'd be capable of murdering a human being if she lets a centipede live."

Bobby grunted and I wasn't sure if it was assent or disagreement. "What about Miguel?"

"No. He's innocent."

Another question, casually tossed out. "Okay, what about Robyn Callahan?"

So he knew the rumors about Robyn sleeping with Jean-Claude when Toby was out of town. "I . . . no. Not her, either."

"If you know anything, Lucie," he said, in a way that let me know that I now had his undivided attention, "you need to tell me. Got that?"

"Yes. Got it."

"Good. Thanks for the heads-up on Miguel. I'll be talking to you."

The phone went dead.

BEFORE I LEFT THE house I took a look at what remained of the quilt that had been wrapped around the skeleton. It had survived better than any of the clothing had, possibly because there were three layers: the beautiful lattice-weave top, the batting, and the back, which consisted of red-and-white-striped linen feed bags that had been taken apart and stitched together to form a single piece of fabric. Plus there was the elaborate quilting—tiny, even stitches that held the three layers together, the handiwork of a talented seamstress.

Maybe Robyn would know about this particular patchwork pattern, with its individual blocks forming a larger series of what must have been eye-catching geometric designs. Whoever made this quilt had had access to a lot of different fabrics. Beautiful, colorful fabrics. I slipped the quilt back into its paper bag and called Robyn's mobile. The call went to voice mail so I tried the house and got Colette.

"I'll let her know about your quilt, Lucie," she said. "She's pretty torn up about Jean-Claude's death and she shut herself into her art studio by herself. Let me figure out when it's a good time to tell her you called, okay? It might do her some good to focus on something else instead of what happened."

I said thanks and wondered if Colette wasn't hinting that there was more to Robyn's grief over Jean-Claude's death than just the shock of a murder and the loss of a valued employee whose family was longtime friends with Toby. Then I yelled good-bye to Persia, closed the door to the library, and drove over to the General Store.

IN SMALL-TOWN AMERICA–IN THE Main Street one traffic-light towns like Middleburg, or the blink-and-you've-missed-it villages like Atoka—there is always a meeting place, a hub where everyone gathers to find out what's going on. It is the heartbeat, the nexus of news, the first place you want to be in good times and bad because the friends and neighbors you care about will be there, too. In Atoka, it was the General Store. Thelma Johnson, who owned the place for as long as I could remember, had her finger on our collective pulse, along with an uncanny ability to know what was going on in the community almost before it happened. If she didn't know, she would sweet-talk—some would say "weasel"—the information she wanted from you before you realized what had happened. She called her special knowledge and prescience her "extraterrestrial psychotic sensibility" and not many people disagreed with her. Thelma, who was certain she could contact people like my mother and father who had passed over to "The Great Beyond" on her Ouija board, lived in a world bounded by otherworldly spirits and soap-opera television. It was an unusual place to inhabit.

Surprisingly there were no cars in any of the four spaces Thelma liked to refer to as "the parking lot" when I pulled up to the store ten minutes later. Maybe everyone else had already stocked up for Lolita. I got gas at one of the two pumps out front in case the power went out as it so often did during a hurricane and took the parking space next to the front door.

The sleigh bells that hung on the door handle jingled when I walked in. From the back room Thelma's reedy voice called, "Coming. I'll be right there as soon as Amber finishes telling Gianni she's getting a divorce from Shay because she loves his identical twin brother."

I looked at the clock on the wall. Nearly 11:30 A.M., which meant *Tomorrow Ever After,* her favorite soap opera, was ending for the day.

She walked out a moment later, wiping her kohl-lined eyes behind thick trifocals with a tissue. "Why, Lucille," she said in a voice that wavered, "how nice of you to drop by. Forgive me, child. I'm just having a moment here."

"Take your time, Thelma. I'll get what I need. Don't worry about me."

She nodded and dabbed her eyes again.

Thelma liked to wear what I called her va-va-voom outfits—dresses that were always a little too short, too tight, and revealed too much of her ample bosom. If she'd been younger—say by about sixty or seventy years—she would have been sent to her room to change into something respectable before she was allowed out of the house. Her age was a more closely guarded secret than the nuclear codes: if anyone dared hint at it, she always patted her bright orange hair, wiggled her hips, and said with a Mae West vamp, "Oh, you'd be surprised, honey. Believe it or not, I'm not as young as I look."

Today she reminded me of an aging canary, in a vivid yellow knit dress, a bright yellow-and-orange scarf she'd wound around her neck, and stiletto sling-backs with pompoms on them that looked like two smashed egg yolks.

I got one of her small grocery carts and filled it with gallon jugs of water, packages of different sized batteries, fuel for the camping stove, and a small plastic tarp to put over a window well so it wouldn't fill up with rainwater. Thelma was composed and back to her usual self by the time I pushed my cart to the counter where she stood at the cash register, although her mascara and eyeliner had smudged, making her look like an elderly raccoon. The *Washington Tribune* lay in front of her folded so the dashing bon vivant picture of Jean-Claude de

Merignac stared up at me. I wanted to either cover it with my hand or turn it over.

"I heard tell you're the one who found Jean-Claude, Lucille." Thelma tapped a bony finger on the photograph. "Who would do such a thing? He was always so sweet to me every time he was in here, I can tell you. And that sexy French accent. Just made my heart go pitter-patter to hear him ask if I had any 'cross-ants' left in the bakery case, so I always tried to keep one by in case he came in. Plus he was so good-looking, a regular Greek Adidas, don't you think?"

"Uh . . . yes." It could be hard to follow the thread of Thelma's conversation at times.

"So it's true? You did find him." She perked up, leaning her chin on a propped hand, her eyes fixed on me. Today even her nail polish was yellow. "Tell me everything, Lucille. Every detail. That poor, poor man. I just want to weep." She got out the bunched-up tissue from where it had been tucked under her sleeve.

"There's nothing more to say besides what you read in the *Trib*," I said in my blandest voice. "He was dead when I got there. I called nine-one-one, of course, but it was too late. That's everything."

She shot me a look that said she wasn't done cross-examining the witness yet.

"I know they're looking for that Hispanic boy," she said. "The one who works over to La Vigne. But my money's on a woman. Could have been a lover's quarrel or maybe a jilted lover."

Her logic seemed to mirror Bobby's investigation, but I was surprised to hear Thelma sound so certain a woman had murdered Jean-Claude. He had been strong and fit after so many years of physical labor working in a vineyard. Whoever plunged those secateurs into him had been quick and must have caught him unaware. He or she had been quite strong as well.

"Who do you think did it?" I asked.

"Why, that was what I was going to ask you."

I shrugged. "No idea. Honest."

"Really?" she said. "Although I can't say I'm surprised or even that I blame you. It's hard not to have blinders on, especially when it involves family, and you feeling all protective of her."

"What are you talking about?"

"Why, your cousin," she said. "Dominique. I heard from one of the Romeos who heard from someone having dinner at the Red Fox Inn last night that she was over to La Vigne yesterday morning right before Jean-Claude was killed. And her throwing him out of her restaurant a few days before that after some big brouhaha. She had to be mad enough to want to do something about that story ending up in the newspaper."

The Romeos, whose name stood for Retired Old Men Eating Out, which pretty much summed up who they were and what they did, were Thelma's henchmen in the information-gathering business. During their daily sojourns to watering holes, diners, and restaurants throughout the county, they served as her eyes and ears, collecting news—or gossip, if you wanted to be technically accurate—about the good citizens of Loudoun County, which they retold over coffee and donuts at the General Store the next morning. Occasionally names, places, and dates got jumbled up—a few of the Romeos had trouble remembering details—so you were never entirely sure what you were hearing was the gospel truth.

I stared at her. Was *that* the rumor that was going around? Dominique killed Jean-Claude over a gossip-column story in the *Washington Tribune*?

"First of all, Dominique did *not* murder Jean-Claude. It's just not in her character. She threw Jean-Claude out of the restaurant because of the horrible way he was treating her staff and she couldn't stand it," I said. "Besides, she wasn't the only woman to visit Jean-Claude the morning he was killed."

Thelma smiled her sweetest "gotcha" smile. "Is that so? Who else was there, Lucille?"

I had fallen for the oldest trick in the book. "I was," I said. "And I didn't kill him, either."

I knew she wouldn't buy my answer. "How about a nice cup of coffee, child? On the house. You can set a spell and we'll have a little chat. I got the usuals, and today's fancy is 'Bean There, Done That.' Kind of a mellow one for a change. Plus I've got one jelly donut left." She gave me a sly look. "Filled with raspberry jam. Your favorite."

When Thelma resorted to bribery, she really meant to interrogate you. But I had questions for her, too, about Charles Montgomery, and I wasn't going to get out of here until she was satisfied she had squeezed every ounce of information I knew about Jean-Claude out of me.

"All right, just a quick cup of fancy," I said. "And I'll take the donut, too. But I insist on paying."

"Nonsense." She walked over to a table where three coffee-makers labeled PLAIN, DECAF, and FANCY sat side by side and poured two cups of fancy. "You know how much I always enjoy conversating with you."

She handed me my donut in a white deli bag along with a couple of paper napkins, and we walked over to the corner of the store where three rocking chairs were placed around a woodstove. Thelma sat in her favorite bentwood rocker and I took the Lincoln rocking chair next to her.

She sipped her coffee and said, "You were about to tell me who else saw Jean-Claude the morning he was killed."

I wasn't about to say any such thing. "Surely the Romeos have already told you everything, haven't they? Honestly, Thelma, no one in Atoka is better informed than you are."

She gave me a tolerant, knowing smile. "I pride myself on knowing what goes on around here. A person's got to stay informed, you know. Besides, people love to tell me things and they're always asking my advice. I think of it as my cervical duty to my community."

I coughed. "I can see that," I said and bit into a blob of raspberry jelly.

"Well," she said, "I did hear that cute little blonde who works for you—Nikki—came by to see him. Apparently Jean-Claude broke her heart when he ended their fling. She wanted to see if they could patch things up, but he told her there was someone else."

"He did?" I said, through a mouthful of jelly. "Who?"

"I don't rightly know, but there were rumors about him and Robyn Callahan." She paused, waiting for my reaction.

I licked powdered sugar off my fingers while I tried to figure out how to respond to that comment. "Robyn's crazy about Toby."

"I have no doubt. But Jean-Claude could be quite the Casablanca," she said. "Just like Humphrey Bogart. A man like that's hard to resist, Lucille."

Didn't I know.

"Bobby Noland's the detective working on the case," I said. "I'm sure he'll find whoever did it."

Thelma set her cup down on a small table next to her rocking chair and folded her hands in her lap. "I'm sure he will, too," she said. Then she added in a quiet, ominous voice, "But what worries me is when he does, it's going to tear this community apart."

Our eyes met. She rocked back and forth, staring at me as if she were seeing someone else. I wiped my sticky hands on a clean napkin while my brain kept repeating *it's not Dominique it's not Dominique it's not Dominique.*

"A lot of people wander into vineyards," I said. "Maybe it's someone no one has considered yet. Jean-Claude got himself into a lot of trouble in France years ago and made some enemies."

Thelma tapped her temple with a finger. "No. I know things, Lucille. I don't know who did it—yet—but I do know it was no stranger."

I believed her. But I sure wished I didn't.

"Now," she said, "something else is on your mind, isn't it?"

I nodded.

"Does it have anything to do with the body that was found on your property?"

The expression on my face gave me away because she said, "I thought as much. What is it?"

"Are you related to someone named Charles Montgomery? Did he own this store once?"

It was her turn to look dumbfounded. When she spoke, her voice quivered. "How in the world did you find out about him?"

"In some family papers among Leland's genealogy records."

"What was in the papers?"

"A letter saying he was going to marry Susanna Montgomery. I presume they were cousins. Susanna was the daughter of Hugh, my great-great-great-grandfather."

"He never married her," she said. "She ran off with someone else, so Charles married my great-aunt. So yes, we're kin, but only by marriage."

"How do you know that?"

"That he married my great-aunt?"

"That she ran off."

"My family kept letters, too, Lucille. It wasn't a pretty story about Susanna, what she did to her family. To your family. I'm not surprised you didn't know about it. She became a *persona not gracias,* as they say. I think your family disowned her."

The donut settled in the pit of my stomach like a rock. "Tell me. Please."

"She took up with a black man."

I thought about my meeting with David Phelps, my half-brother, in half an hour.

"I see."

"In those days it was against the law. You could go to prison for something like that, so the two of them ran off. They were never heard from again," she said. "It was a huge scandal."

I wasn't about to tell Thelma that there was another theory. Susanna never ran off with anyone and perhaps Charles had killed her. Or someone else had, and he buried her. Either way, it explained the blank spaces for her wedding date and date of death in our family Bible.

"Charles ended up marrying my great-aunt. I believe they were happy," Thelma said. "Or maybe I'd just like to believe it. There were no children, so after they died the store passed to my grandmother, who was much younger. It stayed in my family ever since."

"I never knew any of this."

"Sometimes it's just best to leave things lay where Jesus flang 'em, Lucille. The Johnsons don't really talk about it," she said. "And of course your family didn't, either. So who is the body in the grave? Does it have something to do with Susanna?"

"We don't know for sure yet." It was true, though not honest. Yasmin said we couldn't be one hundred percent certain until the results came back from my swab and what could be extracted from the tooth and femur of the skeleton. "The forensic anthropologist who excavated the site said it will take some time—maybe even a couple of months—before she can get DNA results from the lab and we know whether the remains belong to someone related to my family."

Thelma gave me a sharp-eyed look. "Lucille," she said, "please don't lie to me."

She'd been honest with me. I owed her the truth.

"It might be Susanna—the age of the grave and the age of the remains would fit. And a cuff link with the initials CM were found in the grave. Yasmin—the forensic anthropologist—said it probably belonged to whoever dug the grave."

"Charles Montgomery."

I nodded. There wasn't anything else to say.

"I suspect it's impossible for you and me to understand—really understand—how Susanna falling in love with . . . the wrong person, a man of color . . . could destroy a family in those days. Cause so much trouble for everyone involved," she said. "Hugh riding with Mosby as one of his Rangers and all, fighting for the Confederacy and Virginia's right to make our own laws, decide what was right for our own people." She paused and cleared her throat. "Plus, the truth of the matter is that your family owned slaves. So did mine. It's not pretty admitting it now, but you can't rewrite history even if you want to."

"I know. Nor cover it up."

She stood up. "Wait here a moment. There's something you should have."

When she returned, she was holding a leather-bound book. "Susanna's name is in the flyleaf," she said. "You may as well have it, especially after what you just told me. Obviously Charles kept it, though I've no idea why."

I took the book from her and read the title. "*The Journal of John Woolman*. Who is he?"

"He was an absolutionist," she said. "A Quaker who was absolutely against slavery."

"You mean abolitionist?"

"That's what I said, didn't I? Apparently Susanna was thinking about becoming a Quaker. There's an inscription from Samuel Janney, who lived over to Lincoln. He was involved in the anti-slavery movement, helping slaves escape to Canada and the North."

Lincoln was a Quaker village—more like a hamlet—about twenty minutes from Atoka. "Wait a minute. Are you talking about the Underground Railroad?" I said, stunned.

She nodded. "You know it wasn't a real railroad, Lucille, don't you, even though they had conductors and stations and stationmasters and such-like?"

"Yes, of course." Was Susanna helping slaves escape to the North and Charles found out? Or maybe someone else in the family found out? Her father? One of her brothers?

I opened the book and read the inscription.

To Susanna,

Be instructed and enlightened by the words and deeds of this esteemed man who followed the law of the spirit of life in Jesus Christ as an able minister of the gospel, well-endowed with wisdom and an understanding of the mysteries of God's kingdom.

Yrs sincerely,

Samuel Janney

If Susanna had been considering becoming a Quaker and had fallen in love with a black man despite being engaged to her cousin Charles, it wouldn't be hard to imagine why someone might be angry enough to want to stop her from running away. I leafed through the book. Susanna had read it carefully, all right. There were annotated notes in the margins throughout the book that I assumed were hers.

On the back flyleaf I found something that looked like a crudely drawn map. It took a moment before I recognized my farm. Highland House. The cemetery. The pond. The old tenant house—now the Ruins—before Yankees burned it down looking for Mosby. And if I wasn't mistaken, the little house Eli had discovered this morning was marked on it as well, surrounded by woods just as we'd found it. Maybe I'd been wrong about it being a second hideout for Mosby and his Rangers.

Maybe, thanks to Susanna Montgomery, the little stone house had been a secret stop on the Underground Railroad.

Until somebody found out. And killed her.

Fifteen

When Kit and I were growing up, we often met at the Goose Creek Bridge for teenage angst-filled heart-to-hearts, lubricated by a bottle of wine I filched from the winery. In all the years we'd met there, I think we'd only run into someone else once or twice. If you wanted privacy and solitude, this was a good place to find it.

The two-hundred-foot-long stone bridge with its four arches had been built during Thomas Jefferson's presidency to carry traffic from Ashby's Gap Turnpike across Goose Creek. On June 21, 1863, the bridge had been the site of a couple of hours of fighting during the Battle of Upperville as the Confederate and Union Armies moved toward their fateful meeting at Gettysburg ten days later.

But by the 1950s the Goose Creek Bridge fell into disuse when Mosby's Highway—wider and able to carry more traffic—was built farther to the south over the creek. Eventually the site became overgrown and weed-choked until the local Garden Club took over caring for it. People came by every now and then to pay tribute to the role it had played in the Civil War, and historians gave tours on special occasions. Otherwise, it was quiet and deserted.

After everything I had just learned about my family from Thelma, it seemed fitting to be here just now, the place I always came to escape. I'd had no idea I had a relative who might be connected with the Underground Railroad and, until the other day, I'd had no idea I had a half brother, the child of an affair between my father and an African-American woman.

A navy BMW convertible was parked at the end of Lemmon's Bottom Road, which was as far as you could go before a gate kept out vehicles and you had to walk a few hundred feet to the bridge. I leaned down and took a look through the windshield hoping I could tell whether the car belonged to David Phelps. If it didn't, he and I were going to have company. The inside was immaculate except for a glass evil eye hanging on a pendant from the rearview mirror.

I walked toward the bridge down the gravel-and-dirt path that was bordered by a field on one side and woods on the other. My work boots crunched on the stones, the noise eerily amplified in the silence. When the bridge finally came into view I didn't see a living soul anywhere.

Where was he? My skin prickled and I called out, "Hello?"

He popped up from behind the farthest parapet like a jack-in-the-box. An expensive-looking camera hung around his neck. "Lucie?"

"David?"

As David Phelps walked toward me I couldn't help looking for something—anything—that reminded me of Leland. Like my father, he was tall and rangy and there was a looseness about him that said he was comfortable in his skin. But unlike my father who had been cocky and arrogant, David seemed confidant, self-possessed. His jet-black hair was short stubble and he wore at least a day's growth of beard that looked deliberate, not as if he'd forgotten to shave. But it was his charismatic, compelling smile that I noticed most, the way it lit up his face all the way to his eyes.

Until just now I hadn't thought through how this meeting might go, how I would feel meeting the son my father had never spoken about. Now here I was grinning back at this man who—mysteriously—somehow already seemed familiar and known.

He grasped both of my hands. "This is great." His voice, warm and rich, was husky and burred with emotion. "This is really great. I'm so happy to meet you, Lucie."

"I'm happy to meet you, too, David," I said, my own emotions unexpectedly welling up inside me. Before they could spill over, I added, "I wasn't sure you were here."

He looked puzzled and then his face cleared. "I was shooting a few pictures of the bridge while I was waiting. To be honest, I was a bit nervous." This time his smile was guilty, as though I'd caught him doing something illegal.

"So was I. More than a bit," I said and we both laughed.

"Well, shall we sit on the bridge parapet and talk?" His eyes strayed to my cane. "Can you . . . would that be okay for you?"

"It's fine," I said. "You don't need to worry about me."

"What happened?"

The blunt question, thirty seconds after we met, could have

seemed inappropriate or out of line, but it didn't. It was going
to be a no-punches-pulled conversation and that was fine by
me. We had a lot of ground to cover. A lifetime.

"A car accident eight years ago," I said. "I wasn't supposed
to walk again."

"But you did."

"I did."

"Does your bolshie attitude come from Leland or your
mother?"

Bolshie. How odd. That was one of Leland's favorite words.
"Leland could be as stubborn as a mule. Plus he used to say
'bolshie.'"

He seemed surprised. "Well, I guess that's where I get it,
then. The word and the stubbornness."

We walked over to the bridge. "Do you travel everywhere
with your camera?" I asked.

"I do. Not just because it's my profession, but because I pay
more attention to what's around me when I've got a camera in
my hand. I guess it's an occupational habit, but it keeps me
from taking the familiar things I see every day for granted."

I liked his answer. "You would have liked my mother. She
was an artist. She was always showing my brother and sister
and me some new or unusual discovery she'd made, encourag-
ing us to look around and explore the world, push our bound-
aries."

David held out his hand and helped me maneuver onto the
parapet. I swung my legs over the side and he caught sight of
my diamond ring. "You're engaged."

"I am. He's pretty terrific. He's also the winemaker at the
winery."

"Wedding date?"

"Nope. Not yet. We're taking it slow. What about you?"

"No wedding date." A rueful smile. "No fiancée, or even a girlfriend, which would probably be the first step. Right now I travel too much so I'm kind of a solo flyer."

We sat side by side, legs dangling over the bridge as Kit and I had done so often. In a few days after Lolita passed through, the creek would be a deafening, muddy torrent roaring over the edges of the banks, but today it made a pleasant gurgling noise as it moved through the rocks and debris in the streambed.

"You must have a lot of questions," he said.

I did. The first one flew right out of my mouth. "How old are you?"

His lips tightened. "I just turned thirty-two."

"I'm thirty-one," I said, and my heart hurt. "And my brother Eli is thirty-three."

"I'm so sorry," he said. "I wasn't sure if your parents were married when Leland and my biological mother . . . got together."

Somehow I had known David wouldn't be the love child of a relationship that took place before my father met my mother. But it didn't mean I hadn't hoped it would turn out that way.

"It would have been nice to think Leland was crazy about my mother, still devoted to her, when they were starting to have a family," I said, hoping he didn't catch the quiver in my voice, "but I guess even then he had a wandering eye."

He reached over and covered one of my hands, which was resting on the parapet, with his. "My biological mother wasn't married then," he said. "I figured maybe her relationship with

Leland was a fling—or an accident—because she got married a year after I was born. Divorced her first husband not long after that, so maybe it was a rebound relationship. She's been married to the same guy now for something like twenty-five years."

"Have you tried to contact her?"

He nodded. "She didn't reply. I don't think she wants to hear from me. She may have never told either of her husbands about me, so it would be inconvenient for me to show up after all this time. Plus there's her political career to think about."

Inconvenient. It was my turn to say, "I'm sorry."

He shrugged. "What am I going to do? I can't butt in where I'm not wanted. Back in those days no one would have thought DNA testing would be so common, so accessible to everyone and his grandmother. She probably fully expected her secret to stay that way and for her son never to be able to find out who she was."

"But you did."

Yasmin had warned me about this the other day. Not all stories of someone discovering a lost or unknown relative had a happy ending. In some cases, they were traumatic. Heartbreaking.

"She's entitled to her privacy." He said it in a reasonable enough way, but I could tell how deeply it had hurt him to realize his biological mother would not even acknowledge his existence. "The good news, though, is that I found you. And you did want to meet me. You have no idea how happy I am about that."

I squeezed his hand. "Me, too."

Somewhere in the trees a woodpecker rat-a-tat-tatted and

birds chirped. In the silence we could just barely hear the occasional car drive by on Mosby's Highway.

"Who is she?" I asked, finally.

He hesitated so long I wondered if he was going to tell me. "Her name's Olivia Vandenberg," he said. "You might know her. Or have heard of her."

"Congresswoman Olivia Vandenberg? Married to the Treasury Secretary? *That* Olivia Vandenberg?"

"Yep."

She was the House Majority Whip, and there were whispers she was in line to be the first African-American Speaker of the House of Representatives next year when the current Speaker retired. A prominent member of the Congressional Black Caucus and, as if that weren't enough, a glamorous, brainy fashion icon who frequently appeared in *Vogue* and *Ebony*.

"She's your biological mother?" I said.

"Yep."

"My God. I wonder how—or where—she and Leland ran into each other."

"I guess we'll never know." He eyed me. "You're not going to march into her office on Capitol Hill and ask her, are you?"

"Good Lord, of course not. It doesn't mean I wouldn't like to know."

"You and me both. Interestingly, though, she and her husband don't have any kids."

"Huh. Wonder why?"

"I read everything I can find on her. All she ever says is something like 'it just didn't work out.' Who knows what that means?"

I didn't want to say "maybe she didn't want any." "Maybe she couldn't have any more children after she had you."

"Maybe." He cleared his throat. "Anyway, continuing on the subject of who knows what, does your fiancé know about me? Or your brother or sister?"

"Not yet. In fact none of them even know I sent off a saliva sample to the Genome Project," I said. "I thought I'd tell Quinn—my fiancé—first. I think you two will like each other."

He smiled. "Getting to know the family. That would be amazing."

"It's going to be harder for Eli and Mia to learn about you, I'm afraid. Mia was Daddy's little girl when she was a baby. Later she turned into the wild child from the Seven Hells after my mother was killed. Now she lives in Manhattan. She's always been sort of fragile."

"I'm sure you'll know when—or if—it's the right time to tell them," he said. "Please don't think I'm pressuring you in any way. I'm well aware how much of a shock it must have been for you to learn about me."

"Thank you." I shifted on the parapet so I was facing him. "Look, I know we have a lot to talk about, David, but I'm afraid I can't stay much longer. I'm so sorry. With the hurricane coming, there's a million things to do at the vineyard to get ready. But at least we got to meet today."

"Sure," he said. "Of course. We've got lots of time, I hope."

"Absolutely. Perhaps we can meet at Highland House once . . . the others know. You must know where I live . . . I imagine you've checked?"

He nodded. "You imagine right. You're not far from the vineyard where that winemaker was murdered the other day."

"It's next door," I said. "I'm the one who found him."

"God, how awful for you."

"It was worse for him."

He looked startled and then gave me a roguish grin. "I suppose it would be. Have they found the killer yet?"

It was too complicated to go into detail. "Not yet."

"Before we go." He gave me a questioning look and started to lift his camera to his eye. "May I?"

"Of course. Go right ahead."

He clicked off what sounded like ten or fifteen pictures and lowered the camera. "Thanks," he said, checking the viewing screen. "You're very photogenic. I'll send you a couple of these if you'd like."

"I would. Maybe you could send me a few pictures of yourself?"

"I think that could be arranged." He grinned and swung his legs over to the other side of the parapet and stood up. Before I could say anything he reached out a hand to pull me up and automatically passed me my cane as if he'd done this dozens of times before.

I wondered if he was, or had been, a caregiver for someone, and if so, who that person was. Perhaps a conversation for another time.

He picked up an expensive-looking khaki canvas camera bag that had been lying on the ground and looked as if it had been dragged around the world more than once. We started back down the path to Lemmon's Bottom Road. Along the way he pulled at a strand of honeysuckle.

"I know these plants are invasive, but I love the scent of honeysuckle when it's in bloom," he said.

"So do I."

He caught my eye and we both grinned. Was liking the same floral scent one of those weird similar anthropological traits Yasmin had spoken about, like having perfect pitch or red hair? How much *did* David Phelps and I have in common?

"Look," he was saying, "I meant it about not pressuring you to get together again, okay? Besides, it sounds like we're going to get walloped by Hurricane Lolita and I know you've got a lot on your mind running the vineyard."

"That's part of it," I said. "But I also seem to have been inundated by unexpected family . . . relationships . . . all at once."

He gave me a one-eyed squint. "Oh, yeah? You mean, I'm not the only unknown relative to drop into your life?"

I smiled. "Well, the other person didn't exactly drop in. It's more like she turned up."

By now we were back at our respective cars. We leaned side by side against the front fender of my sun-warmed Jeep and I told him about Susanna Montgomery, her fiancé Charles, and what Thelma had told me about Susanna's interest in Quakerism.

"Apparently she fell in love with an African-American man who lived in Lincoln," I said. "They were going to run away together."

"Lincoln, as in the little Quaker village next to Purcell-ville?"

"That's right."

His smile was lopsided. "I guess that means your father and Olivia weren't the first illicit interracial relationship in the Montgomery family."

"I guess not. Susanna and whoever he was fell in love at least a century and a half before they did."

My words dropped into a pool of silence. Neither of us knew whether Leland and Olivia's relationship had been a passing fling, a one-night, forgettable, alcohol-fueled event, or a passionate, forbidden love affair. If I were David, I'd want to think it had been the latter, to be a child of love rather than a careless accident.

"In those days, especially during the Civil War, a relationship like that took guts," he said. "For both of them. Especially in Virginia."

"Because it was illegal?"

"Hell, yeah, it was illegal," he said with feeling. "The statute prohibiting marriage between individuals of different races in America dates back to the late seventeenth century, to when we were still the thirteen colonies. The old word for interracial marriage—miscegenation—was first used in 1863 during the Civil War. In Virginia it remained illegal until the Supreme Court case of *Loving v. Virginia*. Mildred and Richard Loving. That was in 1967. 'Illegal' as in being sentenced to a year in jail because they fell in love with someone they were told they couldn't love. That it was a damned crime."

"I saw the movie about that case," I said. "It was heartbreaking. But the Lovings got the law changed. Something good came of it. Their love mattered, not just for them but for everyone who came after them."

"Took a long damn time," he said, and for the first time I heard bitterness in his voice.

I laid my hand on his arm. "My family owned slaves," I

said. "There are a lot of things that happened in the past that you and I can't change or control now."

He put his hand over mine and I was surprised how hot it felt. Leland had been like that, too. My mother called him hot-blooded. "For the record, they're also my family. And you're right, of course. Plus, we can't whitewash history. Pun intended. Including what happened between Leland and Olivia." He paused. "Which would be me."

"I'm glad you happened, if that doesn't sound too weird."

"Me, too. And it doesn't." He smiled. "Look, speaking of Lincoln, I did some work for the Loudoun Preservation Foundation when they needed a photographer to take pictures for a coffee table fund-raiser book a couple of years ago. I spent some time there shooting the Goose Creek Meeting House, the Quaker school, the burial ground . . . Grace Church, the abandoned African-American Methodist church. It's a pretty little village. Really peaceful. A lot of free African-Americans lived in Lincoln, because the Quakers were friendly and welcoming. Plus they were passionately anti-slavery."

"I haven't been out there in ages—maybe twenty-five years or more. It sounds like it hasn't changed much."

"Not really. Except for the Loudoun Preservation Foundation trying to raise money to restore Grace Church," he said. "Did you know it's one of the oldest black churches in Loudoun?"

"I'd forgotten that."

"If you ever decide you want to go out there, let me know. I'd like to show you around." He roused himself off the Jeep fender. "And now I should let you go. We've been another half hour talking since we left the bridge."

I pulled out my phone. It was nearly three-thirty. And there were two *where are you* texts from Quinn. I thumbed off the display.

"I'd better get back," I said. "I'll call you. Or we can text or email."

"Sure," he said. "Anytime. Take your time."

"I will be in touch."

He nodded. "I know."

"David."

"What?"

"There are some things about Leland that aren't so . . . flattering."

"It's okay," he said. "I'd rather know than not know. I'm not Leland. I'm me. Or as Abraham Lincoln supposedly said, 'I don't know who my grandfather was; I'm much more concerned to know who his grandson will be.' And in my case, that's really true about my grandfather. Good-bye, Lucie."

He leaned in, giving me a sweet brotherly kiss on the cheek. When he pulled back, his eyes held mine for a long time.

After we'd both gotten into our cars, he waited until I turned around and drove down Lemmon's Bottom Road before following me in the BMW to the turnoff for Mosby's Highway. We both turned left headed toward Middleburg, but at Atoka Road I signaled right and he passed me, tooting his horn and sticking a hand out the window in a good-bye salute.

I honked back. After his car disappeared I swiped at tears that were suddenly making it hard to see the road, and headed for home.

. . .

WHEN I DROVE INTO the winery parking lot ten minutes later I was reasonably composed, but not ready to see Quinn. He would know, as he always did, that something had happened, and he would want me to talk about it, tell him what was wrong. Before I said anything about where I'd been this afternoon—first Thelma's, then with David—I needed some time to wrap my head around what I'd learned.

There were no guests in the tasting room when I walked into the villa, which wasn't unusual on a weekday at 4 P.M. I poked my head through the door of Frankie's office. Her computer and desk lamp were on, and a huge ring of keys lay in the middle of her desk, so she was around but not here. Disappointed, I walked down the corridor and stopped outside Nikki's office. Her door was ajar, so I knocked and opened it wider.

She had been crying—that was obvious—but she seemed more angry than upset. Her eyes flashed and she said, "Please don't come into my office. I didn't say 'come in.'"

I stepped inside the room and closed the door behind me. She was sitting in her desk chair, bare feet tucked under her, slim arms wrapped around her knees, which poked through a pair of fashionably ripped jeans.

I leaned against the door and said, "It's a little late for that, plus I'm your boss and this is my winery, so it's my office, too. What's going on?"

Her eye makeup was smeared, her eyes were puffy, and she looked like an emotional wreck. Her blond hair, which she usually wore pulled up and styled with pretty combs or flowers, had been wound into a messy knot and held in place by a pencil that had been stabbed through it.

"I don't want to talk about it, Lucie. Please go away and leave me alone."

It would be Jean-Claude.

"I wasn't asking if you wanted to talk about it, Nikki. You need to talk to me. Bobby Noland told me you were at La Vigne Cellars the morning Jean-Claude was murdered," I said, trying to keep my temper in check. "Not in Culpeper having a discussion with a florist about what colors of alstroemeria or ranunculus were available for Valeria's wedding bouquet, which is where you said you were going to be."

I had come off like a parent lecturing a truant teenager and she gave me a defiant look that said she didn't care.

When she didn't answer, I went on. "Nikki, it's a murder investigation. The Sheriff's Office is looking for a killer. Someone with a motive. You've got one. Bobby knows Jean-Claude broke off your relationship and a scorned ex-girlfriend is always a good suspect. Plus you lied about where you were going to be. That didn't help."

"I didn't kill Jean-Claude," she burst out. "I didn't do it. That's what I told him."

"Told who? Bobby?"

She nodded, her eyes tearing up again. I handed her a box of tissues that were on the corner of her desk. She pulled out half a dozen and blew her nose.

"Then what were you doing there?" I asked. She gave me a stony look and I added, "Trying to patch things up?"

She nodded.

"And?"

"He laughed at me." I couldn't tell whether she was hurt or irate, as in he-doesn't-know-who-he-messed-with.

She was only ten years younger than I was, but right now she came across as a spoiled little girl used to getting what she wanted.

Join the queue. I almost said it. Instead, I said, "I'm sorry he laughed at you. What happened after that?"

Her anger kicked in again. "He told me to go home and find a boyfriend my own age. Can you believe it?"

Oh, yes, indeed. "Did you leave?"

"I told him I wasn't going anywhere, so he came over and grabbed me by the arm," she said, rubbing a spot on her forearm as though she were reliving the memory. "He sort of dragged me out of his office."

"You let him do that?"

"I might have fought back a little. Maybe scratched him. But he was stronger. He just kept laughing and closed the door in my face. Locked it, too. Then I heard him on the phone. Calling someone . . . a woman, of course. Saying *'mon amour'* and *'ma chérie'* and that he wanted to see her. How much he missed her and wanted to make *'looove'* to her. *Faire l'amooouur.* I think he wanted me to hear." Nikki mimicked Jean-Claude's accent, capturing it with wicked perfection. She raised her head and glared at me. "Was he calling *you,* Lucie?"

I started to laugh. "Me? Are you kidding? Of course not."

"You were with him the other day. We both know you lied and made up some story about him helping you with something that had to do with the grapes." If she'd been a cat, her claws would have been out.

I wasn't about to tell her Jean-Claude was worried someone

was trying to kill him and that's why he'd wanted to see me. Not when she appeared to be a prime suspect in Bobby's eyes.

"What we talked about is none of your business, but Jean-Claude and I weren't involved with each other. Okay?" She was . . . *obsessed*.

"You're the one who found him," she said, still insistent. "You went to see him that day. The day someone killed him. Maybe *you* did it."

I shook my head in disbelief. She wasn't going to let it go. "I went to see Miguel Otero to ask him to help with the harvest," I said, enunciating each word as if I were talking to someone who had difficulty understanding English. "And I'm done answering your questions and responding to your silly accusations. You need to leave. Now. You're finished here."

She sat back in her chair as if I'd just physically struck her and her mouth fell open in a big, round O of surprise. "Are you . . . are you firing me?"

"I am. You can come back tomorrow and pack up your things. Frankie will give you your final check. But right now I want you to leave."

In one fluid move, she got up, reached for her purse, slid her feet into sandals, and moved around her desk. Before she got to the door I stepped back and opened it. She breezed by without a sidelong glance, but I caught the scent of her perfume as she brushed past me, head erect, perfect posture. Something seductive and sensuous.

I heard the front door to the villa slam with a vicious force a moment later and leaned against the door to her office once again as though I needed something to prop me up.

What the hell had just happened? A jealous, seething rant

by yet another of Jean-Claude's castoffs. I would have to tell Frankie I'd fired Nikki, who she loved practically as a daughter. Did she know about this dark, possessive side of Nikki's character?

Half an hour ago I would have said Nikki was an unfortunate casualty in the sordid drama surrounding the murder of Jean-Claude de Merignac. Now I wondered whether she could possibly be a killer . . . and I had just let her walk out of here.

Sixteen

called Quinn once I finally calmed down after Nikki had stormed out of the villa. The secrets I'd been keeping these last few days were starting to leak out in all the wrong ways and places—the lies, avoidance, deceptions—until I knew I couldn't keep them to myself any longer without tearing a hole through the heart of my relationship with him. It was time to tell him about David and about what I'd just learned from Thelma about Susanna Montgomery.

"Before you say anything," I said when he answered, "please hear me out. There are . . . things . . . I need to tell you. The red ATV is out in front of the villa. I also want to show you something, so can you meet me there in five minutes?"

"Does this have anything to do with why you disappeared for half the afternoon?"

"Yes."

"I'll be there in three minutes."

I was waiting in the ATV when he sprinted across the

courtyard and ran down the steps to join me. *The Journal of John Woolman* lay on the seat next to me.

"Want me to drive?" he asked.

"I know where we're going."

"Good point," he said and climbed into the passenger seat. "Is this your book?" He picked up *The Journal of John Woolman.*

"It belonged to Susanna Montgomery," I said and slid the gearshift into drive. "Thelma gave it to me."

"Thelma? What was she doing with a book that belonged to Susanna Montgomery?" He set it back down.

"That's part of what I want to explain to you. Is everything okay in the barrel room?"

"No," he said. "Most definitely not. Antonio's so distracted I have to repeat everything at least twice and Benny is going to chain-smoke himself into getting lung cancer. Jesús just looks nervous and doesn't crack jokes anymore, so it's pretty tense at the moment. They're all worried about Miguel."

"Miguel didn't kill Jean-Claude," I said. "And I just fired Nikki."

"You did what?"

I told him what happened. "Bobby seems to be focusing on women who had a romantic relationship with Jean-Claude."

"And Nikki's one of his suspects? Our sweet little Nikki?"

"Yup. And the sweetness might only be skin-deep."

"There's also Robyn, if Bobby's keeping a list," he said. "And Dominique."

"Dominique was not in a romantic relationship with Jean-Claude," I said, snapping at him. "Their affair happened decades ago. You can't count her any more than you can count me."

He held up his hands. "Whoa. I surrender. Don't bite my head off, okay? It's just that she does have a motive, don't you agree? Come on, Lucie, even if she is your cousin, look at it from Bobby's viewpoint."

"She didn't kill Jean-Claude, Quinn."

"Okay," he said. "Truce. Moving on."

"I'm sorry."

"Apology accepted. It's been a hell of a few days," he said, as I turned onto the rutted path that led into the woods and the site for Eli's house. "This is the way to Eli's new place," he said. "Is that where we're going?"

I nodded and he said, "Why?"

"I want to show you the cabin he found in the woods this morning," I said. "It's connected to Susanna Montgomery and this book. At least, I believe it is."

I stopped the ATV outside the stand of trees—including the one with the elbow bend in the trunk—where Eli and I had parked this morning.

"Come on." I picked up the book. "We'll talk on the way."

It was easier and quicker this time to make our way to the falling-down cabin since Eli and I had already beaten a path through the underbrush. I told Quinn what Thelma had told me about Susanna falling in love with an African-American man and planning to flee to New York to marry him.

"What does that have to do with this place you're going to show me?" Quinn asked.

"I wanted to see it again for myself, plus I want you to see it, too. I'd like to know if you agree with my theory."

We stopped walking. The cabin was still hidden by a screen

of deciduous trees, scrubby pines, and wild holly bushes, but now I knew where it was.

"Here we are," I said to Quinn.

"What are you talking about? We're in the middle of the woods."

I opened the back flyleaf of Susanna's book and showed Quinn the map. "It's a map of Highland Farm." I pointed out the landmarks and then showed him the cabin. "And this place here—this little box in the corner with the X through it—is what's right in front of us. On the other side of those trees and bushes. I think the cabin Eli found could have been a stop on the Underground Railroad."

"There's a cabin on the other side of those trees and bushes?"

The sun had gradually disappeared behind banks of heavy clouds that had moved in during the afternoon so now there were no shadows, just thick gray light that was beginning to make it difficult to read the map. Before long it would be too dusky to see anything and the trees and bushes would fade into insubstantial shapes in the autumn twilight.

"Absolutely sure. I'll show you," I said. "Follow me."

I was a couple of steps ahead of Quinn when something— no, some*one*—hurtled through the bushes, broadsiding me and knocking me over. Susanna's book and my cane flew out of my hands and I went down hard on my back.

A few feet away, I heard a man say "Ouf," as he scrambled to recover from our encounter. He was gone in a flash.

"Quinn!" I yelled when I could catch my breath. "Stop him!"

I heard the cracking of branches breaking, followed by a groan and cursing from Quinn.

"Dammit. Too late. I missed him. He's gone."

He was at my side a moment later. "Are you okay?" He helped me up.

I nodded. "That was Miguel. He was hiding in the cabin again. He's here. Somewhere in the woods. Let's find him before he gets away."

"He already got away. And we aren't going to find him in the dark, Lucie. Nor can we go chasing after him. He could be anywhere."

At least he didn't say "and you can't run."

"We can at least talk to him," I said. "Damn. My cane. He knocked it out of my hand."

"It's here." He picked it up and handed it to me. "Lucky it didn't snap in two."

"Thank you, I . . . oh, no. Susanna's book. That's gone, too."

"Hang on." Quinn pulled out his phone and found the flashlight on it. After a moment he said, "It's here. It's caught in some bushes. A bit worse for the wear, unfortunately. I think the cover might be starting to come apart from the binding."

He handed me the book and I saw what he meant. "Maybe I can fix it. Come on. Let's go. Miguel got more of a head start while we've been messing around here."

Quinn followed me to a spot in a small clearing. "Don't tell me you plan to holler at him to come out and show himself like this is some adult version of hide-and-seek? Do you really think that's going to work?"

"Do you have a better idea?"

Within a couple of minutes we had both yelled ourselves hoarse.

"He's not coming," Quinn said.

I cleared my throat and said in my loudest voice, "Miguel Otero, show yourself. *Please*. We know you're in the woods and so does Detective Noland. I've talked to him and he doesn't believe you killed Jean-Claude de Merignac. He thinks it was a woman and that maybe you heard something that will help with his investigation. You're not under arrest and Isabella needs you. All you have to do is talk to Detective Noland, tell him what you know. You have my word that nothing is going to happen to you. *Palabra de Dios*."

I stopped talking and held my breath, listening to the evening sounds of the woods and the faded metallic thrumming of the cicadas. Quinn put his arm around my shoulders. "Come on, sweetheart," he said. "Let's get out of here before it's pitch dark. You tried. He's not coming."

"Wait," I said. "Just one more minute."

He emerged from a thicket of trees and bushes as we were about to leave, a dark form separating itself from the gray-black woods and moving quickly toward us.

"Miguel?"

"*Sí*." He waved a hand, part salute, part surrender. "Are you okay, Lucie? I'm sorry I ran into you. I thought you guys were somebody else."

ICE or a couple of deputies from the Sheriff's Office. That's who he thought we were. He looked hollow-eyed and apprehensive, still wearing the wine-stained T-shirt and jeans he'd had on two nights ago when Quinn and I saw him at Toby and Robyn's. It seemed like an eternity had passed since then.

"I'm fine. It's good to see you, Miguel," I said. "Come on. You must be famished and ready to get home to Isabella. Let's get out of here."

He sat on the flatbed trailer that was hitched to the ATV as Quinn drove us back to the vineyard and I called Bobby. Then I handed my phone to Miguel, whose phone had died, so he could call Isabella and, finally, Antonio. The guys—Antonio, Benny, and Jesús—were waiting as we pulled up in front of the villa five minutes later. Miguel leapt down and Antonio grabbed him in a bear hug, speaking in rapid-fire Spanish. Antonio caught my eye and gave me a tiny nod of acknowledgement. I knew then that he would keep his end of the bargain since I had kept mine. There would be no workers' strike at Montgomery Estate Vineyard.

Miguel wanted Quinn and me to be present when Bobby showed up to question him half an hour later in the villa. At first I thought Bobby was going to refuse since it was against his policy to speak to a witness with other people around, but eventually he relented when it became clear he'd get more information out of Miguel—especially with Quinn as a translator—if we were there. Antonio, Jesús, and Benny, however, were told to wait outside in the courtyard.

Bobby looked almost as haggard as Miguel did, but he was dressed in a dark gray suit, which was unusual for him.

"You've been somewhere," Quinn said while we waited for Miguel, who was sitting at the bar, to finish a sandwich and a soft drink that I'd brought him from the kitchen.

Bobby moved out of Miguel's earshot.

"Dulles Airport and then Salamander Resort by way of the morgue," he said in a low voice. "Escorting the victim's father to make a positive ID on his son, plus I had to ask him a few questions. It's my least favorite part of the job, especially when we haven't caught the killer."

"You were with Armand de Merignac just now?" I said.

"The tenth Baron de Merignac himself. He's . . . uh, quite impressive. The kind of guy who seems like he takes no prisoners. And definitely rich. I bet just one of his shoes cost more than every item of clothing I own put together. Of course you probably already know that since he's an old family friend."

"Our families have known each other in France for generations, but I haven't spoken to Armand—Baron de Merignac—in years. How's he doing?"

"As well as could be expected, considering he just lost his only son. Though I gather they weren't especially close." He glanced at Miguel who crumpled up the paper napkin I'd given him and threw it on his plate. "Looks like Miguel's done eating so we can get this show on the road." He raised his voice. "You ready, Miguel?"

Miguel swung around on his bar stool so he faced us. "I am. Thanks for the food, Lucie. It was great."

"You're welcome. Do you want anything else?"

"Some water, please." I got a bottle of chilled water out of the refrigerator behind the bar and gave it to him. Bobby flipped open a spiral-bound reporter's notebook and pulled a pen out of the inside pocket of his suit jacket, sitting down on the bar stool next to Miguel.

"Okay," he said. "I want you to tell me what happened,

what you know about yesterday morning. Start at the beginning."

In spite of everything that had taken place over the past thirty-six hours, I had a feeling Miguel was glad to get this off his chest, especially now that he realized he wasn't the number one suspect in the murder of Jean-Claude de Merignac. He told Bobby he'd shown up at the La Vigne barrel room around eight o'clock in the morning and discovered Jean-Claude was already there. Almost immediately the two of them had words over Miguel's missing documents.

"He said he had no idea what happened to my papers and it was my fault for leaving them in my car. I smelled alcohol on his breath," Miguel said. "So I left and went to the vineyard to get away from him. So I could calm down—*un poco más tranquilo,* you know?"

Bobby's eyebrows went up. "Alcohol on his breath at eight A.M.? Was he drunk?"

"Not drunk, but he'd been drinking. Maybe he was doing some barrel sampling. I didn't ask."

Bobby let that go, but it was the first I'd heard of Jean-Claude having a little tipple of his own wine for breakfast. It was an occupational hazard in our business. Quinn and I were constantly vigilant about how much each of us drank.

"Then what happened?" Bobby asked.

"I came back when I realized I didn't have my secateurs. I was so mad at Jean-Claude that I'd forgotten to take them with me when I left earlier."

"What time would that be?" Bobby looked up from his notebook. "When you came back the second time?"

"I don't know. I think around nine. Maybe a little later."

"Can you be any more specific than around nine?"

"Sorry. I didn't check. But I think it was nine. A couple of the guys who work in the fields were just getting in."

"All right, that helps. So, you came back to the winery, probably around nine o'clock. Then what?"

"I drove up and parked my car behind the barrel room. It should still be there where I left it. Then I walked over to the crush pad and opened the door to the barrel room. That's when I heard Jean-Claude arguing with a woman." Miguel took a swig of water. "They were angry, really angry. Both of them."

"What were they arguing about?"

"I don't know. They were speaking French. And they were shouting."

Neither Quinn nor I looked at each other and Bobby seemed completely unfazed. Nikki. Robyn. Dominique.

Dominique was the only one among those three whom I knew for sure spoke fluent French. But if Dominique was shouting at Jean-Claude, it didn't necessarily mean that she'd murdered him in anger afterward, stabbing him with Miguel's secateurs . . . did it?

"You didn't pick up a word that sounded familiar?" Bobby was saying. "Something? A name, maybe? Could you recognize this woman's voice if you heard it again?"

"Sorry. Nothing. They were in Jean-Claude's office with the door closed so the voices were . . ." He looked at Quinn and me. "*Apagados.* Sorry, I don't remember the word in English."

"Muffled," Quinn said.

"That's right. Muffled."

"Okay. Then what happened?"

Miguel shrugged. "I didn't want any part of what was

going on with the boss and his lady-friend, you know? So I left."

"Without your secateurs."

"Yes."

"Jean-Claude was alive when you left the wine cellar?"

"Yes. Absolutely."

"Where did you go?"

He shrugged. "Back to the vineyard. Where else?"

"Why did you run?"

Miguel looked uncomfortable. "One of the guys found me and told me what happened. Jean-Claude was dead and you guys found my secateurs with blood on them. I have no papers and everyone knew Jean-Claude and I were fighting the day before he died." He straightened up and looked Bobby in the eye. "If you were me, what would you do?"

Bobby gave him a severe look. "I would have cooperated with us. That's what I would have done. Instead you went on the lam, as if you had something to hide."

"I'm sorry," Miguel said. "But I'm here now, aren't I? And I'm free to go, right?"

Bobby closed his notebook. "Yes. You can go. If you think of anything else . . ." He pulled his wallet out of his pocket, extracted a business card, and handed it to Miguel. "Call this number. Anytime."

"Okay." Miguel slid off the bar stool. "I need to get home. The baby is due any day now." He nodded at all of us. "Thanks, Lucie. Quinn. Good night, Detective."

Quinn left with Miguel, saying he wanted to lock up the barrel room for the night and that he'd meet me at home. I asked Bobby if he could stick around for a moment.

"Can I get you a beer? A glass of wine?" I asked after the others were gone.

Bobby shook his head. "I'm still on duty. What's up, Lucie?"

"Dominique didn't kill Jean-Claude."

"Lucie—"

"She didn't, Bobby."

He gave me a pointed look. "She and Jean-Claude have a long history together going back to when she was still living in France. Baron de Merignac filled me in this evening."

I froze. Had Armand de Merignac known about Dominique's abortion—had he found out, maybe through an indiscreet employee at the clinic she'd gone to? If he knew, he might have told Bobby, especially if Bobby pressed him for information on anyone who held a grudge against Jean-Claude. Plus there was the *Trib* story that appeared yesterday, the morning Jean-Claude was murdered, which only reinforced the enmity between him and my cousin.

"You heard Miguel," Bobby went on. "Jean-Claude had a shouting match with a woman and the two of them were speaking French."

"Dominique's not the only woman around here who speaks fluent French."

"That's right," he said in an even voice. "You do, as well. So were you the one arguing with him?"

Was he serious? Me? "No. Jesus, Bobby. No, of course not."

"Don't worry, your alibi checks out. Unfortunately, Dominique's does not, " he said. "And before we get into this any further—since it is an ongoing murder investigation and I've already said enough—I'm going to see myself out. Good night, Lucie."

He started walking toward the front door.

"Bobby, Nikki Young was with Jean-Claude that morning as well. She told me they argued and he threw her out of his office. Literally."

He spun around. "I'm aware of that. I'm also not any happier about the way this is shaking out than you are, Lucie, but I've got to do my job. That's all I can say."

I nodded, feeling numb, as the front door clicked shut. A few moments later, I heard his tires crunching on the gravel as he left the parking lot, then red taillights reflecting off the wall through the window.

A couple of lights were still on in the villa. I made the rounds, turning them off in Nikki's office, Frankie's office, and the kitchen. It was completely unlike Frankie, who was always so efficient and responsible, to leave for the day without closing up properly.

When I walked into the tasting room she was standing by the door, arms folded across her chest, looking like a volcano ready to erupt. She must have been in the barrel room or somewhere else on the property.

Frankie, who was always so calm and unflappable in the middle of any crisis—I'd never seen her this upset. I wasn't sure how much more raw emotion I could take just now.

"Frankie—"

She cut me off. "What in the *world* happened, Lucie? What did you *do*?"

"It's been a hell of a day. A lot of things happened and I've done a lot of things. Which one are you talking about and do you want a drink?"

"I'm talking about Nikki, and yes, I do."

She stalked over to the bar before I could stop her, uncorked an open bottle of Cab Sauv, and poured two full glasses with a hand that shook badly. I joined her at the bar and sat on one of the stools.

I picked up my glass and said, "I fired her for insubordination."

"She'll apologize. She's just upset about Jean-Claude." She came around from behind the bar and sat on the stool next to me.

"She lied to us, Frankie. She went over to La Vigne that morning instead of driving out to the flower farm. She had it out with Jean-Claude and they argued. Apparently she scratched him up, so it got physical."

"Lucie, she's just a *kid*. She fell head over heels in love with Jean-Claude—show me any woman who wouldn't—and when he dumped her, she came unglued. She'll get over him. I've already spoken to her mother. Apparently there have been . . . other . . . incidents like this in the past," Frankie said.

"Incidents like what?"

Frankie looked uncomfortable. "Nikki can be a bit possessive, maybe a little too jealous. Her mom said she has a hard time letting go when someone breaks up with her."

"Then she needs counseling. Getting your heart broken is a rite of passage. It happens to everyone." I drank some wine. "Look, she even accused me of being Jean-Claude's newest girlfriend. I told her that was ridiculous but she didn't believe me and stormed out of here."

"I know. She called me, crying like the world was about to end. She said you were pretty harsh with her."

I was not going to get into a she-said-she-said arm-wrestling match with Frankie, but I was still ticked off. "I was not. This is a murder investigation and she's got a motive, Frankie."

Frankie gave me a heavy-lidded look that said she knew better. "It doesn't matter, Lucie. Nikki didn't do it. She didn't kill Jean-Claude. I'll bet my job on it."

"Tell me something," I said. "Does Nikki speak French? Fluently, I mean?"

Frankie laughed. "Oh my good Lord, no. I mean, she tried—I think she took French 101 in college, but she gave up. It was like what Mark Twain said about his wife and swearing—she had the words but she didn't know the tune. Franglais with a side of Southern drawl, y'all." She tilted her head and stared at me. "Why do you ask?"

I took a huge swig of wine. "No reason," I said. "I was just wondering."

QUINN AND ELI WERE home by the time I arrived after Frankie and I finished our talk. On her way out the door, Frankie told me she planned to have Nikki spend the night at her house, her way of letting me know Nikki was practically a member of her family, another daughter. She also said she hoped I'd rescind my decision to fire her, maybe put her on thirty days probation as a compromise, if I felt some kind of disciplinary action was really necessary. I told Frankie I needed to sleep on it and would give her an answer in the morning.

I had no idea what I was going to say to either of them tomorrow and just now I couldn't handle any more decisions or confrontations after the tumult of today's events. Then there was this: Miguel had left the La Vigne barrel room while Jean-Claude was in the middle of a heated argument in French with a woman Miguel couldn't identify. In other words, Miguel had no idea if that fight ended when the woman stabbed Jean-Claude in the back with his secateurs, or whether she left and he was still alive.

Though Frankie confirmed that Nikki couldn't say more than "bone-jour y'all," in French, it still didn't mean she hadn't been the one who killed Jean-Claude. She certainly had shown a different side of herself this afternoon—hostile, jealous, possessive—when I confronted her in her office. Plus she admitted she'd been to see Jean-Claude and their meeting had ended badly.

But just how badly? If Nikki turned out to be the killer, it wouldn't matter if I reinstated her or not. She wouldn't be returning here; she'd be heading to a Virginia penitentiary.

Quinn handed me a Scotch as soon as I walked into the parlor and he and Eli made room on the sofa between the two of them. The television was on mute and the mantel clock showed two minutes to six.

"Where's Hope?" I asked.

"At Persia's for the evening," Eli said, unmuting the TV. "I don't want her seeing any of this. Pippa O'Hara, your favorite reporter, has the top story on the six o'clock news on News Channel 3. Armand de Merignac is in town."

"Bobby told us," I said. "He met him at the airport and took him to the morgue."

Pippa O'Hara put on her usual performance hyping the story, showing the de Merignacs' private jet landing at Dulles "so a grieving father can take his only son and heir back to their ninth-century château in France on a final, heartbreaking journey. There he will lay Jean-Claude to rest in the family cemetery next to the legendary grapevines of Château de Merignac in Bordeaux, the most famous wine region in the world."

"That woman," Quinn said under his breath. "Someone ought to spank her."

"Shh," I said. "Listen. She's talking to Bobby."

Her cameraman had panned to Bobby when he was at the airport, looking uncomfortable and irritated as Pippa confronted him and asked why the Loudoun County Sheriff's Office still had not made an arrest for the murder of Jean-Claude. Bobby had given a smart-ass answer that would probably get him in trouble, but it had the effect of momentarily silencing Pippa.

"Because the Sheriff's Office has a habit of waiting until we have definitive proof that someone committed a crime before we make an arrest," he said. "This isn't a television drama so everything wraps up before the last commercial. We also don't answer to the media, Pippa. We answer to the citizens of Loudoun County." Then he'd turned on his heel and walked away.

After that the camera cut to B-roll, generic shots of the airport, La Vigne Cellars, and finally a cameo of Baron de Merignac, looking elated and champagne-soaked along with his Formula One driver after winning the prestigious Monaco Grand Prix last year. Pippa did the voiceover to go with the photos, managing to get in another dig at the Sheriff's Office for being clueless and letting a murderer run loose in Loudoun County. Quinn turned off the television.

"Well, that was entertaining. Anyone for dinner? I'm

starved. I missed lunch," he said. "Persia left slices of cold roast beef and a salade niçoise."

"I had lunch," Eli said, "but it was hours ago. Oh, by the way, Luce, I ran into Kit. She was getting a sandwich at The Upper Crust as I was picking up my order. She wants you to call her."

Quinn set the TV remote on the coffee table and walked out of the room without saying a word.

Eli glanced at me. "What just happened? What did I miss? Was it something I said?"

"No," I said. "It was something I said. I was supposed to have lunch with Kit and . . . it didn't work out. I forgot to mention it to Quinn."

He looked perplexed. "Okay. I see."

Which meant he didn't.

Although I'd taken Quinn out to the cabin in the woods so I could finally tell him about David, my plans had gone awry when Miguel turned up. But right now I wasn't ready to say anything in front of my brother, who I knew would react differently than Quinn to the news that our father had had an affair that produced a son that none of us had known about. Before I told Eli or Mia about David, I wanted to talk things over with Quinn.

As a result of the obvious friction between Quinn and me, the dinner table conversation consisted of Eli talking about the Couple from Hell and the latest progress on the house he was designing for them. We were just finishing dinner when the doorbell rang.

"I wonder who that is." Eli sounded relieved at the reprieve from our tense meal. "I'll get it."

"No," I said. "I'll go."

I stood before he could stop me and left. It was Dominique and she looked like hell.

"Why did you ring the bell?" I asked. "You have a key. Come in . . . is everything all right?"

I pulled her inside.

"I . . . left the key somewhere," she said, her voice shaking. "I don't know where it is."

I heard footsteps and turned as Quinn and Eli walked into the foyer.

"What's going on?" Eli said. "Dominique, what's wrong? Are you okay?"

"She looks like she's in shock," Quinn said. "I'll get her something to drink."

I put my arm around my cousin's shoulders. "Tell me what happened."

"I just left the Sheriff's Office in Leesburg," she said. "I couldn't go back to the Inn tonight . . . I just couldn't . . . so I came here."

"It's okay," I said, but my heart was thumping wildly and my hands felt clammy. "What happened?"

Her eyes were wide with fear. "Bobby's been going over everything I've done in the past few days with a fine-tuned comb," she said. "I think I'm going to be arrested tomorrow."

"You can't be serious," Eli said. "For what?"

"It seems Bobby believes I murdered Jean-Claude." She looked at all of us, still glassy-eyed. "What do I do now?"

Seventeen

t took a while to calm Dominique down and persuade her that she ought to spend the night at Highland House, but truth to tell, her news rattled and upset everyone. The four of us had moved into the parlor and someone plonked the bottle of Scotch in the middle of the coffee table along with four glasses. It was going to be that kind of night.

Eli called Persia and asked if Hope could stay over and spend the night in her apartment. Persia, bless her, hadn't asked why; she just said she'd be happy to take care of her little angel for as long as Eli needed her to help out.

We were in the middle of a heated discussion about whether Dominique needed a lawyer *right now* when my phone rang. The tiff between Quinn and me that had been playing out at the dinner table had been forgotten. We were sitting next to each other on the sofa, his arm draped over my shoulders.

He passed me my phone. "Robyn Callahan," he said, squinting at the screen. "Want to let it go to voice mail?"

Robyn. Why couldn't she be a more plausible candidate to murder Jean-Claude than my cousin? Maybe there were some things Bobby didn't know about her and Jean-Claude. Yet.

"I left a message with Colette earlier today asking if Robyn would have time to look at the quilt Susanna Montgomery's body was buried in," I said. "I bet she's calling back about that. I should take this."

"To talk about a quilt?" Eli refilled his glass. "Now?"

"Yes," I said in a firm voice, "but more important it would give me an opportunity to find out whether Robyn speaks French. Fluent French. Do any of you happen to know?"

There was momentary silence in the room.

"Uh . . . no," Eli said.

"No idea," Quinn said and Dominique shook her head.

I pressed the green button on my phone. "Hey, Robyn, thanks for getting back to me."

Colette had told Robyn enough about the unusual-looking quilt to pique her interest, and she told me she'd be happy to take a look at it if I wanted to bring it by her house in the morning. We settled on meeting at nine o'clock, and then I asked how she was doing.

Her sigh sounded weary and exasperated. "We've still got the press camped out at the entrance to La Vigne and it's driving Toby mad. Plus he had a rather unpleasant meeting with Jean-Claude's father this evening."

"Unpleasant?"

"Baron de Merignac more or less accused Toby of being responsible for Jean-Claude's death," she said. "He said we've turned into a gun-toting, trigger-happy bunch of vigilantes over here and that if we didn't allow everyone and his cousin to buy a gun along with a liter of milk at the grocery store, make it so easy, there would be far fewer deaths in America."

"You can't buy a gun at the grocery store and Jean-Claude was stabbed to death by a pair of secateurs used at a vineyard," I said. "Did he have anything to say about that?"

She sighed again. "No. The man was grieving, so of course you have to forgive that kind of emotional outburst. He just needed some place to vent his anger and sorrow. Toby offered to accompany him to the airport tomorrow night with Jean-Claude's coffin since he's going straight back to France, but he turned Toby down."

"Hopefully Bobby will catch whoever did it soon, and Jean-Claude's family will at least have closure knowing his killer was brought to justice," I said. "Bobby seems to be focusing on anyone who had a romantic interest in Jean-Claude."

"Yes," she said in a tight, clipped voice. "I'm aware of that."

"Miguel turned himself in tonight," I said. "He was hiding out in an abandoned cottage on my land. Quinn and I persuaded him to talk to Bobby, so he did. He told Bobby he overheard Jean-Claude in his office arguing with a woman right before he was murdered."

"Oh?"

"Yes. He said they were speaking French."

"I see. Look, Lucie, I've got to go. It's been a long day. See you tomorrow morning at nine, okay?"

"Sure," I said, "thanks for doing this." But she had already disconnected.

I clicked off my phone and looked around at Quinn, Eli, and Dominique, who had been listening to my side of the conversation.

"Well?" Eli asked. "What happened?"

"She didn't bite when I brought up what Miguel said about someone speaking French with Jean-Claude the morning he was killed," I said. "I'll find out tomorrow if it could have been her or not. But I can tell you this: she got very uptight and nervous all of a sudden."

"Do you think she's guilty?" Quinn asked. "Could she have done it?"

"Done what? Are you saying Robyn could have killed Jean-Claude?" Dominique sounded so startled I reckoned she hadn't heard the rumors about Robyn sleeping with Jean-Claude.

"Bobby seems to think it was a crime of passion, as near as I can tell," I said to her. "He may think you had a motive and possibly the opportunity, but the truth of the matter is you didn't kill Jean-Claude."

"I didn't," she said, "but Bobby's making me so nervous I'm not sure I'm going to answer when he starts asking questions. I'm an American citizen now. I might tell him I've decided to exercise my sixth amendment rights."

"The sixth amendment," Eli said, "is the right to a speedy trial."

"Well, one of the other ones then."

"Before you do anything," I said, "we have to find out who the real killer is."

Though as Bobby said, this wasn't going to end well. Whoever was found guilty, it was going to tear apart our close-knit community.

Because the murderer was almost certainly one of us.

. . .

WE HAD MADE A significant dent in the bottle of Scotch when a deafening crash sounded outside as if the sky had split in two. Between the alcohol and the topic of conversation—finding a murderer—we were all already twitchy enough to jump out of our skin. Dominique, who had been about to pick up her glass, bumped it with her hand and sloshed Scotch on the coffee table.

"*Merde*. Sorry." She swiped the liquid with her sleeve.

"That was thunder," I said. "I didn't know we were supposed to get a storm tonight."

Quinn stood up and walked over to the window. "The sky is lit up with devil's pitchfork lightning. The wind is up, too. You can hear it."

As he spoke a noise like the rumbling of a jet plane passing overhead reverberated through the trees and a blood vessel behind my left eye started to throb. I pushed my fingers hard into my eyebrow, willing the pressure headache I always got when storms like these blew up to go away and leave me in peace for once.

"Dammit, I left a window ajar in the studio. The place smelled of glue since I'd been building a model for the Couple from Hell," Eli said. "I'll be right back."

By the time he returned, the rain was coming down in sheets and Eli's jeans and sweatshirt looked as if he'd gone swimming in them. He sneezed and shook himself like a wet dog. His hair was plastered to his head and water ran down his face in rivulets.

Dominique found paper cocktail napkins in the drawer of a side table and handed some to him. "Here. Use these. You ought to get out of those wet clothes before you catch cold."

Eli nodded and mopped his face. "I will. The rain is coming down so hard it's going to flood the gutters. That wind is wicked. I'll bet you've got a headache, Luce."

"I do."

Another crash of thunder sounded directly overhead followed by a lightning bolt that illuminated the trees and gardens outside like a spooky amusement park house of horrors.

"It's just over top of us," Eli said as the inside lights flickered.

"I hope we don't lose power," Quinn said.

"We ought to get the lanterns and flashlights from the pantry," I said. "Just in case."

"I'll get them," Quinn said.

"I'll get the candles in the dining room," I said.

"I'll change," Eli said.

"What can I do?" Dominique asked.

"Sit there and drink your Scotch," I said. "You've got enough on your plate."

As Eli predicted, the rain soon overran the gutters, cascading like a waterfall down the windows and rat-a-tatting like gunfire as it bounced off the sills. My eye wouldn't stop pulsing. The lights went out for good while Eli was upstairs and Quinn and I were rummaging in the kitchen and dining room. A quiet explosion in the basement followed by absolute stillness meant the heating and air-conditioning system was out.

By the time everyone got back to the parlor, Dominique was on her feet, looking around in the dark for her purse.

"I don't think I should stay here tonight after all," she said. "Thank God we have a generator at the Inn, but I ought to check on everything just in case."

"You have good people working for you who can take care of all that," I told her as Quinn lit two pillar candles and set them in the middle of the coffee table. "You shouldn't be on your own, under the circumstances, and you don't want to be driving in this storm. The low spots in the roads will be flooded and it's too dark to see some of them, so it's dangerous. You're staying here, sleeping in your old room, and no arguing. Got that?"

She gave me a weak smile. "Okay. You win."

"Anyone for another little drinkie?" Eli held up the bottle and waved it back and forth like a semaphore. He was already more than a bit drunk, but then so were we all.

"I've had enough," I said. The swaying bottle was making me dizzy. "I'll pay for it tomorrow."

"Me, too," Quinn said. "I'm beat. Anyone else ready for bed?"

"I am," I said. "First I need to make the guest room bed for Dominique. There are no sheets on it."

"I know where the sheets are and I know how to make a bed," my cousin said, yawning. "This used to be my house, too, remember? Thanks, *chérie,* but I'll take care of it. No arguing. Got that?"

I grinned. "Okay. You win."

Quinn passed out the lanterns and flashlights so we could see where we were going in the dark as we made our way up the spiral staircase in the foyer like a slow-moving caravan. Since Highland House had a well, no electricity also meant the well pump wouldn't function and there would be no water and no flushing the toilet once we used what was in the holding tank in the cellar. The telephone landline had a backup battery capable of lasting only a few hours and everyone's mobiles would work as long as they held a charge. Unfortunately I'd let mine run down until it was nearly dead, but I'd trade no phone for running water any day. And a working toilet.

Quinn and I undressed by lantern-light and opted not to brush our teeth or wash our faces to save water.

"We have to fill the bathtubs and sinks before Lolita arrives," he said, "so we don't get caught off-guard like this again. This storm came out of nowhere."

"I hope the power comes back on tonight or tomorrow morning," I said. "A tree probably fell on a power line or knocked out a generator. They ought to get it fixed in no time. It will be a different story with Lolita. We could lose power for days."

He slid into bed and held the covers for me. I got in next to him and said, "I'm beat. Today felt like it went on forever."

"I know. But I think you still owe me a bedtime story," he said, adjusting his pillow so it was propped against the headboard. He leaned against it and watched me. "Don't you?"

He had turned the lantern down to the lowest setting. Though the bedroom was bathed in soft golden light, the marionette lines on his face looked deep-set and harsh and his silhouette was an angry-looking shadow on the wall. He was still upset with me for lying about having lunch with Kit when I had obviously been somewhere else.

"I'm so sorry," I said. "I meant to tell you everything today at the house in the woods until Miguel showed up."

"Tell me what?"

"I don't want Eli to know about this. At least not just yet. And certainly not Mia."

He frowned, but he said, "Okay."

I took a deep breath and it came out raggedy. This wasn't going to be easy. "Leland had an affair," I said. "After Eli was born and when my mother was pregnant with me. Eli, Mia, and I have a half brother. I have no idea whether Leland realized he had a son or not. I just met him today at the Goose Creek Bridge when you thought I was having lunch with Kit. His biological mother is African-American and his name is David Phelps. His mother gave him up and Phelps is the name of the couple that adopted him."

After a long moment of silence he said, "That must have been a hell of a discovery. Are you okay?"

I nodded and he pulled me into his arms. We lay there for a long time without speaking.

Finally I said, "I want you to meet him. And he wants to meet you. But Eli . . . and Mia . . . I just don't know how I can tell either of them. That's why I didn't say anything tonight at dinner."

"You can't shield them, Lucie. They have a right to know they have a half brother."

I told him about the Genome Project and how I'd learned about David. "They didn't ask for this, Quinn," I said. "I did."

"What are you trying to do? Protect them?"

My voice cracked. "I'm trying not to break their hearts."

"If you're tough enough to take it, so are they," he said, stroking my hair, his touch gentle as a feather. "Look, I'm the last one to give advice on relationships considering what a mess my own family is. But you can't rewrite history. You can't change Susanna Montgomery falling in love with someone she was told she wasn't allowed to love. It seems to me she risked her life, risked everything, for love. And you can't change Leland having an affair that produced a child who is now your adult half brother. You said yourself he's an amazing person. You two have the same father. You share the same blood. So do Eli and Mia."

I leaned into the crook of his arm and blinked back tears. *The blood of your parents is not lost in you.* It was a line from Homer's *Odyssey*. I'd spent an entire semester reading it, one of the most famous epic poems in literature, in an Intro to Lit course in college. My dog-eared marked-up copy was on a bookshelf downstairs in the library. The professor had also gotten into the psychological debate of nature versus nurture: which mattered more in shaping each of us as children into the adults we became? Was it genetic inheritance or environment and experience? Who could say? There was no right or wrong answer, just lots of variables and individual situations that seemed to skew one way or the other.

Except for one immutable fact: in the end blood mattered. No one could change who their parents were or where they came from. DNA was DNA. Family was family.

"I suppose you're right," I said. "I'll tell them, but not just now. There's too much going on. Jean-Claude's murder and Bobby apparently suspecting Dominique. The hurricane. The end of harvest. Let me figure out the right time and place."

"Don't leave it too long. They're both going to want to know when you found out," he said. "And wonder why you waited to tell them. Put yourself in their shoes. How would you feel if either of them discovered bombshell news like this and decided to keep it a secret for a while?"

"You're not making this easy."

"Messy stuff usually isn't easy. Especially when it involves families."

Quinn was right. I was kidding myself that I could spare Eli and Mia from the bewildered hurt and anger I'd felt the first time I learned what Leland had done. And of course there was David, who had charmed me today, and was eager to meet his two siblings. Find the family he hadn't known existed until a couple of years ago, maybe build a future together even though there had never been a past. David was the silver lining that could make forgiving Leland possible.

"I'll do it," I said. "Soon. I promise."

"Good." He leaned over and turned off the lantern. Outside the storm had ended, except for the hypnotic drumming of rain on the roof.

"I hope we get the power back on and the rain stops before morning," I said, stifling a yawn.

"Me, too." He rolled over onto his side so we were facing each other. "Are you okay?"

"I'm worried about Dominique."

"I know. You're all wound up. I can feel it." He leaned in and kissed me. "There's a remedy for that, you know."

I smiled. "Tell me, what would that be?"

"I'm not going to tell you, I'm going to show you . . . for a little while, it would be good to forget . . . everything."

He pulled me into his arms and I felt, as I always did when we made love, as if I was losing myself in him, drowning. But this time was different. This time he was saving me. From the ghost of a dead girl and her lost lover, from the hurt of my father's secret affair, and from a killer who probably had a trusted, familiar face. I surrendered to everything he wanted to do and for the next hour, I forgot all these things that had haunted me.

We finally fell asleep, exhausted, wrapped in each other's arms in a tangle of sheets. Briefly I heard him murmur something about the power coming back on and realized he'd left our bed. Eventually he returned, his body chilled from the night air and wherever he'd been, and I woke up.

"What's wrong?" I murmured. "Where were you? You're cold."

"Shh. Nothing's wrong," he said. "I was just checking on everything, turning off lights we left on. Go back to sleep."

I closed my eyes. The next time I opened them, it was light outside. And it had stopped raining.

DOMINIQUE WAS GONE BY the time I came downstairs a few minutes later after washing my grimy face and brushing my teeth. The grandfather clock in the foyer had just chimed six. My cousin's note was propped up against Susanna's copy of *The Journal of John Woolman* on the demilune table in the foyer. She thanked us for taking care of her last night and said that her bedsheets were already in the washing machine in the basement and our drinks glasses had been washed and put away. If she could have vacuumed and dusted the entire house from top to bottom without waking anyone, she would have done that, too.

I set her note down and picked up *The Journal of John*

Woolman. In the commotion of Dominique's arrival, too much Scotch, and a power outage, I'd forgotten all about it. Quinn had been right that the book had taken a beating when Miguel knocked it out of my hands and it landed open and facedown in the bushes.

I brought it into the kitchen and put it on the table. Quinn had set up the coffeepot the night before to start brewing coffee at 6 A.M. as we usually did, but the power outage had reset the clock to midnight. I readjusted it and hit the brew button. Then I sat down at the table to see what damage had been done to the old book and whether I could do surgery on it myself or it needed professional help. The back flyleaf had started to come away from the cover and the binding was pulling away from the spine. I ran my thumb over the endpaper. It had already been separated from the book once before. The glue that held it to the cover was nothing more than a thin bead around the edge of the paper. Something stiff and rectangular had been inserted between the paper and the book. It felt like a card. Or maybe a photograph.

I got a butter knife and finished separating the endpaper from the cover. When I was done, I knew I was looking at a black-and-white photograph of the man Susanna Montgomery had loved enough to defy her family and reject her fiancé. Noble-looking, light-skinned, dressed in a fine-looking jacket and a white dress shirt, he had large, expressive eyes, full lips, a broad nose, and bushy black hair that was combed back from his forehead like the mane of a lion. I turned the photograph over. The flowery script had to be Susanna's handwriting. It didn't look masculine.

Henry Wells, June 30, 1862. Lincoln, Virginia.

"Who is that?"

I jumped. Quinn was standing behind me, leaning over my shoulder.

"Oh, gosh, you scared me. I didn't hear you come in."

"Sorry." He bent down and kissed my hair. "Want some coffee?"

"Yes, please. According to what's written on the back of the photograph, his name is Henry Wells. I bet he was Susanna's lover, the man she was going to run away with and marry in New York. He lived in Lincoln, the Quaker village next to Purcellville."

Quinn picked up the photograph and examined it. "He looks very . . . I don't know . . . aristocratic. I wonder who he was?"

"Me, too."

"Well, now you've got something to go on. You ought to be able to find out more about him."

"I thought I'd start at the Thomas Balch Library in Leesburg. If any place has information or genealogical records about him, they will."

Quinn got two mugs from the cabinet and poured our coffees. "It would be interesting to know what happened to him. Did he make it to New York, even if Susanna didn't, or did he end up like she did?"

"You mean dead."

He nodded and handed me a mug. "It seems to me the punishment—or retribution—would have been worse for Henry than for Susanna if he got caught. Especially in Virginia, the heart of the Confederacy." He paused. "I wonder if Charles . . ."

"Murdered Henry, too?"

His eyes met mine. "Either on his own or perhaps he had help. He must have been furious when he found out, don't you think?"

I did. Unbidden, an image of men carrying burning torches and pitchforks came into my head. And another of white-robed men in conical hoods on horseback. The Klan. I shuddered.

Maybe Thelma knew whether Charles had exacted some kind of revenge on Henry and chose not to tell me about the man who would not only be my distant cousin but also her great-uncle. I still didn't know for sure whether Charles had killed Susanna or merely buried her in that unmarked grave. Thelma and I hadn't discussed that subject, either.

"David told me yesterday he photographed an old church in Lincoln that was the first African-American church in Loudoun County. It has a cemetery, although apparently it hasn't been maintained. Both slaves and free blacks were buried there. I think I'll call him and ask if he can show me around."

"It would be ironic if Henry was buried there with a proper headstone while Susanna was dumped in a shallow unmarked grave next to your family's cemetery."

"It would. In the meantime maybe Robyn can tell me something about the quilt Susanna was wrapped in. I've never seen one like it," I said.

"Plus I presume you're going to ask her whether she was arguing in French with Jean-Claude right before he was murdered?"

"I thought maybe I could work it into the conversation."

"It's hard to be subtle about murder."

"No fooling."

"So how are you planning to bring it up?"

"I don't know yet," I told him. "But I'll figure out something."

KIT CALLED AS I was in the car driving over to Robyn's.

"I ran into Eli yesterday," she said. "We were getting lunch at The Upper Crust. He was supposed to tell you to call me."

"He did," I said. "During dinner. After that, things got sort of crazy. I'm sorry, I just forgot."

"Is everything okay? How about lunch today? We can catch up."

"Sure, lunch would be fine," I said. "Let's meet at Lightfoot at eleven thirty. I need to pay a visit to the Balch Library afterward and look through their records and it's right down the street."

"Would this have something to do with your skeleton?"

"It would."

"Lightfoot sounds good. I love that restaurant," she said. "Want some company at the library? The *Trib* uses their resources all the time. I know my way around."

"I'd love it," I said. "See you soon."

I disconnected with Kit and pulled into Toby and Robyn's driveway. After last night's torrential rain, the driveway was still wet and slick under a gray, sullen sky that perfectly matched my mood. I got the quilt out of the back of the Jeep, still packed in the paper bag Yasmin had put it in, and rang the doorbell with my elbow.

The housekeeper opened the door and invited me in as

Robyn walked into the foyer, a tired smile on her face. Today she wore faded skinny jeans and an untucked denim shirt, which only emphasized how petite she was. Looking at her I couldn't imagine she would have the physical strength to plunge a pair of secateurs into Jean-Claude when his back was turned. She wore no makeup and dark circles ringed her eyes.

"Good morning, Lucie," she said. "I'm afraid I don't have as much time this morning as I thought I did, so we should get started."

"We don't have to do this right now if it's not convenient," I said.

"It's fine. I wouldn't mind a distraction. After this Toby and I are driving over to meet Bobby Noland at the Sheriff's Office. He has some more questions for us about Jean-Claude's death." She was still smiling, but her eyes were clouded with worry.

"I'm sure it will go just fine," I said. "I spoke to Bobby again yesterday as well. In fact, I think he's been talking to a lot of people for a second time."

"Is that so?" She seemed to relax a little. "Well, I suppose it's our turn next."

I nodded, feeling guilty for offering her false comfort, as she added, "Why don't you let me take that bag from you? We can examine your quilt in my studio. I'm using an old dining room table as a worktable, so there will be plenty of room to lay it out."

I handed over the bag and followed her down the hall. We passed by the closed door to Toby's study and Robyn said in a low voice, "Toby has some pages due to his editor today. He and Colette are working like mad to make his deadline. They got sort of derailed with everything that's been going on the past few days."

By *everything* she meant Jean-Claude's murder. "I can imagine," I said.

Robyn's studio was a window-filled room with a set of French doors that led to a deck overlooking the swimming pool and a rose garden. Mick Dunne, the previous owner, had used it as a glorified man-cave decorated in shades of burgundy, black, and white with an enormous television, an L-shaped sofa piled with throw pillows, a well-stocked portable bar, microwave, and mini-refrigerator. Now the room was distinctly feminine, painted white like the rest of the house to better show off Robyn's artwork. The oak floor, which had been covered with Oriental carpets, was bare except for a tarp underneath a painting easel. The dining room table sat in a corner near a bank of windows and was covered with tablecloths and a protective sheet of plastic.

Robyn set down the bag and removed the quilt. When she opened it up to its full size, she gasped. "My God, this is exquisite. I've never seen one of these before, but I've read about them."

"One of what?"

"This quilt was probably made by an African-American woman," she said. "A very talented woman. It's called a 'kente quilt' because it's based on kente cloth, which is probably one of the best-known African textiles in the world."

"I've heard of kente cloth," I said. "But I've never heard of the fabric being used in quilts."

"Sorry. I didn't mean to confuse you. It's not actual kente cloth that's being used for the quilt," she said. "This is an American version, a quilter recreating the intricate designs of kente cloth—something remembered from home. From Africa."

She walked around the table, one finger pressed against her lips, as she reverently examined the quilt. When she looked up she said, "I can't believe it . . . this is incredible. Kente cloth is associated with the Ashanti people who live in central Ghana. Originally it was considered the cloth of kings, the sacred cloth of royalty. Now, of course, it's more widely available. To this day kente cloth—African kente cloth—is still hand woven in four-inch strips on special narrow looms. The quilter imitated this by interlacing strips of different-colored cloth to form a length of fabric. In Ghana, the men were the weavers, never women."

"Do you think this quilt was made by a man?" I asked.

"No," she said. "Kente *quilts* were an American creation and they were made by women—Ghanaian women—to keep the traditions of their country alive in the New World. The patterns would necessarily be different from those woven in Ghana because no Ashanti commoner would ever dream of wearing a design worn by their king. This quilt belongs in a museum, Lucie. Hanging on a wall by itself. Kente quilts are extremely rare and valuable because so few of them are known to have survived."

"Seriously?"

"Seriously. The history of kente cloth goes back centuries. Originally it was made from cotton until Portuguese traders brought silk to Africa in the fourteen hundreds. The Ashanti unraveled the silk and used the threads to reweave into their own designs. Kente quilts—which originated in America and are more modern—are very much associated with slavery."

Robyn lifted the quilt and ran her hand underneath it. She smiled. "Wow, this is perfect. Your quilt still has the paper-piecing in it. The quilter didn't remove it."

"What's paper-piecing?"

"Just what it sounds like. Templates for individual pieces of a block were drawn on paper, which was then pinned to the fabric so it could be cut very precisely. Paper-piecing is especially useful with a meticulous geometric design like this quilt has, where different pieces are joined together—to make a star or a compass, for example—and the points or intersections must match perfectly."

"Isn't that sort of careless or lazy not to remove the paper?" I asked.

"Not at all. The paper provided extra insulation, which was practical and useful in those days. I'm sure it's part of the reason—that additional layer—why this quilt survived as well as it did."

Robyn turned the quilt over and held it up to the light coming in through the bank of windows. "You can see some of the printing on the paper through the feed sack backing."

I moved closer and squinted at the thin white fabric. "What kind of paper did they use that it still had writing on it?"

"Anything. Don't forget, paper was scarce in those days. So quilters used letters, catalogue pages, sheet music, newspapers—really, anything." She set the quilt down right-side up, tapping a finger on one of the more colorful blocks. "One thing kente cloth and kente quilts had in common was that each color meant something . . . hang on a sec."

She walked over to a floor-to-ceiling bookcase on a far wall, pulling out a large book that she brought back to the table. *African Textiles: A World of Creativity and Color.* On the cover was an intricately woven piece of fabric that reminded me of my quilt.

Robyn opened the book and began turning pages. "Here . . . kente cloth." She pointed to a two-page spread with dazzling, colorful geometric textile designs and began reading. "Yellow stands for royalty or wealth; white represents goodness or victory; red symbolizes anger or violence; blue is for love, and so on . . . every color means something."

"So each piece of kente cloth and each kente quilt has its own story?"

"That's right. The design represents something of importance to the weaver, or in this case, to the quilt-maker."

"It needs to be repaired," I said. "And cleaned."

"I know people—experts—who can take care of that. Don't worry about a thing. It would be a privilege to restore a quilt like this." Robyn paused and tilted her head, giving me a quizzical look. "I also heard the skeleton you found on your property was wrapped in a quilt. I presume this is it?"

I nodded.

"Was he or she African-American?"

"She. Not African-American, but she was in love with a man who was."

Robyn looked startled. "Wow, that was a bold, scary thing to do. I'm sure they both knew the consequences if anyone found out."

"I imagine they did."

"Well, then I suspect this woman had a connection with someone who came to America from Ghana."

"Her name was Susanna Montgomery, at least I'm reasonably sure it was. And she was considering becoming a Quaker."

"Ah, so she's related to you," Robyn said. "Well, it makes sense if she wanted to become a Quaker, especially because they were such strong abolitionists. A lot of free blacks lived near the Quaker community in Lincoln. Quakers and blacks worked together. There was even a Quaker school where both Quakers and the children of free blacks were taught. If your quilt turns out to be local by some chance, it would be an even more exciting discovery." She arched an eyebrow and said in a hopeful voice, "I don't suppose you would be willing to leave it with me for a while?"

Lincoln. It was the third time that town had come up in the past twenty-four hours. David had mentioned it and now so had Robyn. And Susanna had written "Lincoln" on the back of Henry Wells' photograph. Perhaps Henry knew the woman who had made the quilt. Perhaps he had introduced her to Susanna. Or the other way around.

"I'll pay you for restoring it," I said.

"We can talk about that another time. Maybe you'd consider donating it to the Virginia Quilt Museum? Or the African American History Museum in D.C.? A place like the Smithsonian would be over the moon to have it. That would be compensation enough."

"You think it's that valuable?"

"I do. I'll call some of my colleagues at the Virginia Consortium of Quilters and the Virginia Quilt Museum," she said, "and let you know what I find out."

"In that case, sure, hang on to it for a while."

"Excellent. This is wonderful, Lucie. Thank you so much." She started to fold the quilt back up again. "Good Lord. How did I miss this?"

She set the quilt on the table and we both bent down to examine what she had found.

"The thread is faded so it's nearly the same color as the fabric, but there's a name monogrammed in the corner of this block. Rejoice Wells. 1861." Robyn traced it with a finger and smiled. "Rejoice. What a perfect name."

It was. But I was focusing on her surname. *Wells*. I told Robyn about the photograph I'd found.

"I figured Henry Wells was the man Susanna was in love with."

Robyn's eyes grew wide. "Good Lord, Lucie. Maybe Rejoice was Henry's mother. Or his sister. That could mean the quilt *could* have been made right here in Virginia—that it *would* be local. For a quilt researcher that's like finding the holy grail." She pressed her hands together as if she were praying.

"I'm planning to stop by the Balch Library this afternoon to see if I can find out anything about Henry," I said. "I guess I ought to look up Rejoice as well."

"Will you let me know if you turn up anything?"

"Of course."

She glanced at her watch. "Oh, dear, I ought to be going. We're supposed to be at the Sheriff's Office by eleven. I'll have to drag Toby away from his work, though I'm sure Colette can take over for him while we're gone."

"Good luck. And thank you for the help."

"Thank *you* for loaning me this quilt." She paused and added, "But it wasn't the only reason you stopped by, was it?"

No point lying. She knew. "No. Not exactly."

"Does it have to do with Jean-Claude?"

"Yes."

She folded her arms across her chest. "You're wondering if I was the person arguing with Jean-Claude in French right before he was killed," she said in a conversational tone. "I figured that out after what you told me about Miguel last night. I did go see Jean-Claude that morning to talk to him about Miguel's missing papers. Trust me, the conversation was entirely in English. I can barely order from a menu in a French restaurant. I once confused brains with venison when I was in Paris a few years ago. Or as I called it, 'deer.' *Cervelle. Cerf.* Trust me, they neither taste nor look the same."

I smiled, but of course she was right that I'd known she'd put two and two together. "In French we call words like that '*les faux amis.*' False friends," I said.

"I know your cousin went to see Jean-Claude, Lucie," she went on. "She was angry about the story in the *Tribune* and she left our meeting to drive down to the winery and have it out with him. I told her where she could find him because I'd already spoken with him."

"Dominique says she didn't kill Jean-Claude."

"Neither did I," she said, giving me a challenging look. "Besides, what motive would I have?"

"There is a rumor going around that you slept with him when Toby was up in New York."

I think both of us felt the air leave the room.

"Is that so?" She turned pale. "Well, you shouldn't believe everything you hear, you know."

"Is that what you're going to tell Bobby?"

She didn't answer. Instead she closed her book on African textiles and put it back on the bookshelf. When she turned around she said in a low voice, "No. It's not. I'm rather ashamed and embarrassed to say it's true. Jean-Claude came up to the house to talk about something the night Toby left for his meetings at the UN and we started drinking. It's no excuse. I regretted what happened afterward and it has haunted me. I finally confessed everything to Toby the other night after you and Quinn left. Things are strained between us at the moment, but I hope we'll get through it. I love him. I hope he loves me enough to forgive me and we can put this behind us."

"I'm so sorry."

She shrugged. "So am I, but I'm glad it's finally out in the open between the two of us. When Bobby asks me about it— as I suspect he will this morning—at least Toby isn't going to find out in an interrogation room at the Loudoun County Sheriff's Office. At least I will have spared him that indignity."

She walked me down the hall. The door to Toby's office was wide open and the room was empty.

"That's odd," Robyn said. "He told me he would be in his study writing until it was time to go. I wonder where he went. And where Colette is."

When we got to the front door she said, "Thanks again for leaving the quilt with me. I'll talk to someone next week, once we're past everything. I hope it's not going to be as bad as they're predicting."

I wondered if she was talking about Lolita or what the

outcome would be when Bobby finally made an arrest for Jean-Claude's murder. I felt the same way, as if my nerves were stretched like a guitar string about to snap.

"Me, too," I said.

I drove down their serpentine driveway and considered what Robyn had just said. If Bobby believed Jean-Claude's death was a crime of passion, what made him so certain the killer was a woman? The night before he was murdered, Robyn confessed to Toby that she'd slept with Jean-Claude. Maybe she had a motive for murder.

But now, it seemed to me, so did Toby.

Eighteen

On the drive over to Lightfoot, I called David and asked when he might have time to show me Grace Church, the African-American church in Lincoln, and its cemetery.

"I think Susanna Montgomery might have been in love with an African-American man named Henry Wells, who was from Lincoln," I said. "I found his photograph hidden between the flyleaf and the cover of a book she owned, the journal of a Quaker named John Woolman, who was an outspoken abolitionist. I also think Henry was related to the woman who made the quilt Susanna's body was wrapped in. Her name—Rejoice Wells—was embroidered in one of the blocks."

"You learned all that since yesterday?" he said, surprised. "Look, I'm in Berryville taking photos for the Virginia Tourism Corporation this morning so I'm just around the corner from Lincoln. How about if I meet you at the Goose Creek

Meetinghouse at two thirty? Do you know where it is? We can walk over to Grace Church from there."

"I haven't been there for ages, but don't worry, I'll find it."

"Great." He sounded upbeat, cheerful. "See you soon."

LIGHTFOOT RESTAURANT WAS NAMED for Francis Lightfoot Lee, one of the signers of the Declaration of Independence and the man who gave the town of Leesburg its name. The Romanesque Revival Style building, built in 1888, was a historic landmark best known for the two gilded lions on the façade. The restaurant owners had retained its grandeur and elegance so that inside the decor reminded me of something out of La Belle Époque, with hand-painted Venetian chandeliers, numerous fireplaces, carved moldings, and a mahogany-coffered ceiling in the bar.

By the time I parked and walked into the restaurant, it was just after eleven-thirty. Kit was already there, seated at a table next to the fireplace, which, in cold weather, always had a cheerful fire blazing in it. She looked up from texting and smiled, slipping her phone into her purse.

"Sorry to keep you waiting," I said as we exchanged air kisses. "Were you getting some work done?"

"No, just texting Bobby."

Our waitress arrived and we ordered—a Reuben and sweet iced tea for Kit and a wild-berry salad and unsweetened tea for me.

After our waitress left I said, "Then I guess you know by now Dominique is one of his prime suspects for Jean-Claude's murder."

"*What?* Are you serious?"

"I am. She spent last night with us she was so upset."

"Good Lord. Bobby didn't say a word to me, Luce. Not that he would ever tell me he's going to arrest someone before he actually does it."

"So you weren't texting about that?"

Kit leaned toward me as if we were co-conspirators. "You know he can't say anything about an ongoing investigation. But I promise you Bobby would never make an arrest until he's damned sure he's got the right person. If Dominique's innocent she's got nothing to worry about."

If Kit was trying to make me feel better it wasn't working. It wouldn't be hard for Bobby to make a credible case against Dominique as Jean-Claude's killer. She had gone to see him the morning he was murdered and she could have been the woman Miguel heard arguing with him in French. She would have been pissed off by the gossip-column story in the *Trib* that had just appeared that morning and there was long-standing enmity between her and Jean-Claude after she was forced to get an abortion when he got her pregnant and then dumped her.

There had to be someone else who was just as angry with Jean-Claude, or even angrier, someone who lost control in a moment of fury and stabbed him to death.

Kit leaned back against the leather banquette, watching me. "Wait a minute. Don't tell me you're actually worried Dominique did it? Is that what's going on?"

That was the $64,000 question, wasn't it? Our waitress had already returned with our iced teas.

After she left I said, "No, of course not. Dominique didn't do it. She just . . . she *can't* have."

"That wasn't what I asked." Kit gave me a pointed look as she sucked her tea through her straw.

I stirred my own tea and watched the ice cubes swirl around. "I'm afraid she might have enough reasons, enough of a motive—and no alibi for the time Jean-Claude was killed—for Bobby to make a case that she did stab him to death."

Kit reached over and covered her hand with mine. "Bobby's not going to accuse someone of murder just so he can wrap things up with a bow and get the State Department and the press off his back." Her voice was quiet, but firm. "Even one as high-profile as this one. He won't stop until he finds out who really did it and there's not a shadow of a doubt in his mind about that person's guilt. Okay?"

"I suppose so . . . yes."

Our food arrived. Kit attacked her Reuben with gusto, but as good as it was, I picked at my salad.

"We need to talk about something else. Tell me why we're going to the Balch Library," Kit said in her usual blunt way, dabbing her mouth with her napkin. "And eat your salad, kiddo. You'll waste away to nothing."

I picked up my fork, dug in, and told her everything. Susanna Montgomery, Charles, the engagement, his marriage to Thelma's great-aunt, Susanna's interest in Quakerism, and finally about Henry Wells and Rejoice. When I was done I got Henry's photograph out of my purse and handed it to her.

She took a look at it and whistled. "Wow, isn't he the handsome devil."

"I'd like to find out who he was," I said. "And what happened to him."

"The Balch is the perfect place. Anything you want to

know about the history of Leesburg, Loudoun County, and all the surrounding areas is there. They have loads of Civil War documents. A few years ago they were designated as a reference site for the Underground Railroad."

She passed Henry Wells' photograph back to me and my heart skipped a beat. "The Underground Railroad? Really?"

"Yup," she said through a mouthful of Reuben. When she was done chewing she added, "What do you think happened to Susanna Montgomery? How did she die? Do you think Charles did her in because he found out about her and Henry?"

That question still made me squirm. Kit, the journalist, never beat around the bush. Did one of my cousins murder another cousin? Yes or no?

"I don't know. Yasmin said the cuff link she found in the grave almost certainly belonged to whoever dug it. So Charles buried her, at least. Whether he did her in . . . killed her . . ." I shrugged. "Maybe. I don't know. The whole thing is pretty sordid if he did."

"It is, but you can't control what did or didn't happen one hundred and fifty years ago. You're not responsible for the actions of other people, even if they are related to you."

"My family owned slaves, Kit. Susanna's father was one of Mosby's Rangers. To have his daughter fall in love with a black man in those days was probably the worst thing she could do to disgrace her family. The Montgomery family. *My* family."

"Lucie, a lot of people in Middleburg and Leesburg owned slaves. Today it sounds absolutely heinous and unthinkable that someone—anyone—could be considered the property of another person, bought and sold like . . . like animals or farm equipment . . . just because of the color of their skin. But it happened. The times, the beliefs, and people's values were different, and you can't make it unhappen," she said. "I did some research on Bobby's family after we got married. Do you know what I found out? His ancestors owned a place called Noland's Tavern in Middleburg. They used to hold auctions where they sold slaves. Families. Men, women, children. I found a copy of a poster advertising one of the sales. It turned my stomach."

I set down my fork. "I didn't know that."

"Neither did I. But it is what it is. All you can hope—all any of us can hope—is that we learn from the past. Do our best to make sure it doesn't happen again."

I nodded, unconvinced. The world wasn't that simple a place. We both knew it.

"Come on, Luce. I hate to see you look so melancholy," she said. Then she brightened. "How about dessert? We could both do with something sweet."

In Kit's world food equaled comfort and love. The fixer of all maladies, especially if it involved sugar. Or chocolate. I smiled and said, "Sure."

"I think we should each get a homemade ice cream cone. I already asked the waitress before you arrived what the flavor of the day is. It's honey lavender."

"The chef made honey lavender ice cream? I'm in."

I paid for lunch and Kit and I ate our ice cream cones walking the two and a half blocks down West Market Street to the Thomas Balch Library. Like Lightfoot, the library was located in the historic district of Leesburg. It had been built in 1922 and looked more like an elegant redbrick colonial home than a library, with its columned portico, cupola, and two wings flanking either side of the main building, much like Highland House. Originally it had been a subscription-only library until 1960 when it had become a free—but segregated—public library. Desegregation came in 1965. I thought about David—or more accurately, David's birth mother—and tried to imagine what it would have felt like, perhaps as a teenager, for her to be turned away and told to find someplace else to do her research because she wasn't white.

"You're kind of quiet," Kit said, finishing the last bite of her homemade waffle cone.

"Just thinking."

The everyday entrance was around the back, another columned portico that was slightly less grand than the front entrance. Inside the library was light-filled and airy, a series of large, open rooms with floor-to-ceiling bookcases lining the walls. It reminded me of the home of an erudite scholar, with paintings on the walls, fireplaces, comfortable chairs for sitting and reading, and long rectangular conference tables with Windsor chairs pulled around them, a place for spreading out papers and getting work done. All that was missing was the butler and a silver tray with glasses of sherry.

A pleasant-faced woman with short blond hair, clear blue eyes behind librarian horn-rimmed glasses, and a lanyard with a photo ID hanging around her neck smiled at Kit and me from a seat behind the circulation desk when we walked in. "Katherine Noland." She stood up. "How nice to see you again. It's been a while."

Kit smiled. "It's nice to see you, too, Ginna. Lucie, this is

Ginna Underwood, the executive director of the Balch Library. We lucked out meeting the top person as soon as we walked in. Ginna, this is my friend Lucie Montgomery."

Ginna Underwood came around from behind the circulation desk to shake my hand and give Kit a hug. "How can I help?" she asked. "What brings you here?"

"I'm looking for information on an African-American man I believe lived over in Lincoln. He would have been in his twenties, maybe early thirties in 1862," I said.

"You've come to the right place. The library has census records, cemetery records, marriage indexes, and court records for free blacks." She ticked items off on her fingers. "Plus we have thousands of personal documents—ephemera, unpublished papers, manuscripts, diaries, letters. Do you know, by chance, if he was a freeman or a slave?"

"I'm afraid I don't know anything about him, except that he was in love with one of my ancestors. They were hoping to run away to New York and get married. It didn't work out."

Ginna's smile was grave. "I presume your ancestor was a white woman?"

"Yes."

"If he was a slave, they never could have married. In Virginia or anywhere else. It would have been dangerous for them even to have been seen together."

"I know. I believe Susanna Montgomery—my ancestor—may have been murdered because she was in love with Henry. I was hoping to find out who he was and what happened to him."

Ginna frowned. "Henry . . . and Susanna? What's Henry's last name?"

"Wells. I believe he was also related to someone named Re-joice Wells."

She fingered her lanyard, turning it over and over, a look of puzzled surprise on her face. "Henry Wells? We've been working on processing a collection we received a couple of years ago and, frankly, we're just stuck. A real estate agent found a strongbox in the attic of a house she was selling over in Lincoln. The owners didn't want it and the agent saw that it contained a lot of old documents and letters, so they told her she could bring it here and let us see if it was of interest to the library. The family's name was Cooper, but there also were documents belonging to a branch of the family whose surname was Wells."

I couldn't hide my astonishment. "Are you saying that you have papers that belonged to Henry Wells?"

"I'm saying we have papers that belonged to *a* Henry Wells, along with other members of the Wells family. Including, as I recall, someone named Rejoice. The documents span several generations so we have letters that were written home from overseas during both the First and Second World Wars. It would be interesting to see if our papers belong to *your* Henry Wells, though it sounds as if they might. If that's the case, we could use your help."

"Could we see them?" Kit asked.

"Of course," she said. "We keep all our historical records in a room behind the circulation desk. Follow me."

She picked up a set of keys that had been lying on the circulation desk and we followed her around to a door with a sign that said PROCESSED MANUSCRIPT COLLECTIONS.

"You need to leave your jackets and your purses here." She

indicated a small table just outside the door. "Don't worry, they'll be perfectly safe."

Kit and I followed her inside and Ginna closed the door behind us. The room had a faintly musty smell of history and old secrets. Floor-to-ceiling rolling shelves spanned the length of the room and fitted together like a series of interlocking panels forming a false wall. Ginna cranked the handle on one of the panels and, like Aladdin's Cave of treasures, two bookshelves seemed to magically separate along tracks in the floor revealing shelves of labeled archival boxes like the ones Leland had at home, along with stacks of papers, magazines, and old photo albums.

"Pretty neat, isn't it?" Kit said to me. "I've been in here before."

"It's amazing," I said. "Are all the shelves as full of boxes and papers as these are?"

Ginna nodded. "They are. In fact we're nearly at capacity. You'd be surprised the things we get and where they come from. Sometimes there'll be a cardboard box on the doorstep outside when we show up for work one morning with no explanation about what it is or who left it there."

"People just dump things and leave?" I asked.

"They do. In the case of the Cooper and Wells documents, we at least have some context since we know the house where they were found." She walked down the aisle she had created by separating the two bookshelves and pulled out a cream-colored box. "This is what I was looking for. Come on. We'll take a look at the contents in one of the reading rooms."

Kit and I sat on either side of Ginna Underwood at a conference table in a light-filled room called the Divine Room—

named, as Ginna explained, for John Elbert Divine, a local historian who used to give impromptu Civil War talks at the library.

She flipped open the top of the box. Inside it was filled with file folders, each one with a detailed handwritten label.

"Yes," Ginna said, when she saw my surprised expression, "it's all done by hand. No computers for us, at least not until we upload the information to the internet so people know we have these documents."

"It's impressive and it must take a long time."

"Believe me, it does," she said. "Now, as it happens, I'm the one processing this particular collection so you're in luck because I know quite a lot about these families."

"So that's your handwriting?" I said, pointing to the tidy script on one of the files.

"It is."

"Tell us about Henry," Kit said. "Luce, show Ginna the photograph."

I got it out of my purse one more time and handed it to Ginna. "We have a photograph of an older man in this collection," she said after she studied it. "It could be the same person. I'll find it in a minute."

She pulled a sheet of typewritten notes out of a folder and started to read. "Henry Wells was a freeman who originally came from Ghana—the son of a prominent Ashanti village chief—and was sold into slavery in Virginia. However, he was so well-educated, in addition to being multilingual, that it wasn't long before his owner decided to give him his freedom papers." She looked up with a rueful smile. "Although we wish we had those documents here, they are actually in Washington in the

African-American History Museum. You might want to go and see them. We also have documents indicating that Henry was involved in the Underground Railroad."

Kit gave me an I-told-you-so glance.

I caught my breath. "What about Rejoice Wells?" I asked. "Who was she?"

Ginna skimmed her notes. "Let's see . . . Rejoice was Henry's sister, a slave who worked as a seamstress for a well-to-do family in Middleburg. Eventually she and Henry, who was a cabinetmaker, were able to save up enough money to buy her freedom. Afterward she continued to sew and design dresses for some of the wealthier women in the region. Some of her receipts and sketches are among these papers."

A seamstress. That's why there were so many different fabrics in Susanna's quilt, scraps from the dresses and clothes Rejoice made for her rich clients. I told Ginna about the quilt and also what Thelma had told me about Susanna falling in love with an African-American man who I was almost certain was Henry Wells.

Ginna smiled and slipped several files out of the box. She thumbed through them and pulled out a folder. "Then that would explain these," she said. "Love letters from a woman named Susanna to Henry. Until today, we had no idea who she was."

"May I see them?"

"Of course."

I opened the folder. Three letters written in the same flowery handwriting I'd found on the back of Henry's photograph. It would take some time to properly decipher her script so I quickly looked them over, hoping to find any mention of her engagement to Charles or something about her family, who I was certain would be dead set against her relationship with a black man. What I did discover were Susanna's deep feelings of loss and longing for Henry, her acute awareness of how dangerous their love was, and the realization that there were men who were ready to fight—literally—to prevent them from being together.

I looked up. "I feel like I'm reading something out of *Romeo and Juliet*. How sad for them both."

"Isn't it? I think what we should do," Ginna said in a gentle voice, "is set up a time for you to go over the contents of this box on your own, when you don't have to rush. Then afterward maybe you can help us fill in the gaps, things we don't know about Susanna. And this friend of yours—Thelma—perhaps she might be willing to come along as well?"

"I'll talk to her," I said, closing the folder. "Are you quite sure Henry was involved in the Underground Railroad?"

Ginna nodded and removed more files from the box. She opened one that contained a single document. The tissue-thin paper was nearly torn in two pieces and the faded writing was almost impossible to decipher.

"This is a manumission slip," she said. "It's not Henry's, but as you can see it's extremely tattered and well worn."

"What's a manumission slip?" Kit asked.

"The paper a freeman or freewoman had to carry to prove their freedom. What happened, though, was that manumission slips were used over and over again by fugitive slaves fleeing on the Underground Railroad in case anybody stopped them. We believe Henry was probably one of the conductors." She opened another folder. "There were no road maps or plans—everything had to be memorized and runaway slaves traveled mostly at night—but we found this paper among his things."

She moved it into the light so Kit and I could read it. "It's a list of distances between towns in Virginia and Maryland," Kit said.

"That's right." She slid another paper in front of Kit and me. "We also found this diagram. Unfortunately we don't know where it is or what it represents."

My heart skipped a beat. "I do."

Ginna looked up, startled, and Kit said, "What is it?"

I took Susanna's copy of *The Journal of John Woolman* out of my bag and opened it to the back flyleaf.

"It's the same drawing," Ginna said.

I pointed to the house in the woods on both drawings. "I wonder if this cottage could have been a stop on the Underground Railroad. This plan was drawn in the back of the journal of a Quaker abolitionist that belonged to Susanna and you found the same plan among Henry's documents. The cottage is on my land—in fact, my brother and I just came across it the other day. We'd never even known it was there because it's so well hidden in the woods."

"What are you saying?" Kit said.

"I think there's a chance that Susanna could have been helping fugitive slaves escape to the North, most likely without anyone else in our family knowing about it, given that her father was one of Mosby's Rangers. I think it's possible that she and Henry were not only in love, they might have been partners in the Underground Railroad."

Nineteen

left Susanna's book and the photograph of Henry Wells with Ginna Underwood, who asked if I'd be willing to come back to the library when I had more time so we could go over the documents belonging to Henry and Rejoice Wells together. We had looked at her picture of the older man she'd believed was Henry Wells and came to the conclusion that both photos were of the same person. I also promised to look through Leland's records more thoroughly, in case I'd missed something.

Last but not least was Thelma. Did she know what really happened to Susanna? Did she have letters or documents belonging to Charles Montgomery that explained how Susanna died? And if so, did Thelma want that information brought to light, especially if it proved Charles had played a role in his fiancée's death—maybe even murdering her himself? At the end of the day, whether Thelma chose to release information that had come down through her own family was her call, not mine.

David's birth mother did not want to acknowledge him and, as difficult and heartbreaking as that was for him to accept, she was within her rights to do so. As I realized when I opened Pandora's box and explored my DNA and my family history, I couldn't stuff what spilled out back inside. Sometimes—like now—you just had to live with *knowing* and that's it. I told Ginna I wasn't sure Thelma would be eager to share what information she had about Charles.

"It's all right, Lucie," she said. "Everyone needs to follow their conscience on matters like this. Who wants to reveal alcoholism, physical abuse, pedophilia . . . all sorts of unpleasant details about ancestors and relatives? Many people want the past to be dead and buried, so to speak. I happen to believe that these are the things that need to be out in the open. To make sure the next generation is aware of less-than-desirable character traits in order to change the paradigm. And also to be aware of good traits—a generous and giving heart, kindness to the less fortunate, a teacher or doctor who was beloved by students or patients, someone who adopted foster children or a disabled child. It cuts both ways."

I could live with a philosophy like that. *The blood of your parents is not lost in you.* But it didn't have to define you.

"I'll talk to Thelma," I said. "And see what she says."

"Let me know," she said. "And call me when your schedule is a bit less hectic."

"You might not hear from me for a while—at least until harvest is over."

"Take your time," she said. "These documents aren't going anywhere. But I will tell you that this could be a very exciting discovery for the library—for historians—especially if we're able to establish that the house on your land was actually a stop on the Underground Railroad. Plus you also own a rare kente quilt made by Rejoice Wells. A lot of people will be interested in it." She smiled and sighed. "Including, I'm sure, the Smithsonian."

Robyn Callahan had said practically the same thing. *A very exciting discovery.* Now all I had to do was tell the people who really needed to know about this: my own family. Plus I needed to tell Eli and Mia about David, our half brother. As Quinn said last night, do it sooner rather than later. Keeping that secret was no different than lying to them.

On the way back to our cars Kit said, "Where are you off to now?"

"Meeting a friend who might know something about Henry and Rejoice."

"Oh?" She waited and when I didn't elaborate she said, "Well, good luck, then."

"Thanks. And thanks so much for introducing me to Ginna. She was terrific."

"You're welcome. Look, Luce, don't worry, okay? Everything is going to work out."

I hugged her and said, "I hope so."

I waited until I saw her taillights disappear in my rearview mirror before I started the Jeep. Kit and I told each other everything. She knew I was holding something back.

It had been a week of secrets, deceptions, and outright lies. I wanted it to end and I wanted the truth to come out.

Except for knowing the identity of Jean-Claude's murderer.

That truth still scared me.

. . .

THE NAVY BMW CONVERTIBLE was parked with the top up on the grassy lot behind the Goose Creek Meetinghouse, which was located at the intersection of four roads in the tiny Quaker village of Lincoln. I pulled in next to it and got out of the Jeep. Except for our cars, the place was deserted.

The Meetinghouse, a long, low redbrick building with its white-columned flagstone front porch, reminded me more of someone's home than a place of worship. I climbed the steps to the porch and opened the screen door. David was inside, sitting on one of the long wooden benches, eyes closed as if he were meditating, his camera lying next to him.

A rush of memories flooded my mind. A sweltering summer day years ago when my mother brought me here seeking a sanctuary after Leland had come home drunk once again and they'd argued over where he'd been . . . and who he'd been with. The large room was exactly as I remembered it, open-armed, nonjudgmental, and welcoming as an old friend. Wooden benches were still arranged as three sides of a rectangle surrounding a fireplace with a much-used woodstove and a basket of logs and kindling ready for the next chilly meeting day. No ornamentation on the whitewashed walls except an antique clock above a doorway that led to rooms used for classes and socializing. The small one-room library was directly opposite that doorway on the other side of the meeting room.

David straightened up and turned around so he was facing me, his irresistible smile lighting up his face. "You found it."

I grinned and went over to join him. "I've been here before." I leaned my cane against the bench and sat down.

"For a meeting?"

"No, my mother was looking for a peaceful place to come for a while. She brought me with her. We sat here quietly until she was ready to leave."

He nodded, without asking the logical question: *Why?*

"The Friends call their meetings 'expectant waiting,'" he said. "An entire meeting can pass in total silence. There's no leader and everyone is welcome. But Friends also believe the still, small voice they hear in that silence may be the voice of God coming from within."

"I think that's lovely."

"Want to sit for a few minutes right now?" he asked.

"I do."

He leaned back, stretching out his long legs and crossing them at the ankles. Then he closed his eyes. I followed suit, closing mine. Unbidden, the names came into my mind, crowding my thoughts. Susanna. Charles. Henry. Rejoice. Jean-Claude. I had no control over what had happened to any of them—how they lived and how they died. Quakers believed that God was present in all of us and by quieting our minds and listening deeply we could directly experience that divine presence. All I could do, as Ginna had said, was follow my conscience. And try to quiet my mind.

"Lucie?" David laid a hand on my arm and my eyes flew open. "I didn't mean to disturb you."

"Was I asleep?"

"More like in your own zone." We both stood and he added, "Before we go to see Grace Church and the cemetery, I thought I'd show you the Goose Creek Burying Ground across the street."

"You really know your way around."

"I photographed this place for *National Geographic*," he said as we stepped outside onto the porch. "This meetinghouse was built in 1817. It's not the first or even the second place of worship." He pointed to a little stone house across the street. "That was the second, built in 1765. The first was a log cabin built in 1750. The caretaker lives there now. He looks after this place, the burying ground, and the one-room school, which is that redbrick building over there."

"That's a school?"

"Oakdale School," he said. "It was built in 1816 to educate Quaker children and the children of free African-Americans. It was one of the first integrated schools in Virginia."

We crossed the quiet country lane and followed a gravel path shaded by an enormous pine and surrounded by woods until we reached the cemetery. It was a large, flat, grassy area with trees that had clearly been around as long as the burying ground had been there. Many of them now sheltered well-worn mossy headstones, all of which were small, simple, and unadorned.

"You didn't have to be Quaker to be buried here," David said. "Anyone was allowed—slaves, Indians, indigent or homeless people. But whoever buries someone is required to follow the rules. No ostentation or display of wealth at any grave and no flowers. That's why the headstones all look so similar. Generally there's just a name and a date of birth and death. Sometimes only the name of the deceased."

The last time I'd been in a cemetery talking with someone like this—and not standing over an open grave as I had with Yasmin—I'd been with Jean-Claude when he told me someone wanted to kill him. And then someone did. I shivered. I seemed to be spending a lot of time in graveyards these last few days. Looking for answers from people who couldn't give them, trying to divine their secrets. Just like I was doing now.

"Is something wrong?" David asked.

We'd known each other for a little more than twenty-four hours but it was uncanny how astute he was at reading me.

I smiled. "Just thinking. All of the Montgomerys—including Leland—are buried in the family cemetery at Highland Farm. You should come and see it."

He nodded, the realization of what I'd just said sinking in. He would see his father's grave. "Thank you. I would like to do that."

"Susanna's remains are going to be reburied there as soon as the forensic anthropologist finishes taking DNA samples. I'm going to talk to Hunt & Sons Funeral Home since I've never done anything like this before, but I'm sure we'll have some kind of service. Maybe you could come?"

"I'll be there," he said. "You told me on the phone you think you know the name of the man she was in love with?"

"Actually I found out a lot more since I spoke to you."

I told David what I'd learned at the Balch Library about Henry and Rejoice Wells. "They came from Ghana," I said. "They were both Ashanti, which explains the quilt that she made that was wrapped around Susanna's body. My neighbor, who is an artist and knows a lot about textiles, told me it's called a kente quilt. Apparently it's quite rare."

We had made a slow loop around part of the cemetery and now David was leading us over to an opening in the low stone wall that seemed to lead farther into the woods. The sky was the color of gunmetal and I wondered whether it was going to rain again. The air even smelled like rain. At this rate, by the time Lolita arrived in two days the ground would be so saturated the water would have no place to go except to immediately begin flooding riverbanks and streams, inundating low spots and washing out roads.

"Have you ever been to Ghana?" David was asking me. "This is the back way to Grace Church, by the way."

I followed him through the open gate and we clambered down a grassy hill to a narrow gravel road. He had slowed his pace to match mine. We still hadn't seen a soul, as if we were the only two people for miles around.

"No, I've never even been to Africa. Have you?"

He nodded. "Also for *National Geo*. Ghana, which was and still is Africa's largest producer of gold, as well as diamonds and bauxite, has a famous series of castles and fortresses along their magnificent coastline. Hundreds of years ago they were used as warehouses for trading goods, but eventually those places—which also contained dungeons—were used to house slaves before they were sent to America. There was a door on the seaboard side that everyone called the 'door of no return.' From there, slaves were put on boats to be taken to slaving ships farther out to sea where they were loaded like cargo for the journey to America."

He spoke in a matter-of-fact way, but my stomach churned.

"That's horrible . . . it's inhuman." My protest sounded feeble, even to my own ears. It had happened for decades and decades and no one had done anything to stop it. It was reality.

"If Henry and Rejoice came from Ghana, they would have

come through that door," he said in a quiet voice. "The door
of no return."

We turned into a small driveway leading to an old fieldstone building. A sign at the entrance to the driveway said it
was the Mt. Olive Baptist Church and it sat between two cemeteries.

David pointed to another small building in the distance
that looked like a twin to the one in front of us. "That's Grace
Church," he said. "Unlike the Baptist Church, which is still in
use, Grace Church was abandoned in the 1940s when the con-
gregation moved their place of worship to Purcellville.

"The cemetery is still in use, though," he went on as we
walked through the cemetery toward Grace Church. He
pointed to a patch of rusty red Virginia clay soil that looked
freshly disturbed. "They're still burying people here. The
older graves are farther from the church. We'll take a look at
them after we see the church."

"Do you think Henry or Rejoice worshipped there?" I
asked.

"It's possible. They also might have come for other reasons.
The basement was a vocational school where Quakers taught
all kinds of useful skills—sewing, cooking, shoe repair," he
said.

The church windows were boarded up, there was a protective tarp over part of the roof, and someone had hung a
now-desiccated twig-branch wreath with artificial flowers
twined through it next to the front door. A NO TRESPASSING
sign had been nailed to the door and the stone steps were
moss-covered. No one had been here in a long time.

"It's a pity the place was abandoned. It was the first legal black church in Loudoun County, built by Quakers and freed slaves, so it has a lot of history," David said. "Come on, let's take a look at the gravestones in the cemetery."

Unlike the Goose Creek Burying Ground with its plain, unadorned headstones, many of the graves here were decorated with bouquets of plastic flowers and the headstones contained epitaphs like RAMBLING MAN or GONE FISHING. A lot of the bouquets had become separated from their plastic holders so they now were scattered across the cemetery. By the time we got to the older part of the cemetery, some of the smaller markers had fallen over and whatever had been etched on them was worn away.

Of the headstones we could read, none had the name Wells or Cooper on them. The sky had grown darker. More rain was coming.

"Maybe the files in the Balch Library will have something that will help." David sounded hopeful as we walked back to our cars, which were still at the meetinghouse.

"Maybe," I said. "There are also Thelma's family papers. If she's willing to let us take a look at them."

He threw his arm around my shoulder and gave it a friendly squeeze. "We're just starting to look. We'll find answers. I'm sure of it."

I smiled at him. "I hope so."

We leaned against my Jeep as we'd done yesterday while I told him about Rejoice's quilt and how I believed the cottage on my land could have been a stop on the Underground Railroad.

"I'd like to document all of it," he said. "Photograph the

house and the quilt. And Susanna's gravesite. If you don't mind."

"I think that would be a great idea. First, though, you need to meet Quinn. And Eli and eventually Mia."

"Your call," he said. "Just let me know." He squinted up at the sky through the canopy of trees. "We probably ought to get going before this storm breaks."

"I know. I'll be in touch. I'm not quite sure when . . . but soon." I knew it sounded lame but I hadn't told him about Dominique, how worried I was that she was going to be arrested any day now for Jean-Claude's murder.

"It's okay," he said. "I understand. Take your time, Lucie."

He kissed me on the cheek and once again waited for me to leave before he did. This time, though, I didn't see the blue BMW in my rearview mirror. He must have taken one of the three other roads at that intersection.

I drove down Lincoln Road, thinking about what he'd said about the door of no return on the seaboard side of the slave fortresses on Ghana's coast. Henry and Rejoice had probably passed through such a door and their lives had changed forever. Because of what they had done in America, their actions had reverberated through generations, changing my family's narrative. Susanna had been gutsy and brave. So had they.

I would have liked to know them all. And I still wanted to find out who killed Susanna and what had happened to Henry and Rejoice.

PURCELLVILLE WAS PRACTICALLY DUE north of Middleburg and Atoka, so I cut across the county to the Snickersville

Turnpike and came through the village of St. Louis. By then it had started to rain, not the lashing downpour we got last night, but still a steady rain that required headlights and caution on slick, winding country lanes. At the intersection of St. Louis Road and Mosby's Highway, I could turn left to go home or right and about a quarter of a mile down the road I'd be at the turnoff for Hunt & Sons Funeral Home.

I turned right.

If anyone would know what to do about burying Susanna's remains—which Yasmin had told me would essentially be a cardboard box filled with bones—it would be B.J. Hunt. He'd been my mother and father's close friend and when the time came, he had taken care of every detail of their funerals as if they were his own kin. After their deaths, he had been like an uncle to Eli, Mia, and me.

I wasn't expecting the black Lincoln Town Car that sat in front of the entrance with the engine running and a bored-looking driver, but as soon as I saw the car and got over my shock I knew why it was here and realized it should not have been a surprise. Baron Armand de Merignac was supposed to return to France today with the body of his son. Who else would he come to but B.J.—the Sheriff's Office had probably steered him to Hunt & Sons—to handle the arrangements for preparing Jean-Claude's body?

I parked next to the Town Car and got a sideways glance from the driver, who returned to fiddling with his phone. The rain was coming down harder now and I had forgotten an umbrella. By the time I climbed the steps onto the porch of the old Victorian gingerbread house, I was thoroughly soaked.

The front door opened and Armand de Merignac nearly ran into me.

"Excuse me, miss. I'm so sorry." He held the door for me, a perfect gentleman.

"Baron de Merignac, you probably don't remember me," I said in French. "I'm Lucie Montgomery, Chantal Delaunay's daughter. I'm so sorry for your loss."

He let the door close and stared at me as if I'd just told him I came from Mars. He looked older and more heavyset than I remembered, perhaps how Jean-Claude would have looked in another twenty-five or so years had he lived. Snow-white hair, thick jowls, deep-set eyes, and a face gray with fatigue and grief, but the aristocratic bearing of someone used to being accommodated and getting what he wanted because of his wealth and title.

"Lucie?" He stepped back, frowning. I was wet, bedraggled, and leaning on a cane. He hadn't seen me since I was thirteen. Maybe he didn't think I'd aged any better than he had. A faint look of disapproval crossed his face. "Is it really you? I was told you were the one who found Jean-Claude."

"That's true. I'm so sorry," I said again.

He flicked his hand, irritated. "I plan to speak to the French ambassador as soon as I return home. He's an old friend. I want him to insist that something be done to find out who murdered my son. Your sheriff ought to have arrested someone by now. I don't understand why the detective I spoke with hasn't done anything. I won't tolerate incompetence."

"Bobby . . . Detective Noland is *not* incompetent and he's done plenty," I said, my own anger flashing. "He'll find out who did this. Forgive me, Baron de Merignac, but Jean-Claude managed to make more than a few enemies in the short time he was here. And who's to say his killer wasn't someone from his past? It's an open secret that you paid off people to keep quiet about the trouble he got into over the years."

For a moment I thought he might spit on me. The contempt and anger on his face was visceral. "Including," he said with venom, "your cousin. I knew about her abortion after her affair with Jean-Claude. Your friend Detective Noland is now well aware of that fact, too."

"She said you never knew about it," I said, stunned.

"Then she was naive to believe I would not learn what happened. I found out when I took care of the other one, the American girl. The nanny. Dominique, at least, had the grace to keep her mouth shut. The bloody nanny wanted money. So American and greedy. I gave her enough to satisfy her but I made her sign papers that she would forfeit everything if she ever bothered us again."

"What American nanny?" I asked.

"Some young woman. Coco, her name was. She was working for another family," he said. "She managed to meet Jean-Claude and flirt with him. It wasn't long before she got him into bed with her. Of course he had no intention of the relationship being anything more than a *divertissement,* an amusement. She had other ideas."

"What happened to her? Do you know?"

He shrugged and said with disdain, "Why would I keep in touch with a servant? They move on, go elsewhere. Presumably she went back to America." He flicked a hand, summoning the driver of the Town Car who emerged, opening a large black umbrella. "My jet is at the airport and my son's coffin will be accompanying me. I have to go. *Adieu,* Lucie."

In French you said *adieu* to someone you expected never to see again. *Au revoir* meant "until we meet again."

"*Adieu*. And please give my sympathy to Baroness de Merignac."

The driver helped him down the stairs and into the car. I watched as it made a sweeping U-turn before heading down the long driveway. As the Town Car passed in front of the entrance to the funeral home, Armand de Merignac turned his head briefly and glanced at me, his face impassive. Then he looked away.

The nanny. Coco . . . short for Colette?

The other night Robyn had explained that Toby met Colette when he and his first wife lived in Bordeaux and she had been working as a nanny for a local family.

Could Colette have been the other girl who had an affair with Jean-Claude that summer? Did he get her pregnant as well? What were the odds that Toby would unknowingly hire both of them within a few weeks of each other—Jean-Claude as his new winemaker and Colette, his longtime secretary whom he needed to help him write his memoirs? If Colette had kept her pregnancy a secret, Toby would never have known about her relationship with Jean-Claude. *If* Colette was the nanny Armand de Merignac had been speaking of.

Somehow I thought she just might be. I ran back to the Jeep and called Bobby. His phone went to voice mail.

"Bobby," I said, "I think you might want to find out whether Colette Barnes ever knew Jean-Claude de Merignac before Toby hired her a few months ago. Armand de Merignac just told me his son had an affair with an American nanny whose name was Coco years ago and got her pregnant. She extorted a lot of money from the de Merignacs to keep quiet about the baby and terminate the pregnancy. I think you were right about this being a crime of passion. But it wasn't Dominique who was angry with Jean-Claude. I think it was Colette—who I suspect speaks fluent French—who confronted Jean-Claude the other day in the barrel room. Just before she killed him."

Twenty

Robyn Callahan's car was in the parking lot next to the villa when I got there just after five o'clock. So was Nikki's. Certainly by now Robyn and Toby would have finished talking to Bobby. We were closed but maybe Robyn had come by to discuss something about the kente quilt. Nikki, who was supposed to be packing up her office, must have let her in. Maybe Robyn knew something beyond what she'd said the other night about Colette's early days when she'd first met Toby—though I doubted she knew about the affair with Jean-Claude.

The door to the villa was unlocked but no one was in the tasting room. I set my purse on the bar and called Robyn's and Nikki's names. A muffled noise like two people scuffling came from the corridor where the offices were located. I started to head back there and for the second time in an hour nearly collided with someone in the doorway. This time it was Colette.

She was wearing jeans and a La Vigne Cellars T-shirt. One hand was behind her back.

"Lucie," she said with a genial smile, "I'm glad to see you. I stopped by because I heard you might be shorthanded for help tomorrow. I'm no expert at picking grapes, but I thought I might be able to help out in some way. Toby just finished with a big deadline for his editor so we're taking a day off before plunging in to the next part of his memoirs."

She was fiddling with a gold chain around her neck with the hand that wasn't behind her back.

"Thanks for the offer." I tried not to let my eyes stray to that hidden hand. "What were you doing just now?"

"Looking for someone so I could tell them that I'd be willing to help out, of course."

There was another noise from the back, this time a moan of pain.

"What's going on?" I said, raising my voice. "Nikki? Are you okay? Move out of the way, Colette."

The blade of her hunting knife flashed as she brought it around and brandished it in my face. There was blood on it. "Not so fast," she said. "Nikki's a bit tied up at the moment."

I took a step backward. "What have you done to her?"

"Never mind. Let's go." Colette moved closer, lowering the knife so the blade was aimed at my heart. "Don't try anything, Lucie. I'm not afraid to use this."

"Like you did when you killed Jean-Claude? What did you do to Nikki?"

"Shut up," she said. "And move."

I cast a quick sideways glance at my purse on the bar. Why hadn't I hung on to it?

"Where's your phone?" Colette read my mind.

"In my purse."

"Good," she said. "That makes things simpler."

We walked outside. The rain had stopped, but the sky was still leaden and gloomy and the air was damp with humidity. Everyone was either in the barrel room or out in the field. Even Frankie had called in sick, her way of letting me know she was upset about my decision to let Nikki go. There was no one around but Colette and me.

I tried to stall. "What do you have in mind? We can't go very far, you know."

Colette's eyes fell on the red ATV parked at the bottom of the stairs. Antonio had put roofs back on both vehicles the other day after Quinn and I got soaked.

"Come on, we're going for a drive," she said. "Let's go. Before someone shows up."

"You're crazy," I said. "Someone is going to show up. They're going to find Nikki and then they're going to come after you."

"Hopefully not until after I've taken care of you." Her voice was menacing. We had reached the ATV. "Get in. You're driving."

"Where am I going? It would be useful to know."

"Don't be a smart-ass," she said. "Drive to your cemetery."

My throat closed. Why would she want to go there? And then I knew. Susanna's grave. No one had filled it in.

Yet.

"How could you work for a good man like Toby all these years and he never figured out about you and Jean-Claude?" I put the ATV in gear. "Never knew that you extorted money from the de Merignacs in return for keeping quiet about your abortion."

I shouldn't have provoked her. She flicked her knife blade along my arm and an angry bright red line appeared. It stung like hell. I shut up.

"If you keep talking like that," she said in a calm voice, "I'll keep cutting you. I didn't have the abortion. My son, John, is alive and well and living in Boston. He's the sole heir to the de Merignac fortune and the title, now that Jean-Claude is dead."

We had reached the cemetery.

"Drive up the hill," she said. "Park next to the shed."

The cut on my arm was bleeding freely. Colette shoved me out of the ATV.

"You're going to remove the tarp over that open grave," she said. "And be quick about it."

"I'm not quick."

She touched the tip of her knife to my heart and withdrew it. "You'd better be."

I could only move so slowly before she would grow impatient and use that knife again. Finally I pulled the tarp away from Susanna's grave.

"Now, get in," she said.

"You're not going to bury me alive." My voice quaked but I made sure my words came out as a statement, not a question.

"I said get in." She walked over and gave me a rough shove. I lost my footing and stumbled backward, falling into the grave and landing hard on one shoulder. At least it wasn't the side that was bleeding. At least I hadn't hit my head and passed out, making it easy for her to quickly fill the grave with dirt.

Yasmin had said that most graves dug in haste were usually too shallow and too short. I couldn't get out of this hole
easily without someone helping me, but it wasn't so deep I
couldn't stand up with my head and shoulders aboveground. I
scrambled to my feet as Colette set down her knife and found
the shovel that Charles had used to bury Susanna.

The first shovelful of dirt caught me full in the face. I spat
dirt, coughing and gagging. "Don't. Please stop."

She ignored me and turned back for more dirt. My cane had
fallen into the grave with me. I picked it up and held it down
at my side, ready for her when she threw that next shovelful
at me.

"Hey." I was still coughing. "There's something down here.
You'd better see it."

She fell for it. She came over to the edge of the grave and
before she could react, I hooked my cane around her ankle and
yanked hard. The ground was slick and slippery from the rain.
She landed on her back with a dull thud. For a moment I
thought I'd knocked her out, but then she swore and started
to move. I held on to both feet and pulled her into the grave
with me.

Somehow she had managed to grab the knife before she fell
in. It flashed, lethal and deadly, as she raised her arm to plunge
it into my chest. I grabbed my cane and swung it hard at her
arm. It connected with her wrist with a loud crack and the
knife flew out of her hand into the air. I moved and the blade
landed between Colette's neck and shoulder. She screamed as
a bright bloom of red appeared and quickly grew. I grabbed
the hilt and pulled it out, shoving her against the wall. A small
geyser of blood erupted and she moaned.

My turn to give instructions. "Give me your phone," I said. "Now."

"No."

"You'll bleed to death. It looks like the knife struck an artery. You won't last long. Give it to me or you're going to die."

She fished the phone out of her pocket and moaned again, slumping down the wall until she was sitting on the ground. Her face was ashen and I suspected she was going into shock.

The sirens sounded in the distance before I even made the call to 911 for the third time this week. Bobby's unmarked cruiser and Quinn's truck arrived together with a screech of brakes and a lot of shouting. Someone called for more ambulances at the cemetery, in addition to the one that was already at the villa.

It was Quinn who lifted me out of the grave and pulled me into his arms. "You're bleeding. Thank God you're safe."

Someone in a uniform—I don't remember who it was—took my place next to Colette and began tending to her.

"It's just a superficial cut. It hurts like crazy but it'll be okay. Better than being buried alive," I said.

"My God."

"What about Nikki?"

Bobby joined us and heard my question.

"Nikki lost a lot of blood but she's on her way to the hospital," he said. "Frankie is going to meet her there. Colette wasn't expecting to find Nikki when she showed up at the villa. She came over to plant the nitrile gloves she used when she murdered Jean-Claude in Nikki's office. She stabbed Nikki a couple of times but she may have missed any vital organs. At least

Nikki was lucid enough to tell us what happened. She heard Colette talking about going somewhere with you. Once Quinn realized the red ATV was missing, we came looking. Looks like we got here just in time."

"I'm glad you did," I said. To Quinn I added, "As soon as Lolita's finished with us, I want to fill in this grave and take down the rest of the shed. Then I want to plant something in memory of Susanna before we rebury her in the cemetery."

He kissed me. "We'll do that," he said.

Twenty-one

t will be a long time before any of us forgets harvest this year. Hurricane Lolita thrashed us, but by the time she arrived in Virginia she had been downgraded to a Category 3 hurricane, which still made her a powerful storm but didn't wreak the kind of devastating damage folks in the Caribbean and Florida had to deal with. One of the two bridges that ran over Goose Creek on Highland Farm was washed out and destroyed and we lost power for four days. But I think we got off lucky, considering.

As soon as Nikki was released from the hospital, she decided to go home and work in her mother's florist shop for a while. So Frankie, Valeria, Isabella, and I put together the flowers for Antonio and Valeria's wedding, which took place in the courtyard on a spectacular Indian summer Saturday in October. The dancing and partying went on until the wee hours.

I told Eli about David one evening a few days before the wedding when just the two of us were sitting on the veranda with a bottle of wine. Hope had already gone to bed and, by a previous arrangement, Quinn said he wanted to do some stargazing at the summerhouse. Eli took it better than I'd expected—in fact he'd come across an old photograph of Olivia Vandenberg hidden under a false bottom in a hand-carved box Leland used for his keys and spare change that sat on his dresser for years.

"I always wondered who she was," he said. "And why Leland hid her picture."

"Maybe he really did love Olivia," I said. "Since she won't talk to David, or even acknowledge him, David has no idea if he was the result of a one-night stand or an affair of the heart."

"Based on how well Leland hid that picture—keeping it on his dresser in a box he used every day of his life—I'd say it was the latter," Eli said. "It stinks for you and me and Mia, and especially Mom, but I bet David would probably like to know his father loved his mother."

"Are you going to give him that photograph?"

He nodded. "I thought I might."

"Why didn't you tell me about it when you found it?" I asked. "I would have liked to know."

He poured more wine for both of us. "For the same reason you didn't tell me as soon as you found out about David, Captain Obvious."

"Ouch. Touché."

We picked up our glasses and he clinked his against mine. "Every family has a story," he said. "Welcome to ours."

• • •

THE REBURIAL CEREMONY FOR Susanna Montgomery at
the end of October was more like a celebration than a funeral.
David came to lunch at Highland House with Eli, Quinn, and
me beforehand and that's when he met them for the first time.
After a few awkward moments, the talk got around to sports,
the bonding language of all males. The three of them got along
like a house on fire after that—though I knew there would be
other sessions where we would discuss the painful subjects
that were still too raw to bring up on Day One.

We had invited everyone to the cemetery: Robyn, Toby,
Ginna, Thelma, Yasmin, Kit, Bobby, Frankie, all the tasting
room staff and the workers. A few days earlier the results had
come back from Yasmin's lab with a DNA match, and although
it was good to have that confirmed, I think we'd all long ago
made up our minds that the remains belonged to Susanna.
Ginna had gone over her files one more time, eventually track-
ing down the descendants of the Cooper-Wells family, an
elderly African-American couple living in New Jersey, who
confirmed that both Henry and Rejoice had managed to make
it to New York and were buried in a cemetery in Queens.
Henry never married.

The subject of whether Charles had killed Susanna before
burying her remained a touchy one with Thelma, who assured
me no kin of hers—and mine as well, for that matter—was a
murderer. Someone else must have done it. She did, however,
produce a photograph of Charles, which Ginna was able to en-
large enough to determine that the cuff link Yasmin found in
the grave belonged to him.

As for the ceremony, we agreed we would keep it simple. Antonio, Benny, and Jesús had dug the new grave near Susanna's parents and siblings the previous day; they were going to fill it in after everyone left. It was still traumatic for me to watch dirt being thrown over a casket in the ground after what had nearly happened with Colette.

Frankie bought enough white roses for everyone to place a flower on the pine box we had chosen for Susanna. Eli read Psalm 23. I read a poem by Mary Elizabeth Frye, which seemed to me to sum up everything that had happened.

Do not stand at my grave and weep
I am not there; I do not sleep.
I am a thousand winds that blow,
I am the diamond glints on snow,
I am the sun on ripened grain,
I am the gentle autumn rain.
When you awaken in the morning's hush
I am the swift uplifting rush
Of quiet birds in circled flight.
I am the soft stars that shine at night.
Do not stand at my grave and cry,
I am not there; I did not die.

Acknowledgments

As usual, many people were generous with their time and knowledge in sharing information and helping me get my facts straight for *Harvest of Secrets*. The usual caveat applies: if I got something wrong, it's on me, not them.

Rick Tagg, assistant winemaker at Delaplane Cellars in Delaplane, Virginia, has been answering questions, strategizing, and researching arcane wine facts on my behalf, either on the phone or in a vineyard (usually after offering me a glass of wine), for the last ten years. "Thank you" doesn't begin to do justice to my debt to him. Detective Jim Smith of the Fairfax County (Virginia) Police Department has fit in time to see me around the demands and crazy hours of his job ever since he showed up on my doorstep at dawn years ago to help with an animal-control issue. One thing led to another—he's an avid reader—and eventually to lunches at local restaurants where I continue to ply him with crime scene and law enforcement questions. Over the years I'm sure we've alarmed more than a few folks sitting near us, especially the time I wanted to know how to stab someone so there would be a lot of blood, or what a body abandoned in a car in a hot parking garage would look and smell like after a week. (The head would fall off.)

Marc Leepson, author, historian, and good friend, introduced me to Lee Lawrence, a resident of Lincoln, Virginia, who is an expert on Quakerism and the fascinating history of Lincoln, especially during the Civil War. Lee and I sat in the Goose Creek Meetinghouse one sultry summer morning not long after the riots of August 12, 2017, had occurred in Charlottesville, talking about Confederate memorials and the uncomfortable dialogue that was going on about their place in our society. In Virginia, the epicenter of the Civil War, that discussion includes monuments, schools, and highways in probably every town and village in the Old Dominion. It wasn't lost on either of us that we were having this conversation in a Quaker house of worship, a faith that advocates pacifism and tolerance.

Lee, in turn, referred me to Mary Robare, a dance teacher and instructor at Shenandoah University, who is also an expert on Quaker quilts and the author of *Quilts and Quaker Heritage: Selections from an Exhibition, Virginia Quilt Museum, May 3–September 22, 2008*. Thanks to Mary for suggesting I invent a rare and unusual quilt for the purposes of my plot, and to my son, Peter de Nesnera, who travels extensively in Africa, for his suggestion to use kente cloth. Sharon Stout, my cousin-in-law, a practicing Quaker, discussed her faith and its history with me over lunch.

I'm especially indebted to Dr. Tal Simmons, forensic anthropologist, chair of the Department of Forensic Science at

Virginia Commonwealth University, and an expert in postmortem interval estimation (time since death) for describing in basic layman's terms how to go about excavating human remains. She also explained what would—or could—realistically be learned or discovered from a grave site after nearly a century and a half. Alexandra Gressitt, director of the Thomas Balch Library in Leesburg, Virginia, gave me a tour of the library's wonderful historical archives and offered valuable advice on how Lucie might turn up information on the fictitious Wells family.

Donna Andrews, John Gilstrap, Alan Orloff, and Art Taylor are my monthly partners-in-crime who help make my writing better with their comments and suggestions. Our critique group, affectionately known as the Rumpus Writers, has met every month without fail for the last eight years. Enormous thanks to Rosemarie Forsythe for art and inspiration. Peter de Nesnera designed the gorgeous new map of Montgomery Estate Vineyard, a true labor of love for his mom, and I love it.

At Minotaur Books, thanks and gratitude to Hannah Braaten, my charming and amazing editor, for the deft use of her blue pencil and wise advice, and to Nettie Finn, her assistant. Thanks, also, to the many people at Minotaur who do so much to make this book the best it can be: Kelley Ragland, Keith Kahla, Sarah Schoof, Allison Ziegler, Joe Brosnan, and Megan Kiddoo, among others. And special thanks and love to Dominick Abel, my agent, who makes it all happen.

Last but most important, it is said that writing is by nature a solitary occupation. In part that's true, but no author writes in a vacuum—at least this one doesn't. So much thanks and love to André de Nesnera, my husband of thirty-five years, for cheerleading and encouragement when I've been sure the words are all rubbish or I can't remember how to begin a new book, for being a sounding board and my first reader, for dinners cooked and glasses of wine or cups of tea brought to my desk, and, mostly, for being the love of my life and the man who still makes my heart skip a beat. You, my love, make it all worthwhile.